SERPENT

SERPENT

A JACK CURTIS MYSTERY
BOOK 4

TRISHA HUGHES

PREVIOUSLY BY THE AUTHOR

Autobiography
Daughters of Nazareth

Historical Fiction
Book 1
Vikings to Virgin – *The Story of England's Monarchs from The Vikings to The Virgin Queen*

Book 2
Virgin to Victoria – *The Story of England's Monarchs from The Virgin Queen to Queen Victoria*

Book 3
Victoria to Vikings - The Circle of Blood

The Story of England's Monarchs from

Queen Victoria to The Vikings

The Tartan Kings - *A Powerful & Rich Story of Scotland*

Crime/Mystery
Beware of Beautiful Days

Dragonfly

Chameleon

Scorpion

Copyright © 2024 Trisha Hughes

The right of Trisha Hughes to be identified as the author of this work has been asserted by her in accordance with the Copyright, Design and Patents Act 1988.

All rights reserved. No part of this publication may be reproduced, transmitted, or stored in a retrieval system, in any form or by any means, without permission in writing from the publisher, nor be otherwise circulated in any form of binding or
cover other than that in which it is published and without a similar condition being imposed on the subsequent purchaser.

This work is fiction based on real events in history.

1

Here's how you destroy a life. You stand over his bed and watch him sleep. You know how long he'll sleep because you've been watching him for weeks and you know his routine. You've prepared. You don't take chances. There is no reason to rush. Anticipation is the spice of life. I remember my father saying that to me. It's a cliché but it's stuck with me. Not because it's true but because it's not far wrong.

Because you are well prepared you know his girlfriend is working tonight and won't be here. You also know he likes a Jack Daniels before he goes to bed. If he hadn't had one tonight, you would have postponed. Don't be in a rush. Don't take chances. Don't make mistakes. Be patient and get your target with little or no risk.

It's all about preparation and patience.

Because you've been watching him, you know he has a dog that sleeps on the covered back veranda. You're prepared for that. A large juicy steak full of drugs will put the dog to sleep for the night. And because you've been watching him, you know where the spare key is hidden. That's how you gained access to the house this morning and spiked his whisky. That's how you gained access again tonight while the dog and his owner sleep. Neither of them will be waking up for a long time.

You are wearing gloves. He, of course, is not. You pull out a glass from the backpack you're wearing and wrap his fingers around the glass in the right spots. You carefully put the glass in a sealed bag and put it back in the back pack. Then you pull out your tissues, you always carry them, and you dab the tissue against his mouth, making sure to get his spit on it. Then you put the tissue in another plastic bag and put it in the backpack with the glass. It may be overkill, and you may not need it, but overkill seems to work.

He remains on his back snoring and you can't help but smile. You enjoy this part as much as the kill. A kill is the end of the game but this, the set-up part, is a work of art.

His mobile is on the night stand. You pick it up, put it on silent, then type her address in it so there's a record of it in his map searches. Then you put that in your backpack as well. You leave his bedroom. His Audi keys are on the side table near the front door. He's meticulous about that. He comes home, he puts the keys on the table. Every time.

You grab the keys and you drive off in the Audi towards her. You know where she lives because you've been preparing.

You park on the street houses away. You break in by a window in the home office. You spill some potpourri but you clean up. This shouldn't look like a break in. You get one of her tea towels and then you wait for her to come home. You know she'll be home soon because you're prepared. She is sitting in the bar of a hotel waiting for the client who will not show. She doesn't know that client was me and that I am lying in wait for her to get home.

You hear her come in and head into the kitchen. You hear the light switch click and you see the light threading under the office door. Another click means she is boiling a kettle. You take the time to peek through the crack of the door and there she is. You have a tea towel ready and you take a metal container out of your back pack and empty some of the contents onto the towel, careful not to bring it close to your face. Chloroform works fast.

She sits alone at the table, with a cup of coffee about to open her mail. She's a beautiful woman, even with her dirty blonde hair cut into a elfin style. She looks thin in the satin dress but that's probably because of the stress. She is totally focussed on the letter.

Slowly and carefully, you push the door open and step into the kitchen. And then she raises her eyes and sees you. Her eyes open wide in surprise and she is about to scream. You don't want that.

Careless. Despite all the planning, you almost made a mistake.

You don't hesitate. You charge her and grab her head, placing the towel over her face. Seconds pass as she desperately struggles but then she goes limp and drops into your arms. You drag her into the lounge room and tie her to a chair, both arms and legs. Then you place a gag in her mouth while she sleeps, taking care not to suffocate her. That would be another mistake. One is enough.

You go back to the kitchen and pull the glass from the backpack with the man's fingerprints perfectly placed on it and set it on the dish drainer. Then you take the tea towel and the tissue and drop them in the trash can. Juries love DNA. They've grown up with CSI and TV shows that exaggerate the miracles of technology. They expect it in a murder trial. If there's no DNA evidence, a jury wonders about guilt and the defender concentrates on it.

You are in and out of the house within minutes. There is no need to hang around. You hurry back to the car. You don't worry about being seen. If worse comes to worst and someone remembers a man running away, it'll be someone running back to an Audi registered to him.

It will, if anything, help.

You start to drive, feeling a little excited about getting back to her house to start the best part. You check the clock. He and his dog should be passed out for hours more. You arrive at his house and park the Audi where you found it.

You smile. This is the true rush you were waiting for. The Audi has a tracking system so the police will see where it went tonight. You enter the house. You drop the keys on the table. You head to his bedroom and take the phone off silent before placing it back on the night table. You even plug it in to the charger for him. Like with the Audi, the police will get a warrant for his phone locations that will prove he took the journey from here to her house and back again on the night of the murder.

The Audi. The phone. The tissue. The DNA. Any three will be enough to convict him.

When he eventually goes to her apartment, and you are sure he will, you will make an anonymous call to the police informing them of a break in and give his number as the contact.

I touch the vial of tablets in my pocket. The chloroform is only a temporary anaesthetic. For what I have planned for her tonight, ketamine is the ideal drug. I want her helpless but fully conscious while I have my fun.

For her, the horror is about to begin.

For him, it's not too far away.

2

MARTIN

SATURDAY 31ST AUGUST

A writer never forgets the first time he accepted money or a word of praise in exchange for a story. He will never forget the sweet poison of vanity in his blood and the belief that, if he succeeds in not letting anyone discover his lack of talent, the dream of literature will provide him with a roof over his head, a hot meal at the end of the day, and what he covets most: his name printed on a piece of paper that will surely outlive him.

Lunch that day was my agent's idea. I hadn't even known Rick was in Brisbane, Sydney was his hometown, until he rang me the night before and insisted we meet at his club. It wasn't actually *his* club, but he was a member of a similar club in Sydney whose members had reciprocal rights Australia wide. At lunchtimes, only men were admitted and everyone had to wear a suit and tie. As I looked around, everyone was over sixty and I hadn't felt this young and out of place since university.

"You've come along way, Martin," Rick grinned, holding his half-full wine glass up to me.

And I had.

My first book was written at twenty-three when I worked in a small weekly newspaper in the hinterland of the Gold Coast, thirty kilometres and a forty minutes' drive west of Surfers Paradise. The newspaper was based in a languished barn of a building that had once housed a manure factory. The walls still oozed the vapour that stayed in my clothes and hair and at times, made my eyes water. The building rose behind a forest of angels and crosses of the Canungra Cemetery and from afar, its outline merged with the mausoleums silhouetted against the horizon. On the bright side, the building was quiet and secluded, ideal for the newspaper, and because the cemetery was so close, we were fortunate enough to get a discount on the rent. From afar, its outline merged with a skyline stabbed with chimneys and in the distance, the perpetual twilight of light that could be seen from the city that never sleeps. Surfers Paradise.

On the night that was about to change the course of my life, the newspaper's deputy editor called me into his dark cubicle that he called an office just on closing time. He was a forbidding looking man with a bushy moustache who subscribed to the theory that the liberal use of adverbs and adjectives was the mark of someone with a vitamin deficiency. Any journalist prone to florid prose would be sent off to write funeral notices for three weeks. If, after this penance, the culprit relapsed, he would ship him off to the "House and Garden" pages. We were all terrified of him, and he knew it.

I remember standing timidly in his doorway. "Did you call for me, Max?"

The office smelled of sweat and tobacco in that order. He barely acknowledged me and continued to read through one of the articles lying on his table, a red pen in hand. For a couple of minutes, he machine-gunned the text with corrections and amputations, muttering sharp comments as if I weren't there. Not knowing what to do, and noticing a chair placed against the wall, I slid towards it.

"Who said you could sit down?" he muttered without raising his eyes from the text.

I stayed standing and held my breath, waiting for him to finish. He sighed and let his red pen fall to the desk, then leaned back in his armchair, crossed his arms over his ample stomach and eyed me as if I were some useless piece of junk.

"I've been told you can write, Martin."

When I opened my mouth only a ridiculous, reedy voice emerged.

"A little, well, I mean, yes, I do write but…"

Serpent

"Well, I hope you write better than you speak. And what do you write if that's not too much to ask?"

"Uh. Crime stories, mostly. I mean..."

"I get the idea," he sighed. "Woods says you're not too bad. He says you stand out."

I was surprised. Mark Woods was the star writer of our newspaper, however small it was. He penned a weekly column on local crime and lurid events, although I might add there were precious few of those in Tamborine Mountain, but his column was the only thing worth reading in the whole paper. He was also the author of a couple of thrillers about gangsters carrying out bedroom intrigues with ladies of the night, if you know what I mean. He was still waiting for an agent and publisher to pick them up but that didn't stop him from writing more of them.

Mark Woods was the first person to whom I had dared show rough drafts of my writing to after I'd carried cups of coffee around the staff room. He always had time for me and he read what I had written and gave me good advice.

Max stared at me over the top of his glasses. "It would seem that Woods is a sentimentalist because he says that if I give you a break, I won't regret it."

I gaped open-mouthed, waiting for him to continue.

"Woods is leaving the paper and I want you to take over his column."

An involuntary gasp escaped my lips and my eyebrows shot up high on my forehead. I inched slowly towards the chair again and sat down heavily before my legs gave out.

"You are to cover the story of the five small skeletons who were unearthed in the rainforest over the past few days," he continued, watching me. "And you are to hound the lead detective, Jack Curtis, for any information you can. He's tough and doesn't suffer any fools so shut that mouth of yours and try to pretend you know what you're doing."

"Thank you so much Max. I promise you won't regret it."

"I'd better not. But don't get too carried away. What do you think of the indiscriminate use of adjectives and adverbs?" he asked, unfolding his arms and leaning forward in his chair.

"I think it's a disgrace and should be set down in the penal code," I replied, a small smile spreading across my face.

Max grinned back, nodding in approval. "You're on the right track, Martin. Now, sit down and concentrate because I'm not going over this twice."

Those days are behind me now. I did indeed cover the story, doing as Max told me to do, and hounded Jack Curtis endlessly. The story hit national headlines and a year later, I finished off the true crime book and a decent agent picked me up and found a publisher for me in Sydney who published it.

That was four years ago now. The royalties have dwindled which means I'm always looking for the next story that will supplement my income. As I mentioned before, the sweet poison of vanity is in my blood now and I love seeing my name, Martin Farrow, on my book in bookstores.

But the moment I heard how Peter Marshall died I should have walked away. I almost said to my agent, "Rick, I'm sorry. This isn't for me. I don't like the sound of it." I almost finished my drink and left then and there. But he was such a good storyteller – I've often thought he should have been the writer and I the agent – that once he started talking, there was never any question I wouldn't listen.

By the time he had finished, I was hooked.

Outside the rain continued to drizzle making the wintery skies as dark as a tombstone, and just as cold. But inside, the electric lights from three enormous chandeliers glinted on dark polished tables, plated silverware and glasses of ruby red wine.

The story as Rick told me over lunch that day went like this.

Peter Marshall had been working on a storyline for his own next book involving the same detective, Jack Curtis, who had left the police force after my book was published to start a private practice of his own. I had been keeping up with what Jack Curtis was doing by reading the Brisbane papers, especially a case involving a lawyer who killed his mistress which Curtis was instrumental in solving, despite the entire Surfers Paradise police force running around chasing their tales.

Rick had heard on the grapevine that Curtis was once again helping the police on a case involving child prostitution and biker gangs in Surfers. His ears pricked up because Curtis is not someone who messes about. Rick made it his business to follow him because Jack Curtis was worth the effort. Since I was busy with signings and finishing my own book, Rick got hold of Peter Marshall and told him to follow Curtis everywhere and that there was a good book just waiting for someone to write. And of course, Peter Marshall took the bait.

I read in the papers that the night Curtis caught the criminal was like a Spielberg movie. He and a female detective chased the criminal, with three young boys bouncing around in the back seat, through the streets of Surfers Paradise. The car crashed and the perp, (I love using that word), the perp died at the scene. Needless to say, Curtis was once again a hero who had saved the lives of three boys and Marshall elbowed himself through the media circus to get close enough to shove his business card into Curtis' hand before he was jostled aside by reporters.

While I nursed my beer, Rick told me that Marshall had been writing a new book in the solitude of Stradbroke Island and had caught the last ferry back to the mainland two Fridays earlier. I worked it out afterwards that it must have been 17th August. Rick found out later that it had been touch and go whether the ferry would sail at all. A gale had been blowing since mid-afternoon and the last few crossings had been cancelled. But towards 9 o'clock the wind had eased slightly and at 9.35 pm the master decided it was safe to leave the dock. The boat was crowded and Marshall was lucky to get a space at all for his car. He parked and then apparently went for a walk to get some air.

No one saw him alive again.

The crossing from the island usually takes about forty-five minutes but on that particular night the weather slowed the voyage considerably. Docking a 200-foot vessel in a fifty-knot wind is nobody's idea of fun, Rick said. It was nearly 11 o'clock when the ferry landed at Southport and the cars started up their engines. All except one: a brand new white Ford Escape SUV. A loudspeaker appeal went out for the owner to return to his vehicle as he was blocking the drivers behind him. When he still didn't show, the crew tried the doors, which turned out to be unlocked, and freewheeled the big Ford down to the dock to let the other cars pass.

Afterwards they searched the ferry with care: the toilets, stairwell and even the lifeboats. Nothing. They called Stradbroke Island to check if anyone had disembarked before the boat sailed or had perhaps been accidentally left behind. But again, nothing. That was when they finally contacted the Coast Guard to report a possible man overboard.

A police check on the Ford's licence plate revealed it to be registered to one Samuel Price of Surfers Paradise, although Samuel Price was eventually tracked down to his penthouse apartment in Broadbeach. By now it was almost midnight.

"This is *the* Samuel Price?" I interrupted, now fully interested.

"That's right," Rick replied, his eyes locked on the ice swirling around in his Scotch.

Apparently, Samuel Price confirmed over the telephone to the police that the Ford did indeed belong to him. He kept it for when he was holidaying at his house on Stradbroke Island for the use of himself and his guests in the summer. He also confirmed that Peter Marshall was one of several guests staying there at the moment. He said he would get his assistant to call the house and find out if anyone had borrowed the car. Half an hour later, she called back to say that Peter Marshall had indeed been at the house but had taken the car, intending to return to Surfers that night via the ferry.

There was nothing that could be done until first light. Not that it mattered. Everyone knew that if a passenger had gone overboard it would be a search for a corpse.

I watched Rick swirl his ice some more. He is one of those irritatingly fit people in his early forties who looks about twenty-five and does terrible things to his body with bicycles and canoes. He also knows that stretch of water well. He once spent two days paddling a kayak the entire sixty miles around the island and he knows the dangers without even mentioning the gale as well.

Rick shook his head. "No one could survive," he stated.

A local woman found the body early the next morning, thrown up on the beach about four miles down the coast. The driver's licence in the wallet confirmed him to be Peter James Marshall, aged 43, from Julia Creek in Northern Queensland. I remember feeling a sudden shot of sympathy at the mention of that dreary, unexotic town. The police took his corpse to the morgue and then drove over to the Price residence to break the news and to ask for someone to come and identify the body.

"It must have been quite a scene," mumbled Rick with a smirk. "I bet the morgue attendants will be talking about it for quite a while to come."

Apparently there was one patrol car from Surfers Paradise Police Station with a blue flashing light, a second car with four armed guards to secure the building and a third vehicle transporting a bodyguard along with the instantly recognisable man who, up until eighteen months ago, had been the Local Labour State Parliamentarian for Surfers Paradise who had been charged with being implicit in the child exploitation gang that Jack Curtis had infiltrated and who had been summarily fired as a result.

"I'm amazed this hasn't been in the papers," I commented. And I *was* amazed. Samuel Price, child prostitution and biker gangs sold a lot of papers.

"Oh, but it has been. It's not a secret."

And then I realised I *did* vaguely remember reading something. But I had been working fifteen hours a day for a month to finish my new book, the autobiography of a footballer, and the world beyond my study had become a blur.

"What on earth is the ex-parliamentarian doing identifying the body of a man who fell off the ferry from Stradbroke?" I asked.

"Peter Marshall," announced Rick, with the emphatic flair of a man who has flown a thousand kilometres north to deliver his punchline, "was helping Samuel Price *write his memoirs.*"

He glanced up at me from the wine glass on the table. "And that's where you come in to the picture, Martin. He was nearly finished and I want you to complete it."

And this is where, in a parallel universe, I fold my linen napkin, finish my drink, say goodbye and step out into the chilly evening with the whole of my undistinguished career stretching safely ahead of me. Instead, I excused myself, went to the toilet and studied an unfunny cartoon on the wall while urinating thoughtfully.

"You realise I don't know anything about politics," I said when I sat back down at the table.

"Did you vote for him?"

"Price? Of course I did. Everybody voted for him."

"Well that's the point. It's a sympathetic, professional writer Price wants to exonerate him to the world."

He glanced around. It was an iron rule of the club apparently not to talk business on the premises which was a problem for Rick and me because we never talked about anything else.

"Samuel Price was paying $1,000,000 to Marshall to write his tell all," speaky signs, "memoir on two conditions. Firstly, it was to be in the stores within one year. Secondly, he wouldn't pull any punches about the war against child prostitution and to show how Price was framed."

"Rick," I sighed. "I don't write political memoirs. You know my track record. Give me another footballer and I'm yours. But this?" I shook my head. "One million dollars? How much do you think he'll get back from this?"

"It's not about the money. This is about Price's reputation and his opportunity to speak directly to history."

"Sure. But the last thing he needs is to produce a book that nobody will read. How will it look if it ends up on the trash pile?"

I hated sounding whiny but I really didn't want to do this. Peter Marshall had supposedly committed suicide after researching the book and I had no want to end up the same way. Why would I want to go down that same road?

Rick was smiling as he spun his glass. "The fact is a big name alone doesn't sell a book. We've all learned that the hard way. What sells a book is *heart*." He thumped his heart theatrically.

"Then find someone else, Rick, because my heart wouldn't be in this. Everyone knows political memoirs are the black hole of publishing. The name outside the tent may be big but everyone knows that once you're inside you're going to get the same old tired show."

"But whose story has more heart than the guy who starts from nowhere in a family that is struggling to survive and ends up almost running the State Government? It was even rumoured he was heading to Federal."

"Rick. I repeat. I know nothing about politics."

"You can learn on the run." He smirked. "$1,000,000 Martin. Think about what you can do with that amount of money in the bank. A holiday. A new suit." His eyes travelled up and down the only suit I owned.

I leant forward. "I cherish my ignorance, Rick. Why not get Brendan Scott. He's a political genius and in my humble opinion he does what every movie star, or a rock star, needs. He's an experienced writer who knows how to ask the right questions and draw the correct answers out of the client's heart."

There was silence. I was shaking. Rick leant over and patted my hand. "That was a lovely speech."

Outside the freshly cleaned windows, traffic was backing up along the street and a light drizzle of rain was continuing to fall.

Rick folded his napkin and placed it gently on the table beside his empty wine glass.

"Let me finish my story. Price gave Marshall the use of his vacation house on Stradbroke Island so that he could work without any distractions. I guess the pressures must have gotten to Marshall. The medical examiner found enough booze in his blood to put him four times over the limit."

"So it was ruled an accident?"

"Accident? Suicide?" Rick casually flicked his free hand in the air and shrugged one shoulder. "No one will ever know. And what does it matter anyway? It's the book that really killed him."

I snorted. "Well, gee thanks. That's very encouraging. Maybe you should work on your pitch a little."

While Rick went on with his 'pitch', I stared at my plate of untouched food and imagined the former parliamentarian looking down at Marshall's cold white face in the morgue.

How did it feel? I always pose that question to clients. I must have asked it a hundred times a day during the initial interview stage: *How did it feel?* And mostly they can't answer, which is why they hire someone to write their memoirs for them. Most of them can't put a sentence together.

By the end of the book, I am more them than they are themselves. My job is to make them shiny and glossy when they never were.

To be honest, I rather enjoy the process of being someone else. It may sound arrogant but real craftsmanship is required to not only extract their boring life stories from them but to shape those stories into something that readers will actually want to read. It gives these people exciting lives they never realised they had. If that isn't art, what is?

"Should I have heard of Marshall?" I finally asked, coming out of my reverie.

"Don't pretend you haven't. You know you have. Before Marshall began writing books, he was Price's speechwriter in the early days when Price was still in office. Price was the member for Surfers Paradise for over ten years but before that, he was a local councilman, paying Marshall to write his speeches for him. When Price moved up the ladder, Marshall stayed with him for over a year, continuing to write his speeches and doing political research. It's why I chose him to write this book."

I sighed. "I don't know Rick."

Throughout the lunch, I'd been half watching an elderly television actor at the next table. He'd been famous when I was a child for playing the single parent of teenage girls in a sitcom. Now, he rose unsteadily to his feet and started to shuffle towards the exit. He looked as though he'd been made up to act the role of his own corpse. *That* was the type of person whose memoirs I now write. Not crime novels as I'd once dreamed of writing. I wrote about people who have fallen a few rungs down the celebrity ladder, or who had a few rungs left to climb or who were just about clinging to the top rung by their fingernails and were desperate to cash in while there was still time. I was abruptly overwhelmed by the ridiculousness of the whole idea that I might collaborate on the memoirs of an ex-parliamentarian, whom I knew nothing about except he was a suspect in a child prostitution ring.

"Rick, I seriously don't know…" I began again.

Rick interrupted me. "Price Inc are getting frantic because they're helping to fund this book." While he was talking, he pulled out his mobile and sent a quick message away. "And Price is sending the lawyer up who negotiated the original deal for him, the hottest lawyer in Sydney,

Serpent

a very smart guy by the name of Preston Crane. I have other clients I could put on this, so if you're not up for it, just tell me now. But from the way they've been talking, I think you're the best fit."

"Me?" I was incredulous. "You're kidding. I'm the best one you have for this?"

I chuckled but noticed Rick was serious, maybe a little annoyed.

"First off, we need this wrapped up in a month," he continued. "That's Price's view, not mine."

"A month?" I gaped. "You want a book in a month?"

"An almost completed rough manuscript already exists," he admitted. "It just needs some work."

"Where did they find it? If he jumped overboard, I mean," I asked.

"It was found in the boot of his car, under the spare tyre."

I raised my eyebrows. "You mean hidden under a spare tyre."

Rick shrugged. "Who knows. Okay. Yeah. Hidden."

"Have you read the manuscript? Why did he need to hide it?" I stopped to think for a second before continuing. "Who even knew what he'd written?"

"I'm leaving that to you. See. You're already working on it in your mind. If he discovered something, all the better. You love true crime, don't you?"

"But maybe his death had something to do with what he found," I suggested to him.

"You're being a drama queen. He got drunk and fell overboard. End of story."

He clapped his hands together like a game show host ready to start the show with the questions. "So. Taking it backwards, they want to publish in December so it's in bookstores by Christmas, which means they edit in October, print in November, which means the manuscript has to be at the publishing house by the end of September. The publicity tour has to be fixed and in place well in advance. We need to book a space in stores so that's it, you have until the end of September."

I snorted incredulously. It was already the fourth week of August and they wanted it by the end of September? I hadn't even seen the manuscript yet.

"I promise you, you're the best fit," he said straight-faced. "You're quick and experienced and they need to do something radical because this book needs to be on the shelves within three and a half months."

He reached down to his briefcase resting at his feet, scraped back his chair with a screech on the marble floor and pulled it on to his lap. His face was hidden behind the lid for a few seconds before he pulled out the typed manuscript.

"Take good care of this, Martin. It's the only copy. If Marshall was on to something this is a hot piece of property. Someone might do anything to get their hands on it." He wiggled his eyebrows. "Maybe even Random House." He handed it to me with a grin.

"You were so sure I'd do it?" I asked, lifting my eyebrows high on my forehead. Was I that desperate?

"It's a great opportunity for you and perfect timing, now that you've finished with the footballer. And the money will be good. The kids won't starve."

"I don't have any kids."

"No," said Rick with a wink, "but I do."

3

JACK

Saturday mornings and soggy sports fields seem to go together like acne and adolescence. That's how I remember my childhood, standing ankle-deep in mud, freezing my bum off while playing rugby for the school's third grade team and listening to my father yelling, "Don't just stand there like a warm bottle of piss. Call yourself a winger? I've seen continents drift faster than you!"

Now I'm doing the same. Not yelling at my daughter, Jazz, on the soccer field, but watching her play on Saturday mornings. At almost fifteen, she was a late starter to the game but it keeps her away from the computer and out into the reasonably fresh air. These days, you're not supposed to take too much notice of the score. It's all about having fun and getting every child involved. But tell that to the parents standing nervously on the side lines.

Truth is, I'm not much help. My knowledge of the round ball game could fit on the back of a coaster. All I can do is offer them a small level of advice for when they lose. 'No matter how miserable the defeat, always shake the opponents' hand and smile with the hook through your cheek.' Sadly, that happens too often with Jazz's team.

What I'm here for mainly is to show support and keep myself in her life, as much as she'll allow me anyway. She still sends barbs my way on how I was out of her life for two years. Sally, my ex-wife, left me to move to Surfers Paradise with Jazz while I stayed behind in Tasmania for those two years licking my wounds and waiting for a transfer to come up that would take me closer to them. I've tried telling Jazz that it was her mother who took her away from me but that falls on deaf ears so I've swallowed my pride and I'm doing everything I can to rectify it.

It was almost half time and the opposition had just scored again. Jazz's team, the Tigers, were trudging back to the halfway line, debating on who was going to kick off. Under my breath I was praying, "Just one goal." No such luck. By halftime, we were down four nil, the kids were sucking on orange quarters and the coach, a mid-twenty-year-old by the name of Annie Burton, was lying to them by saying the other team were undefeated and the Tigers were holding their own.

She put Josie, our strongest kicker, in goal for the second half and put Nicki, our leading goal-scorer, a term I use very lightly, as fullback.

"But I'm a striker," I heard Nicki whine.

"Danielle is playing up front," Alison stated firmly.

They all looked at Danielle, who has only just worked out which direction we were running, and she looked terrified.

My belief has always been that at this level, soccer is all about momentum, not skill. Once the ball is moving forward the whole game moves in that direction. "Forget about dribbling, or scoring goals or passing," I yelled loudly, my hands cupped on either side of my mouth. "Just go out there and try to kick the ball as hard as you can." To this, I received foul looks from both Annie and Jazz. I glanced over at Sally on the other side of the field in a multi-coloured gypsy dress and high boots that Stevie Nicks would have been envious of and she was shaking her head in annoyance as well.

What do I know?

My grandfather, a Major in the Australian Army, had played rugby with gusto. His son, my father, followed in his footsteps and my elder brother Adam, followed on the Curtis tradition in both sport and career. This is where I come in. I was expected to be a soldier as well, certainly not as good as Adam, but close to it. I broke the tradition by becoming a policeman. So when Adam was killed in Afghanistan, the Curtis legacy disintegrated and my father never forgave me.

He should have seen it coming. My failure to play Rugby with either passion or aptitude like Adam should have tipped him off. All I can say is my flaws mounted up and he always regarded me as his personal failure. I was the dropped stitch in our family's history.

In her gypsy dress and loose hair blowing in the wind, Sally looked nothing like my mother had looked when I played school rugby.

My mother had a pretty face with straight hair that she wore in the same style all her life that I could remember, pinned back with silver clips and tucked behind her ears. Sadly, I inherited my father's tangle of hair. If it grows half an inch too long it becomes completely unruly and I look like I've been electrocuted.

Everything about my mother pointed to the fact she was an officer's wife, down to her box-pleated skirts, plain blouses and low-heeled shoes. She could arrange a dinner party for twelve in the time it takes to boil an egg and was always a contributor to school fetes, church jamborees, charity fundraisers and funerals.

Every time I contemplate my mother's life, I am appalled by the waste and unfulfilled promise of it. At eighteen she began her Batchelor of Economics at University of Tasmania and at twenty-three had written a thesis that had other universities knocking on her door. What did she do? She married my father and settled down to a life of convention and endless compromises. I'd always hoped that one day she would suddenly toss aside her correctness and go dancing barefoot in a grassy park while singing at the top of her voice. But those were my wishes and certainly better than watching her grow old listening to my father rant at the TV screen about some crime that had been committed or simply just complaining. Before she had a chance to fulfil my wishes, she died of breast cancer a year after my father died.

For the first few minutes of the second half, nothing changed. The Tigers may as well be chasing shadows. Then the ball reached Josie and she hoofed it up the field. Danielle tried to run out of the way but fell over and brought down two defenders with her. The ball rolled loose and Jazz, being the closest, looked warily down at it. I bellowed at her, "Nothing fancy. Just take the shot!!"

Call me biased but what came next was the sweetest struck, curling, dipping, swerving shot over the goalkeeper's head. Shell-shocked by our new strategy, the opposition fell apart. Even Danielle scored when the ball accidentally bounced off the back of the goalkeeper's head.

Thirty minutes later, with a win five goals to four, ecstatic parents were wrapping their children up warmly to look like mini Michelin people and putting muddy boots into plastic bags. As I gazed across the field, I noticed a man standing alone with his hands in the pockets of a jacket. I recognised him instantly and inwardly groaned because I knew he was about to ruin a perfectly good day.

My day had started out wonderfully, watching Sam doing her stretching exercises and yoga at the foot of the bed. She is an early riser and combat-ready for work as a police detective by 6.30 am. She'd padded barefoot over to me in nothing but a camisole top and skimpy pyjama shorts and bent to kiss me.

"You had a restless night," she whispered letting her fingers tap-dance up my stomach until she felt me shiver.

My relationship with Sam is in its early stages. After moving to Queensland, and for more than two years, we were partners at Surfers Police Station until a case involving the murder of five ten-year-old boys on Mount Tamborine came up.

The events of that final case for me as a policeman play regularly in my mind like a surrealistic film filled with horrifying images. It was Hiroshima for my career. Days after solving the case, I resigned from the police force when I should have listened to Sam and Inspector Grayson who both told me to see a psychologist. That's my big problem. I never listen to anyone.

That case was four years ago, but it seems like a lifetime, and for barely four months now, Sam and I have been 'a couple'. There isn't a day I don't pinch myself to see if I'm dreaming.

"Come back to bed," I muttered, grabbing her wrist.

She laughed and slid away. "Not today. I'm too busy."

"C'mon," I begged. "I could grow to be a much better person if you stayed with me."

She raised one eyebrow and smirked. "A hard-on doesn't count as personal growth, Jack."

I'd stared in wonderment at the beautiful, curvy brunette as she dressed. White bikini pants snapped into place. She raised the camisole above her head and shrugged her shoulders into a bra. Next came a pair of trousers and a shirt she buttoned up the front. There is nothing sexier than watching her dress. It was almost as wonderful as watching her undress. She didn't risk giving me another kiss. I might not let her go.

I snapped back to reality as I walked slowly towards the man who had replaced me as Sam's partner at Surfers Paradise Police Station almost three years ago. I didn't dislike the man but if I was being honest, I was miffed at being replaced by someone as capable as this man. Call it vanity.

"What brings you out here, Detective Cavanaugh?" I asked when I reached him.

While I pulled my jacket close to my body in the cool breeze, he unwrapped a boiled sweet and popped it in his mouth, rattling it against his teeth.

"I need you to come into the station with me."

For a moment I wondered if he'd discovered my recent clandestine employment with Sandra Burton.

Sandra Burton is a heavy-set woman with greying hair pulled back into a ponytail with eyes the colour of freshly brewed coffee and she is the most unlikely person to run a secret organisation handling situations involving degenerate men who abuse children. She and her people take matters into their own hands when the police have their hands tied. She actively works to uncover these men, mostly people high up on the food chain, who think they are so smart they can lure young boys into online chat rooms with nothing but perverse and disgusting intensions.

I'm not a hit man by any means. But I know how to destroy careers. And so does Sandra. In a secret room behind a video game parlour, she has four men who infiltrate chat rooms disguised as young teenagers, along with a handful of others like me as dedicated as she is. They sit behind monitors and participate in the chats and more often than not, they uncover someone who is doing the same, only their purpose is to harm not defend.

After my last case, Sandra asked me to join her organisation.

I'm not one for theatrics or even feeling much of what might be labelled astonishment. I have seen a lot in my forty-plus years. While being a policeman, I have killed and I've nearly been killed. I have seen depravity that most would find difficult to comprehend and I have learnt over the years to try and control my emotions and reactions during stressful and volatile situations. These useful qualities have saved me from time to time. But when she asked me to join her organisation, I was shocked. Not just because she asked *me*, an ex-policeman, but because I was actually considering it.

What I did know was it would change everything for me forever if I accepted. My principles. My morals. My rules. My life. And I would have to keep it a secret from everyone I knew. Especially Detective Samantha Neil. Not just because she is a policewoman but because our relationship has moved from ex-partners, to friends and recently to lovers and I didn't want to lose her from my life. I instinctively knew she would not be able to accept my new line of work so I have to stay under the radar.

In the end, after much thought, I accepted and I have never regretted that decision. Which is why I have to be careful around people like Cavanaugh.

I stared past him and thought hard while he waited for me to answer. I was sure I hadn't been careless.

"How did you find me?" I eventually asked.

"Nosy neighbour."

Near the club house, Sally and Jazz were both warming themselves in the late-morning sunshine and watching us, Sally shading her eyes against the glare of the sun and Jazz impatient as ever with her hands planted on her hips. No one could mistake Cavanaugh for anything but a policeman and I knew Sally had recognised the look as well.

"And why do you need me to come into the station?" I asked.

It wasn't just curiosity. Considering my present occupation, it was essential I didn't put myself in a tricky situation that would be awkward to get out of.

He moved the sweet from one side to the other with his tongue before answering.

"I need you to help identify a body," he finally said.

I cocked my head on the side. "Really? Why me?"

"We think you may know her," he stated simply. "She could be a prostitute."

I blinked a few times. "A prostitute?" When he didn't elaborate, I asked, "And you thought to ask me? Why is that?"

I feigned wounded but my curiosity was getting the better of me now. I may dislike Cavanaugh but he was a smart cop. Nothing he did was accidental. Everything was planned and had a connecting web. He may look like someone from a Gucci magazine, but he had a decent brain inside that pretty head.

I sensed a piercing calculation as he sucked his sweet. "Like I said, you may know her."

His answer made me curious because for the life of me, I couldn't think who he was referring to.

"How do you know I know her?"

He sucked some more and I knew he was weighing up how much he could tell me. There's a fine line between getting my attention and telling me too much. He wanted me to come with him but he couldn't give away too much and risk compromising his investigation or the identification. I knew that for a fact. I'd been a policeman myself for twelve years and done the same thing hundreds of times.

I waited as his eyes stared over my shoulder for a while as he thought. When they flicked back to me, he looked resigned.

"We found a piece of paper in her handbag with a message saying *'If something happens to me, ring this number.'*" He began. He wiggled his eyebrows. "Have you checked your phone recently?"

I reached into my back pants pocket and pulled out my phone. The screen said *'1 missed call'* from an unknown number.

"That's from you?"

He nodded. "That's from me."

That stopped me short. My number on a scrap of paper in the handbag of a dead woman had implications, for sure. But if that dead woman was in fact a prostitute, and she had my number in her possession, there were very few names I could hazard a guess at.

"Come on," I said, tucking my hands and phone in the pockets of my windbreaker. "I'm a private investigator. A lot of people have my number. I'm not going with you until you tell me more."

He swallowed noisily, which surprised me. It caused me to let my eyes travel up and down his body while he thought about how much he could tell me without telling me too much.

Cavanaugh was a clotheshorse. At a glance, you would put him at around thirty-five but on closer inspection, there was a Tom Cruise innocence about him. There were grey streaks in his blondish hair, crow's feet around the blue eyes and lines on either side of his nose leading to his mouth, adding ten years to my original estimation. Under his double-breasted suit, the subtle blue pinstriped shirt and the loosened Calvin Klein tie, he has the build of a man who works out three or four times a week. Not big but muscular. He is the kind of man who never passes a mirror without glancing into it. He might stop at mirrors, but I doubt he ever missed anything going on behind him when he did.

But something subtle had changed. The clothes were the same but maybe it was how he wore them today. I know that sounds like I'm familiar with the fashion scene, and I'm not. But I'd seen enough of Cavanaugh to know something was a little off. Perhaps the way he was carrying himself. His usual style was loose and wary at the same time, with hard caution in his eyes even when he was smiling. A wolf in sheep's clothing. The sense you get from him is that you could go from being his friend to his enemy in a split second. It didn't matter either way to him, it was your choice, but once that decision was made, he would act accordingly and immediately.

Then it struck me. He was being pleasant today and it irked him.

He looked at me, arms crossed over his chest. "Don't be stupid, Curtis. You know I can't tell you more." He snorted air through his nose derisively. "I've already told you more than I should."

I knew that. He knew that. He knew that I knew that.

Serpent

His snarl wasn't quite evident but I knew it was inferred. My good angel and bad angel were having a battle at the moment and it wasn't looking promising for the good guys. I said nothing for a moment, letting the silence hang as I thought of a witty retort. It was on the tip of my tongue when he asked, "How many prostitutes do you know?"

Then it hit me. Christine Buchanan. Otherwise known as Elizabeth Delaney.

I froze, my mouth open in shock, as my blood paused in my veins. I could hear my heart thumping through my shirt and I had an unpleasant taste in my mouth. Suddenly, I felt a little light-headed and there was sweat on my face that wasn't there an instant ago. I felt it in my hair, on my forearms and behind my knees. Even the skin on my forearms tingled.

My previous case as a private investigator in Queensland had ended up with me chasing a lawyer in a car through the back streets of Surfers Paradise with three pubescent boys bouncing around in the back seat of his car. Together, Sam and I had exposed the paedophile ring and saved the three boys from further exploitation. The lawyer however did not survive. These boys were the latest kids to be abused and it was only with my connection to Sandra Burton that I was able to uncover the truth.

I kept my face neutral enough, although a long-dormant horror began to churn inside me. Christine Buchanan had been instrumental in helping me solve that last case involving the paedophiles. She had been a prostitute and overheard a hushed conversation concerning young boys one night before leaving her client. Putting two and two together, she knew she was in deep trouble if they realised she'd overheard them talking. Overnight, she changed her identity and became Elizabeth Delaney and began a new life. She changed her appearance, found a job and put her past behind her. Until that client spotted her in a bar in Broadbeach. That was the moment it all unravelled for her. It was Sam and I who stepped in and exposed the paedophile ring with her help.

After that, Christine joined up with me in Sandra Burton's organisation. She had names that were invaluable to Sandra and over the past year had worked as Elizabeth Delaney to expose more deviates. It was only Sandra and I who knew her true identity. Then again, I had a vague memory of mentioning it to Sam during that last case but I had no idea if she had told Cavanaugh. I had to trust she hadn't.

I spoke quietly, my eyes intent on holding his gaze as my stomach clenched. "Is it Elizabeth Delaney?"

He snorted. "That's *my* question for you."

He doesn't know her real name, I thought.

Blinking rapidly, I asked, "Where was the body found?"

"In bushland near Dreamworld."

Fifteen minutes from my house? A message? Was I being paranoid?

We stared at each other in silence, different thoughts running through our minds. I wanted to know when she had died but I knew Cavanaugh would jump on that and ask me why I wanted to know. The answer to that was I'd had a call from her over a week ago at 9 pm to say her latest client had not arrived at the proposed rendezvous, Star Casino, at 8.30 pm. I'd been held up in a meeting with Sandra and I told her I'd call her back later. When I tried later on, there was no answer.

"Let's not turn this into a pissing contest," Cavanaugh finally growled, impatient with my silence. "Like I said, I would like you to come in and identify the body." He smiled, all teeth. *What big teeth you have grandma.* "Please," he added.

"I have to say good-bye to my daughter first, Cavanaugh," I said. I spun around and began walking towards Sally and Jazz. "You can meet me in the car park if you like," I called over my shoulder. "I assume you know where that is too."

The walk to Jazz, who was now scowling furiously at me, took me several minutes through the damp clods of upturned, wet grass, giving me plenty of time to regret my decision to come today. Behind me, I could hear Cavanaugh silently cursing as he ignored my direction and made his way through the mud as well.

I reached Sally and Jazz, both wearing matching scowls, and introduced them to Cavanaugh.

"This is Detective Cavanaugh, Sally."

The walk through the field had ruined his shoes and mud was splashed on the cuffs of his expensive pants.

"I remember him." Short and curt as always. "He was at Joe's trial with the female detective."

The trial she was referring to was the murder trial three years ago of my friend, Joe Banner, for the murder of his fiancé, Shannon Connor. It's fair to say Joe is not a friend anymore, not just because I helped to put him away for Shannon's murder, but because Shannon and I were having an affair under his nose. The female detective she was referring to was Sam.

Sally shot me a look that I tried hard to avoid. "You were going to take Jazz to McDonalds for lunch. Is that off now?"

Beside her, Jazz was shaking her head angrily as if she already knew the answer.

Cavanaugh would have been stupid not to see where this was going. Ex-wife and 15-year-old daughter pushed aside yet again. I could almost hear Jazz saying to her mother, "I told you so."

I turned to Jazz. "I'll make it up to you, Jazz. Tomorrow, my place, and a trip to Dreamworld. How does that sound?" Tomorrow was Sunday and I knew she'd jump at the chance for a day at Dreamworld.

Jazz's scowled deepened but behind it, there was a gleam in her eyes. There was no gleam behind Sally's scowl however.

"I'm very sorry to intrude, Mrs Curtis," Cavanaugh purred.

Anger flared in Sally's eyes. "It's Nolan now."

"Sorry. Ms Nolan. But this is vital to my investigation."

I should take lessons from Cavanaugh. Sally's anger visibly subsided with his softly-spoken, earnest voice and puppy eyes. Even Jazz looked mollified.

Cavanaugh turned to me and placed a hand on my shoulder as if giving me a Papal blessing. "We appreciate your help here, Mr Curtis. Having you, with your knowledge and experience to assist us, will make things so much easier for me."

He even managed to sound sympathetic and I knew I'd have to thank him later. Maybe I should take notes.

We left Sally and Jazz chatting to a group of women and began walking towards the car park.

I glanced sideways at him. "You already know whose body it is," I stated. "Forget the garbage you said to Sally and Jazz, why do you need *me* to come in?"

He hesitated long enough for me to know he was at a dead end. "I want your take on it."

"It?" I don't know why I was making it deliberately hard for him. As usual, something about him irked me. It was mutual, I guess.

His voice hardened. "You were a profiler once. And a good one. Or have you lost that skill now that you're in private practice?" he smirked.

It was the smirk that did it. I stopped walking and turned to face him. "You were a country boy who wore second-hand clothes while growing up on a farm milking cows and collecting eggs. You played soccer, or some such sport, until some injury ended your escape plan and you needed another one. You entered the police force and came to the big city where you could buy all the expensive clothes you wanted. You like going to the gym and by the look of your hands," I nodded at his hands clasped in front of him, "you like to punch bags. Your hands are also calloused from gripping dumb bells and even your fingers are muscled. The clothes you wear are all Italian which would indicate you have a little Italian in your background, although you hate Italian food because it's messy. You're proud of your heritage, almost to the point of being arrogant, and you love letting the folks back home know how well you are doing." I hesitated. "You glance in mirrors and shop windows a lot checking out your appearance, making sure your image is perfect. You're smart, ambitious, vain, and you've learnt the art of getting what you want by observing and playing nice."

I was surprised at how cold and indifferent I sounded.

The colour had risen in his face and I knew I'd hit a nerve or two along the way.

"Very impressive. Is that a party trick?"

"No." I wanted to apologise but had no idea where to start. I'd gone too far and I knew he wouldn't forget it.

We walked for the rest of the way to our cars in silence. He had parked his car just a few spaces away from Sally's Nissan which was a few spaces away from my Audi.

He turned to look at me over his shoulder as he opened his door.

"Follow me. You'll need my clearance to get in the morgue at the Southport Hospital."

I nodded unlocking my own door.

"Curtis," he called out, still standing beside his opened door. "You were wrong about one thing."

"What was that?"

"I love Italian food."

4

MARTIN

We parted on the steps of the club. Rick had a car waiting with the engine running but he didn't offer to drop me off anywhere. It made me suspect he was off to see another client to whom he would make exactly the same pitch he had made to me since I was sounding hesitant. Rick had plenty of ghosts, which is what I was actually called – short for ghost writer – on his books. Book stores were full of books written by ghosts. What is the collective noun for a group of ghosts? A haunt? We are the ones who keep the publishing business going, writing for celebrities who can't put a sentence together. We are the worker bees who scuttle along the subterranean tunnels of celebrity, popping up here and there, never sharing the limelight the celebrity receives when the book is on the bookshelves.

"See you in a week with the first draft," he called out and in a puff of exhaust fumes, departing as dramatically as he intended.

I stood for a minute, undecided what to do. I was close to a stretch of Surfers, just on the outer of a trash-strewn strip of empty alleys, red lights, snack bars and the odd bookshop or two. I often drop into any bookstore along the way to see if any of my titles are still displayed and that was what I did that drizzly afternoon.

Once inside the first one I came to, it was a short step across the worn carpet to the Biography & Memoir section. I saw neither of my two books displayed so on a whim, I moved along to the Politics section.

I was surprised to find a couple already on Price, both by the same author. I took one down from the shelf and opened it to photographs: Price as a toddler, Price as Macbeth in a school play. Price in a football uniform. Price with his wife and children on the doorstop of a house. Price dramatically waving from an open-topped car when he was elected as state member for Surfers Paradise. Price with his staff gathered behind him. Price with the Premier and Prime Minister and then with several actors from Movie World. A bald customer next to me glanced over at the cover of the book I was holding and held his nose with one hand and mimed flushing the toilet with the other.

I flicked back through the photographs and went back to the staff photo. The caption identified Marshall as the slightly out of focus figure in the back row – a pale, dark-haired, unsmiling smudge in a group of happy faces. I squinted closely at him. He looked exactly the sort of unappealing, inadequate person that is congenitally drawn to politics and makes people like me stick to sports pages. And this was the person chosen to ghost a $1,000,000 memoir? I felt affronted. Insulted even.

I sat and read the manuscript in the warmth and solitude of the bookshop for a while, tucked away in a deep armchair, then bought myself a small pile of research material that would fill in a few gaps. With everything now tucked safely back in the satchel, I headed out into the watery sunshine with the conviction that Rick was right: perhaps I was the man for the job.

Unable to catch a cab, I walked along the busy road in the hope one would magically appear. My arm was aching from carrying the manuscript and judging by the weight, I reckoned it must have been close on a thousand pages. If so, I'd have to cut it down.

Eventually, I waved down a cab and settled myself in the back seat.

The cab smelled of stale sweat and takeaways. The driver was huge with hair lank with sweat which dribbled over the greasy collar of his shirt. He seemed to fill the whole front of the cab as if he had grown inside it, to the point where it was no longer possible for him to leave. The cab was his home, his castle and his bulk gave me the impression that it would eventually be his tomb. While he complained about illegal immigrants sneaking into the country and making the housing situation worse, I settled the satchel on my lap and thought as I stared out the window. Maybe this wasn't such a bad idea after all. Martin Farrow. Ghost writer to the Stars.

It had a certain appeal.

5

JACK

For some reason, the bald, thickset supervisor at the morgue took an instant dislike to me.

"Who said you could come here?" he growled.

"I meeting Detective Cavanaugh."

"I haven't been told. Nobody made an appointment."

"Can I wait for him?"

"No. Only family of the deceased are allowed in the waiting room."

"Where can I wait?"

"Outside."

At the beginning of the conversation, I'd decided to give him leeway. His sour breath and sweat stains under his arms meant he'd probably worked all night, maybe doing overtime. He was tired, cranky and probably hungry. A trifecta for anger. Plus it must be a lousy job.

I was just about to say something when Cavanaugh arrived. The supervisor began his spiel all over again but before he finished, Cavanaugh leant across the desk and picked up the phone.

"Listen, you lazy shit. I see a dozen cars outside on expired meters. You're going to be very unpopular with all your workmates when they get clamped."

I hadn't seen this side of Cavanaugh before; the nasty, bullying one. I'd have to keep this new one in the back of my mind for future reference.

A few minutes later, I was following Cavanaugh through narrow corridors with renewed respect as my shoes clip-clopped on the polished tiles like horse's hooves. Occasionally we passed doors with frosted glass windows and occasionally one would be open. Stainless steel tables stood in the middle of the room with a central channel leading to a drain. Halogen lights were suspended from the ceiling, alongside microphone leads.

It wasn't my first time to a morgue. In twelve years of police work, I'd lost count of the number of times I'd seen a dead body on a steel table.

Personally, I hate them. Sure, they're all white, cool and clean but it's the mixed odours of blood, alcohol, disinfectant and death permeating the cold air that I hate. Maybe it's the formaldehyde. Maybe it's the blood. But whatever smell it is, it infiltrates everything. It's a mixture of decay and chemicals unique to this world. But then again, maybe the thing I hate most about morgues was just the silence that has little to do with the absence of noise. It's a silence that comes from a failed heartbeat, a voice silenced forever and all the senses that have shut down.

While we walked, Cavanaugh talked.

"The body was found at 11 am yesterday morning. Fifteen minutes earlier, an anonymous call was made from a burner phone. The call came from the Dreamworld area from a caller who claimed his dog had discovered it. No name was left and we now believe that call came from the killer."

We pushed through double plexiglass doors and dodged a trolley being wheeled by a technician in green coveralls who totally ignored us. A white calico sheet covered what I knew would be a body coming from an anteroom with a large glass door. Through it we saw an operator with short blonde hair sitting at a desk and when Cavanaugh tapped lightly on the window, she looked up and buzzed us in. In the bright halogen lights, her dark roots were clearly visible as were her eyebrows that had been plucked to the thinness of dental floss. Behind her were filing cabinets set on either side of a door marked STAFF ONLY.

Serpent

Cavanaugh handed her a sheet of paper. She ran her eyes over it before asking, "Do you want me to set up a proper viewing?"

"The fridge is fine," he replied.

The heavy door unlocked with a hiss like a pressure seal and Cavanaugh stepped aside to let me go first. I expected to smell formaldehyde but instead there was the faint odour of antiseptic and industrial soap.

Trolleys were parked in rows and the metal crypts I knew held bodies took up the three remaining walls with large handles big enough to accommodate both hands.

I realised Cavanaugh was talking. "According to the pathologist, she's been dead for seven days," he said checking the label on a drawer. I was thankful for he wasn't looking at me. He would have seen the horror in my eyes. While in the car driving here, I'd backtracked to when I'd last heard from her. It was the call to my phone seven days ago.

He gripped the handles on a drawer and said, "She was naked except for a gold chain around her neck and her bra and knickers. Her handbag was beside her but we're still searching for her phone and her clothes. There was no sexual assault but I think you'll see why we've narrowed down the cause of death."

The door slid soundlessly open on rollers and my head instantly snapped back in shock.

Cavanaugh watched me silently. "As you can see, the left side of her face is badly bruised and swollen, her nose is broken, as were her teeth, and the eye is completely closed. She is almost unrecognisable. Someone gave her a real workover. There are twenty-one stab wounds, not one more than an inch deep. This means that the wounds were a form of torture rather than a means of killing her. They were slow and methodical but eventually her heart gave out. She died in agony, I'm sorry to say."

Raising my head, I saw Cavanaugh's face reflected in the polished steel and in that reflection I saw confusion. In his career, he must have investigated dozens of crimes, but this one is different because he didn't understand it.

My stomach was empty and I was perspiring in the cold. Nothing had been done to restore her dignity. She was stretched out with her arms against her sides and her legs together. Her dull whiteness made her look like a marble statue that had been vandalised with slashes of crimson and pink. Where the skin was pulled taut, the wounds gaped like empty eye sockets while others glistened slightly.

By now I knew the post-mortem had been done. She would have been swabbed and photographed and her organs would have been removed and weighed. Her stomach contents would have been analysed and flakes of dead skin and dirt from her fingernails would have been sealed within plastic slides. This once beautiful, vibrant woman had been reduced to Exhibit A.

"What made you think she was a prostitute?" I asked.

"We weren't sure but it's been a week and no one has reported her missing. You know how prostitutes move around, looking for work. They take off and turn up at a totally different area. If the girl had a strong network of friends and family, somebody would have reported her missing by now."

He had a point.

"I'm not sure how I can help you," I muttered, my eyes wandering over her face. "She resembles Elizabeth Delaney but who can be sure with so much damage to her face. Maybe that was the point."

We all have hidden talents but as Christine Buchanan, Sandra Burton had found a diamond hidden in her depths as Elizabeth Delaney. Her reinvention came at her lowest point after nearly dying at the hands of a client when she worked as a prostitute. It was with her help that Sam and I had uncovered the paedophile ring. After solving that case, she disappeared. Out of the blue, months later, she left a message on my answering machine, simply giving her address and no other details. When I met her, she was still beautiful but she'd returned to being a blonde and had her hair cut short in a practical style that was easy to wash and dry and didn't need constant brushing. She wore little make-up and she looked like a junior executive in a dark blue skirt and jacket.

As we talked, she told me what she wanted to do. She wanted to set up a drop-in centre for young girls on the street, to give them good advice about personal safety, health and accommodation in a drug rehab programme. She had some savings and had rented a house in the back streets of Ashmore.

The drop-in centre proved to be just the beginning. Soon she set up job search network and it amazed me at the number of people she could call upon for advice – judges, barristers, journalists, social workers and restaurateurs. I always wondered how many were former clients until I found out that one of the judges was her father. Judge Buchanan. Because of her previous employment, he wanted nothing to do with her but she knew his contacts.

It seemed natural to introduce her to Sandra who welcomed her into the organisation with open arms.

Although I could hardly bear to look at her swollen face, I was already collecting details. Her body and her looks had been her only means of income, so she had cared about them. She kept her hair short so that when she needed to, she could don a wig and became virtually unrecognisable. That was her disguise. Her fingernails and toenails were modestly trimmed and well cared for and her eyebrows had been tidily shaped. Her bikini line had been waxed recently, leaving a neat triangle of pubic hair.

"Was she wearing makeup?" I asked.

"A little eyeliner. If she was wearing lipstick, the killer removed it with his fists."

"I need to sit down," I mumbled shakily. "Is there a report I can read at the same time?"

Ten minutes later, I was alone in an empty office staring at the stack of ring-binders bulging with post-mortem reports and results from blood and toxicology analysis.

CITY OF SURFERS PARADISE CORONER

Post-Mortem Report
Name: Unknown. Post-Mortem No. FJ- 61 729

DOB: Unknown
Date of Death: Unknown
Age: Unknown
Sex: Female

Anatomical Summary

1. Twelve lacerations and incised wounds to the chest, abdomen and thighs, penetrating to a depth of 1.2 inches with a width of half an inch.
2. Five lacerations to the upper left arm.
3. Four lacerations to the left side of the neck.
4. Sharp force injuries tend to be downward with a mixture of stabbing and incised wounds.
5. Heavy bruising and swelling to the left cheekbone and right eye socket
6. Broken nose and broken teeth
7. Slight bruising to the right forearm that could be defensive wounds and abrasions to the right tibia and right heel.
8. Oral, vaginal and rectal swabs are clear.
9. An old scar on her left cheek.

Preliminary Toxicology Report
Blood drug screen: Ketamine hydrochloride detected
Blood ethanol: None detected
Sexually transmitted disease: None detected
Pregnancies: None detected

Cause of Death
Post-mortem x-rays reveal air in the right ventricular chamber of the

heart, indicating a massive and fatal air embolism due to the stab wound to the carotid artery in her neck.

The intensity of the attack took my breath away. I scanned the report quickly looking more for particular details rather than *how* she died. What I was looking for were clues that related to her death. Was there evidence of drugs? Recent sexual activity? When did she have her last meal?

The reference to ketamine hydrochloride in her bloodstream stopped me. Ketamine was an unusual drug, a special type of anaesthetic used for some minor surgical procedures. No one was too clear on its precise affect apart from the fact that it was similar to PCP and worked on sites in the brain affecting the central nervous system.

It was fast becoming the drug of choice these days in clubs while I was on the force, usually in capsules or ketamine crystals. Users described a ketamine trip as 'swimming in the K pool' since it distorted the perception of the body, creating a feeling that the user was floating in a soft yet supportive medium. Other side-affects included hallucination, distortions in the perception of space and time and out-of-body experiences. Ketamine could also be used as a chemical restrainer on animals, since it induced paralysis and dulled pain while allowing the normal laryngeal reflexes to continue. I had a terrible feeling that whoever had done this had deliberately kept Christine alive while they systematically and continuously stabbed her. That simple fact meant she hadn't died where her body was found.

I glanced at the crime scene photographs again to confirm my theory. There was little signs of blood around and under the body and with a carotid artery being severed, there should have been a massive amount of blood. That there wasn't meant she'd been killed elsewhere and her body dumped there.

I tried to calm my emotions by focusing on Item 9 in the Anatomical Summary. *An old scar on her cheek.* There was no doubt in my mind now that it was Christine Buchanan. The scar had been caused by the very lawyer who died in the car crash while driving the three boys away from a house where they were being abused in a paedophile ring.

Then came the photographs. I was a policeman for twelve years and seen countless bodies, but I will never get used to seeing a human being reduced to a bloody corpse. This corpse was worse than any of them because I knew who she was.

Cavanaugh entered without bothering to knock.

"I figured no milk no sugar."

He put the plastic cup of coffee on the desk and then lifted his own cup to his lips. "So what can you tell me?" he asked while he sipped.

"Sadly it's Elizabeth Delaney. The scar on her cheek confirms that for me, but she wasn't a prostitute anymore." I couldn't tell him Elizabeth's real name just yet. I had to talk to Sandra first. He would be angry at me for hiding the fact from him but that's the way it goes sometimes.

He frowned. "How do you know that?"

I had to be careful what I said. It had to be my observation I referred to, not the truth of *how* I knew. "The median age of prostitutes is sixteen. Elizabeth is," I hesitated, "was, about twenty-two, maybe a bit older. Plus the report says there is no evidence of recent sexually transmitted disease. Abortions are common with prostitutes but as far as I know, Elizabeth has never been pregnant."

Cavanaugh tapped the table three times with his knuckles. "Go on."

"Prostitutes at the high end sell fantasies. They take great care of their appearance and presentation and they enhance them. They have to. But it looks like she now kept her fingernails short, her hair short and her pubic hair was modestly waxed. She wore low shoes since there were no callouses on her feet from standing in stilettos."

Cavanaugh walked around the room listening to me talk, his brow puckered and lips pursed, deep in thought.

"She still took care of herself. She exercised and ate healthy food. She was probably still concerned about putting on weight which would have been a leftover trait from when she was a prostitute."

I heard Cavanaugh pacing behind me.

"I can tell you that as an ex-profiler, I don't think this is the first time this person has murdered," I said over my shoulder.

Cavanaugh stopped pacing. "Why is that?"

"Going by the number of wounds inflicted, he took his time killing her. That takes practice. It also shows enjoyment at inflicting pain. It definitely wasn't a crime of passion."

From behind me, Cavanaugh said, "I didn't take any pleasure from dragging you into this, Curtis."

I smiled my smartass smile. "Yes, you did."

He grinned. "Well, just a little." His eyes seemed to smile but there was no self-congratulation in them. The impatience I had noticed was gone.

"When you were a detective, the success of your career was based on how many crimes you solved," he said sipping his coffee. "Nowadays it depends on how few complaints you generate and whether you can stick to the budget."

"That was only beginning when I left," I acknowledged.

He nodded. "Nowadays they talk about pro-active policing. Do you know what that means?"

I shook my head. I had an idea but I let him talk.

"It means the number of detectives they put on a case depends on how big the tabloid headlines are. The media runs these investigations now, not the police."

"I haven't read anything about this case," I said.

"That's because everyone thinks the victim is a prostitute. If she turns up to be a politician's daughter, I'll have forty detectives instead of five. Then Grayson will take personal charge because of the '*complex nature of the case.*'" He did 'speaky signs' with his fingers.

"Why did they give it to you?"

"Like I said, they thought we were dealing with a dead prostitute. '*Give it to Cavanaugh*', they said. '*He'll bang heads together and put the fear of God into the pimps. So what if any of them object.*'"

"And now?"

"I'm keeping this little bit of information to myself for a few days and I'll work on it alone." His eyes never leave mine. "I don't want anyone knowing." He stared some more. "Got it?"

I had the feeling he was intimating Sam. He knew we were friends, but he had no idea it had progressed to a lot more than that. For a second I wondered how he could keep her out of the investigation if she was his partner.

Nonetheless, I theatrically zippered my mouth and pushed my chair back.

"Your secret is safe with me. Like I said, I didn't want to get involved in the first place."

6

MARTIN

The journey home took about half an hour. I had plenty of time over the next few days to think about how I would start the book. What I wanted most to do was to put my own personal stamp on it somehow.

I had taken a cab to lunch knowing alcohol would be included and I'd just paid the driver and was crossing the pavement towards my unit, head down searching for my keys in my pocket, when I felt someone touch me lightly on the shoulder. I turned and felt like I'd been hit by a truck. Some great force slammed into me and I fell backwards. I crumbled and felt the gritty wet stone of the gutter against my cheek and gasped.

One of the most inadequate words in the English language is 'winded', suggesting something light had caused breathlessness. But I hadn't been winded, I had been whumped and whacked and knocked to the ground, finally banging my head. My solar plexus felt as though it had been struck with a knife and stars burst into my eyes. Gasping for air, I was convinced I had been stabbed.

My fingers must have gripped the handle of the satchel with involuntary tightness because I was conscious, though in a great deal of pain, as a foot ground into my hand. Even in my pain, I knew the satchel was being wrenched from my grip. Then suddenly, the tension was released and the satchel fell back in my grip.

I was aware of people taking my arm and pulling me up into a sitting position and propped against a tree on the footpath with the hard bark digging into my spine. When at last I managed to gulp some oxygen into my lungs, I immediately started patting my stomach for a gaping wound and my intestines strewn around me on the ground. I inspected my fingers for blood but there was only dirt. Next I patted my jacket. I still had my wallet, my phone and the Rolex my parents had given me on my 21st birthday was still on my wrist. So not a robbery. It seemed the only thing the mugger was interested in was the satchel.

People gathered around me, producing mobile phones and calling for the police and an ambulance. I heard filtered comments about how the mugger had been hanging around for some time but the words came to me as if through water. The word *ambulance* however registered in my brain. The prospect of waiting ten hours in casualty waiting for a doctor, followed by half a day spent hanging around the local police station making a statement was enough to propel me out of the gutter. Instantly, my head swam and I was back, still clutching the satchel tightly to my chest.

Maybe a hospital wasn't such a bad idea after all.

7

Being brought in an ambulance with a head injury apparently gives you preference over others who have been waiting in casualty for many hours. The paramedics had me on a gurney rushing me through the corridors until I was positioned in a small cubicle and seen within ten minutes. I was told I had a bump on my forehead the size of an egg so I was rushed off to x-ray and back again within another ten minutes.

When half an hour passed, they must have realised there was no serious injury despite my dizziness. I was given a bag of white tablets and told to take one every four hours for the next two days but please *do* come back if the dizziness continued.

The casualty doors whooshed open as I walked towards them. I was moving now out of euphoria rather than shock, still clutching my prized satchel. I sat down heavily on a bench outside and pulled out my mobile phone.

Rick answered on the second ring. I could tell by the inflection in his voice that he was smiling.

"Rick," I said trying to sound natural. "You'll never guess what happened."

"Some guy tried to steal the manuscript?"

For a moment I couldn't speak. Then I mumbled, "Well yes."

"WHAT!?" His voice changed abruptly. "Jesus. I was kidding! Is that what *really* happened? Where are you? Are you okay? Is the manuscript okay?"

I explained what had happened. I explained how I hung on to the manuscript along with my wallet, watch and phone. Rick made all the appropriate sympathetic noises but the moment he learned I was well enough to work, the anxiety left his voice and happiness replaced it.

"This manuscript must be GOLD," he enthused. "Someone doesn't want it published. For your trouble, I'll make sure you get a collaborator's credit."

"On the title page?"

"In your dreams!" I could hear him chuckling down the phone. "In the acknowledgements. But it'll be noticed in the press. I'll see to that. A whole new world is opening up for you, my boy! Get to work on it asap."

"But how did they know about the manuscript?" I asked in a puzzled voice. "It's obvious that's what they wanted. You only just gave it to me."

I could almost see the shrug. "No idea. Maybe someone had heard about the book and was watching the publisher's office, then followed me when I left. It was in that big brown satchel. Whatever, Martin. The main thing is that someone doesn't want it published so it must contain something of huge value. The publishers are going to be over the moon when I tell them you just got mugged."

I snorted. "Gee thanks, Rick. Don't forget to tell them I'm okay though."

"Stop being a sook. You're okay, aren't you?"

Grudgingly, I said I was. "But what if Marshall's death has something to do with the book," I asked. "And it's beginning to look like he was. That puts *me* in danger, doesn't it?"

I heard a groan and a tsk on the other end of the line.

"I've glanced through this book," I continued. "It's a boring cock of shit." Even as the words were leaving my mouth I knew I sounded petulant. "Why would someone steal it?"

"You're not getting paid to enjoy it. You're getting paid big bucks to write the ending to it. You're making it sound like some conspiracy. That someone knew..."

"All right," I interrupted. "Let's leave it."

"... where you lived. Because you said he came up behind you, didn't you?"

"Forget it!"

"Okay. I'll see you in a week for the first draft. Get back to me if anything else happens." Then he rang off.

I stood there holding my silent phone. It was true. I was sounding weird. The trouble is once you start thinking down these lines, it's hard to stop.

But Rick was right. The line between suicide and accident isn't always clearly defined. The mere act of leaning over the railing too far whilst drunk was enough to tip you over. You'd hit the icy black water with a smack that would take you ten feet under and by the time you came up, *if* you came up, the ferry would be a hundred metres away. And no one would have heard him fall. That was another thing. The weather was bad and there probably wasn't another soul on deck.

So why was *he* on deck?

I walked back inside the hospital lobby and went to the men's room. The bruise and lump on my forehead where I'd hit the pavement was ripening, like some exploding supernova in an astronomy textbook. All I wanted to do was get home and lay on the couch with a bottle of Scotch.

I jammed my hands in my pockets, hunched my shoulders, and walked back outside. And that's when I saw Jack Curtis walking towards me.

8

JACK

All I wanted to do was see Sandra Burton. It was 2.30 pm and I had a lot to tell her. She did not know that Christine was dead and we needed to talk about the implications. I'd already texted her and asked if she was available for me to come over and she said to come at 4 pm.

I put my phone back in my pocket as I turned the corner and a tall man who looked familiar was standing outside the emergency ward with a giant egg on his forehead. The man hesitated, then began walking towards me.

"Jack Curtis?"

It was my turn to hesitate. "Do I know you?" His face looked familiar but I wasn't sure.

He shrugged one shoulder. "You probably don't remember me. I'm a journalist." His grin was sheepish. "Author actually. I wrote a true crime book on your Tamborine Mountain case. The five boys found in graves?"

"Ah. Now I remember. You're Martin Farrow. You followed me around for a while asking questions."

He looked surprised. "You remember me?"

I nodded. "And I read your book. It was pretty accurate. And well-written."

"Thank you," he said with a trace of colour rising up his throat to his face. "Writing the book was long and arduous, and took me almost six months to write because it was so complicated. It did, however, make me a bit of money."

When I grinned, he hurried on nervously. "Not much, but enough. This next one," he patted the satchel slung over his shoulder, "will be much bigger."

"Ouch," I laughed.

He blushed even deeper. "I didn't mean it like that. But my agent has big plans for it."

"Another true crime?"

He shook his head. "The autobiography of a politician. Or rather, ex-politician," he stated. "I don't usually do these sort of autobiographies. I don't know much about politics. I'm more into sports. But this is a 'tell-all'," he put his fingers up in speaky signs, "and the money I'm being offered is astounding. Thanks to your book."

His face changed expressions, like a light bulb moment. "Hey. I think you might know him."

"Oh? What's the name?"

He hesitated. "I'm not supposed to talk about it. All very hush hush at the moment." His mouth twisted. "But you might be able to give me some insight into its authenticity." He smiled. "And I think I owe you a drink."

I glanced at my watch to check the time. I had plenty of time to waste before meeting Sandra and if he was buying me a drink on the basis of how much money he'd made on the book from my case, it wouldn't be a big drink.

"No, you don't," I said. "But I won't say no." I didn't feel much like socialising and I wasn't looking forward to telling Sandra what had happened but I had time on my hands and I was curious.

"I came here by ambulance," he said. "Here's the deal. You give me a lift and I'll shout the drinks and food."

"You're on," I grinned.

Before we left, I took the time to text a colleague of mine by the name of Frank Fitzroy, asking him if he could meet me at Sandra's in a couple of hours as well. Frank needed to hear what I had to say as well.

The reply pinged back instantly with a thumbs up.

9

The closest pub to the hospital was The Grand Hotel at Labrador. Looking out over the ocean, you can just see Wave Break Island on the horizon, the water looking like dark blue ink.

The last time I was at The Grand was with Frank and a lawyer by the name of Karen Sawyer after Joe's guilty verdict came in for murdering Shannon. Saying Shannon was Joe's fiancé was a tad incorrect because Joe was still officially married to Sarah, a beautiful woman who was twenty-five years his junior with a taste for diamonds, the good life, and re-decorating. Stupid was a word that came to my mind when I thought about their marriage, but I would never say that to Joe's face.

But maybe stupid wasn't the correct word to use because Sarah wasn't just any woman. Sarah was stunning, no doubt about it, but it was her family connections that would have been the deciding factor with Joe. Her father owned a prominent law firm in Surfers Paradise and within weeks, Joe went to work for him. But instead of advancing in criminal law as Joe had imagined, even hoped, his father-in-law buried him in a corporate office and as far as Joe was concerned, he would never leave it.

This wasn't where Joe saw his career going and his health began to worsen as his drinking increased and weight increased. In that time, his weight ballooned up to 90 kilos mainly due to the amount of alcohol he consumed. Enter the beautiful Shannon, dark, mysterious and alluring. Joe never had a chance. He left Sarah and began living with Shannon. It was all downhill from there.

There's something disturbing about recalling a warm memory and feeling utterly cold, but that's how I feel when I remember the moments when I thought I'd found my soul mate in Shannon. Moments when I believed I had caught a true glimpse of what lay beneath that beautiful shell. And there were moments, when I thought the solution to Shannon's sadness might just be me. There had been a deep sadness in her and it had been delusion on my part to think that I could change everything and make her happy. It turned out I never understood or knew her at all. Everything she did had an ulterior motive.

That afternoon, after the guilty verdict, Karen, Frank and I were going over the result. Frank bought all the drinks and at one stage, a waitress bought out a platter of prawns, split and grilled, a wild assortment of antennae and legs sticking helter-skelter from the shells. It looked like some bizarre Klingon meal but we all dived in and ate like it was our last meal.

Most people find Frank Fitzroy a hard person to like. He has a reputation for being a weasel but no one has been able to pin him down to any crime. Frank was the investigator for the law firm where Shannon worked and one morning while I was having breakfast during Joe's trial, he sat down at my table and smiled at me, showing off crooked teeth with a large gap between the two front ones. His face was soft and round and his ears stuck out like handles. His nose was a blob and there were scars from stitches on his jawline. He was so ugly, I found myself staring.

At the time, I didn't trust him, giving him the nickname of Frigging Frank Fitzroy but over the past two years, he's grown on me and helped me out when there was no one else I could depend on. He's shifty, coarse, rough and crude but he has proved himself to be solid and reliable. Like most people, I started out hating him, I even had a suspicion he was somehow involved, but he soon became a trusted friend. As well as being an investigator for a law firm, he does part-time undercover work for

Sandra Burton as well, trying to rid our patch of earth from creeps who prey on children. If that isn't a true friend, I don't know what is.

Today, Martin and I were sitting on the same bar stools on the same veranda watching the storm clouds build on the horizon. Across the road in front of Charis Seafoods, surf lapped softly on the smooth sand and a dog barked as he shook water from his coat while pelicans drifted quietly on the water. The sky was beginning to darken and pretty soon, lights would be coming on, blazing yellow as businessmen with well-defined hairdos made their way home talking into their mobile phones with one hand and carrying their laptops protectively in the other. In my youth, laptops were a whole other pleasure.

Martin settled back a little on the stool as he talked, resting on the backrest and twisting his beer glass on the table leaving wet rings. Resting at his feet was a brown satchel which I knew contained his manuscript and between us sat a plate of potato wedges and nachos that we were eating with our fingers while sipping our beer. Around us, people were laughing and shooing away seagulls that were squawking nearby.

"This book I'm writing was originally started by Peter Marshall," Martin began as he glanced up at me. "Do you remember him?"

I shook my head, sipping my beer. The name was vaguely familiar but I couldn't place it.

"After your last case, Peter Marshall followed you around trying to get you to give him an exclusive for a book." Martin smiled. "He pushed his card into your hand once but you never called him."

"Huh. I remember someone doing that. That was Marshall?"

"Yep," he nodded as he watched the circles forming under his glass. "We share the same agent and because I was writing a memoir for a footballer at the time, Rick," he glanced up at me, "that's my agent," his eyes dropped to the circles again as he spoke, "told Peter Marshall to see if he would write a book on the case. He didn't end up contacting you because Simon Price stepped in first with an offer."

My head jerked up at the mention of Simon Price's name.

"Simon Price?" I didn't like hearing that name now any more than I had a year ago.

Serpent

He smiled smugly. "Thought that would get your attention. The book is Simon Price's 'tell-all' memoir about how he was wrongfully accused of being a part of the paedophile ring you uncovered."

I snorted. "He wasn't wrongfully accused," I reminded him. "He was guilty as hell."

Martin shook his head from side to side. "Maybe so but that's not the way he tells it. He claims he was innocent and it was he who suffered the fallout by losing his position and career. Guilty or not, that's his story. Price contacted a publisher who contacted Rick who contacted Marshall because I was busy. Must have been my lucky day."

The waitress who appeared to take our empty beer glasses was in her mid-twenties, dressed in a tight black miniskirt, a white blouse and sensible black walking shoes. Her hair was the brightest red I'd ever seen but at least it matched her nail polish. Parts of her spilled out of every item of clothing she wore, making her look as if she had swollen mysteriously sometime between dressing for work and arriving here.

Martin sculled the last of his beer and asked me, "Same again?"

I nodded absently, upending the last of my beer and handing it to the waitress.

There's a subtle sixth sense that most experienced investigators have developed over their careers. Most times it's a feeling that something isn't right. I have always taken advantage of these thoughts and impressions.

I don't believe in coincidences so seeing Martin so soon after identifying Christine's body in the morgue and then hearing that he was writing Price's memoir that denounced his part in the same paedophile ring that Christine had a big part in sent shivers down my spine. The odds on that occurring must be astronomical. What bothered me was they seemed connected in some strange way that I couldn't see right now. Could Simon Price be involved in her murder? Did he silence her in case she challenged him? He certainly wouldn't do it himself but that didn't mean he couldn't pay someone else to do it. But why would he put himself at risk like that if he was publishing a book that said he wasn't even involved? It didn't make sense.

"The same again when you're ready," Martin said, smiling up at the waitress. "My card's at the bar."

When the waitress was on her way to the bar, I asked, "What do you mean it must have been your lucky day?"

He leaned back in his chair. "Marshall was writing this book in Price's holiday house on Stradbroke Island. Right over there, at Amity Point."

I followed his finger to the shadow on the horizon. I could barely make out Stradbroke Island. In the distance, a foghorn sounded, and I knew it was the Southport ferry on its way to Stradbroke. To get there, you have to pass through a collection of other small, forgotten islands that grip the sea in hard tufts of mangroves, sand, wiry trees and rock formations. This ferry was one of two ways to reach the island, apart from a private boat – one from Southport, the other from the bay area of Cleveland. As the ocean roared, I noticed the sea had lashed the beach in recent days. It was strewn with shells and driftwood, mollusc skeletons and some dead fish half eaten by scavengers. Empty cans and sodden paper had blown down from the streets as well.

"His house is pretty secluded near Amity with no distractions," he continued his story, interrupting my thoughts. "About two weeks ago, Marshall caught the last ferry back from Stradbroke to the mainland. Rick found out later that it had been touch and go whether the ferry would sail at all due to bad weather. He parked and then apparently went for a walk after a few drinks to get some air. No one saw him alive again."

As I listened, I remembered a story I'd heard many years ago about the history of Stradbroke. Today, there is North and South Stradbroke Islands but apparently Stradbroke was once a whole island. Around the late 1850s, Dunwich had become Moreton Bay Quarantine Station and only weeks after this proclamation, the immigrant ship *Emigrant* arrived with typhus on board. Sadly 56 people died, many of whom are buried in Dunwich Cemetery. Around then, a stricken vessel by the name of *Cambus Wallace*, carrying a cargo of dynamite, ran aground 15 miles north of Southport and had been detonated for safety reasons. The explosion destabilised the fragile sand mass and when a strong gale blew through the area two years later, the South Stradbroke and North Stradbroke were created.

"Maybe it was suicide but they're treating it as an accident at the moment," Martin continued.

Serpent

He was intent on finding a nacho with the biggest blob of cheese on it so he didn't see the look of surprise on my face. Again shivers were running up and down my spine.

"I haven't seen anything about it on the news," I frowned.

"Not newsworthy enough, I'd say. A drunk takes a walk on the deck of the Stradbroke ferry and falls overboard." He shrugged. "Hardly page one news."

"Still," I muttered. "You hear all sorts of nonsensical things on the news these days. Surely this deserved some sort of mention."

He simply shrugged.

Curiosity got the better of me. "Tell me about the book," I asked.

"Like I said, it's Price's 'tell-all' memoir. From growing up in a poor household with four brothers and sisters, with barely enough money to pay for the shoes on their feet. A bit of a 'rags to riches' story."

"And people read that garbage?" I said reaching for a wedge and dipping it in sauce.

Our drinks arrived and we waited again until the waitress left.

"Some people do," Martin said, taking a sip from his glass and wiping the froth from his lip with a the back of his hand. "It's mainly out of vanity these people want their lives on display. But Simon Price has another motive. What makes this story different from the others is when he moves on to the paedophile ring you accused him of being a part of."

I snorted, then sipped my own beer. "Prisons are full of people who say they're innocent."

He smiled and nodded in agreement. "Some people's life stories are just lies. How could they be the heroes of their lives if they told the truth? They shade an incident here, invent something there, leave out a telling detail and change everything. Is there anything less reliable than a memoir? Hermann Goering was only following orders, he said. Richard Nixon did absolutely nothing wrong, he thought. Some life stories are just the greatest works of fiction."

"Maybe your job with this book should be to go behind the lies," I said.

"Maybe it should," he agreed. "I've had a quick glance through the book this morning while I was in a book store doing some photocopying," he continued, "and from what I've read, he names people who helped him advance his career. Later he names them as some of these people involved in the paedophile ring you uncovered. Some were prosecuted, some weren't. Have you heard of the Lachlan brothers? Andrew and David Lachlan?"

"I've heard a little about them," I replied. "Not much. Just that they're not the sort to take home to meet your mother."

Martin smirked. "Price didn't exactly say the brothers were involved," he explained, "but the implication was unmissable. He devoted a whole chapter to them."

I knew who the Lachlan brothers were. Their mother was the sister of a family in the western suburbs of Sydney you didn't want to cross if you wanted to keep the use of both legs. There were violent clashes with other families because they were all competing for the same limited amount of work and income. As the brothers grew, they learnt the business and moved out on their own to the Gold Coast with money their grandfather left them. Neither of them were young men, both in their mid to late thirties, but they supported Price when he was in office and by doing that, they advanced their careers.

I'd heard Andrew Lachlan was the brains while David was his go-for, doing anything his brother told him to do. Andrew was a smart land developer with plenty of cash and ambitions to buy up properties and build luxury blocks of units for people who also had plenty of cash. Which is where Price came into the story. Price helped him out by approving applications he made and in turn, Lachlan put money into Price's campaign fund.

"There's still a good bit of work to do on the book but my deadline is to have the first draft available for my agent in a week."

They say alcohol loosens tongues. I grinned because an hour ago, Martin told me the book was hush hush but after one beer, he had given me the whole basis of the book.

"Don't laugh," he chided me, misinterpreting my humour. "It's hard work. Instead of the usual six to twelve months to complete, I've got one month. It's an incredibly difficult task."

"I wasn't laughing at you," I lied. "I think they're expecting you to do the impossible."

"You're right," he agreed, mollified. He picked up a potato wedge and chewed for a few seconds before continuing. "Price couldn't state definitively the Lachlan brothers were involved in the ring and not get sued for slander or worse, but he certainly pointed a finger at them and their dubious friends, especially the ones in high places. Which implied that they were all tarred with the same nasty brush. From what I've read so far, Marshall was trying to find the right pitch to make and how to make it work by making Price look like a wrongfully accused angel."

"Price is playing a dangerous game if he's involving the Lachlans. I've heard Andrew is vicious. He's ruthless and violent and into gambling and prostitution, maybe some drugs. And he wouldn't hesitate to protect his family. He'd certainly not want his family name muddied especially when friends and family have skeletons in their closets."

"You're right about that," he agreed. "But it all comes back to Price stating his innocence," he said without a flicker of a doubt.

"Mmm," I nodded.

"I don't normally work this way," he said brushing salt from his hands.

He saw my questioning look and added, "Finish someone else's work, I mean. For my own book, I'd normally do fifty or sixty hours of interviews. That would give me a couple of hundred words, which I'd then edit down to a hundred thousand."

I knew where he was going. "But you already have the manuscript," I stated.

"Yes, I do," he acknowledged. "A partially completed one. But frankly, it's rough at the moment and it's not very publishable. No matter what my agent says, it's mainly research notes, not a book. It doesn't have any kind of voice."

I pulled a face.

He grinned. "I've only got a week to get the first draft back to my agent, so it's going to be tight. Marshall's manuscript isn't entirely wasted though. He's already done the interviews and I can ransack it for quotes and facts. The structure is good at the moment," he added. "I just need to add my personal touch to it."

While he talked, I glanced at my watch. I had about half an hour left before seeing Sandra. I couldn't be late.

"I'll open differently, though."

Martin looked like he was happy to sit back and talk all afternoon, sipping his beer while running through in his mind his personal layout for the book.

"I want something more intimate as the beginning. Something to catch the reader's attention. And every chapter has a dreadful beginning. Which could mean going back to Price this week with some more questions so I can plug in the holes."

I downed my drink and put the glass back on the table. "Martin, it's been nice catching up but I have an appointment I have to keep. Thanks for the drink."

As I stood up, I watched his eyes pop open. "What? You're leaving? Do you have a card or something? I thought we had a bit more time. I want to run through what Price said in his manuscript to see if it ties in with what actually happened."

He sounded like a whinny ten-year-old who'd been told to pack up the picnic early.

"I don't have time right now but maybe in a day or so when you're a bit further on into the book." I added, glancing towards my car.

I really didn't want to get involved in what he was writing. No matter what Price said, he was a criminal in my opinion and I had no want to read his self-serving story. What I wanted was to find Christine's murderer and leave Martin to handle Price's ego.

"Can I get a lift back home with you then?"

I hesitated. "Where do you live?"

"Near Harbour Town in Southport." Harbour Town was just a five minute drive away. It was in the opposite direction but I could drop him off and still make my appointment with Sandra in Surfers in half an hour.

I glanced at the egg on his forehead that was ripening. I was surprised he wasn't told not to drink alcohol in case of concussion.

"If we leave now," I stated.

Serpent

He downed the last of his beer and stood up. "Then let's go amigo," he said, slapping me on the back. "I'll just pick up my credit card at the bar and we're off."

I had an awful feeling I was going to regret accepting the offer of drinks.

10

Sometimes, you have a feeling you're being watched. There's no reason for it, just a sense that someone's attention is focused on you. The feeling is never the same for everyone but when it happens, there's no mistaking it. Maybe it was just paranoia but I kept glancing in my rear vision to make sure I wasn't being followed. With deliberate slowness, I took the back streets to Adventureland and kept changing lanes, but I couldn't detect any tails.

Sandra Burton's hideout is hidden in plain sight, tucked at the back of a video game parlour in Surfers Paradise called Adventureland. As usual when I entered, there was the digital ding-ding and siren sounds coming from machines as kids scored, together with the artificial noises of virtual planes being struck down and monsters dying under heavy armed assault. There were flashing neon lights, racing car simulators and claw cranes trying to snag generic stuffed animals from within a glass cage. Towards the back there was a ping-pong table and a pool table. Together, the noises were chaotic. And there were a lot of hooting teenaged boys taking the noise up another level.

I weaved through the room towards an area called Laser Maze, which looked like one of the scenes from *Mission: Impossible* where someone tries to move without crossing a beam and setting off an alarm. Walking towards me from behind the pool tables was Jimmy Croft with a smile on his face, dressed in faded jeans, battered Nike hi-tops, a t-shirt that had not felt an iron since it left the factory many years before and a loose corduroy jacket.

Almost a year ago, at the age of nineteen, Jimmy had walked into the game parlour and applied for work. Sandra took to him straight away with his easy smile and tousled hair. She laughed and said he looked like someone from a boy band. He was assessed, his background checked out, and was finally given the job. He had recently been accepted by Sandra into her inner sanctum as a go-between.

"Good afternoon, Mr Curtis. And how are you today?" he chirped as he fell into step with me.

"Well enough, Jimmy. And you?"

"Can't complain. Who'd listen," he grinned and shrugged.

As we walked, I commented, "Judging by the noise level, you're busy today."

He kept in step with me, his head and eyes level with mine. "As always. If we were allowed, I'd put in a Roulette Wheel. We could use the added revenue."

"You'd be using the money for bail, Jimmy. Gambling is not allowed."

"I know," he smiled again. "I'd get no work done either. I'd be trying my luck all day. Red is my favourite colour and twenty-one is my lucky number."

"As the ads on TV say, Jimmy, you lose more than you win. Is Sandra in her office?"

"She is."

We'd reached the back of the room. Behind a door marked EMERGENCY EXIT, two security guards stood with their hands folded in front of them, like they were protecting their family jewels from an imminent attack.

Jimmy stood between the guards and looked up at a surveillance camera. Then he motioned for me to do the same. Seconds later, there was a clanging noise and the door, made of reinforced steel, swung open. Jimmy walked through first and I followed.

A faint, sweet odour wafted up as I followed Jimmy. Something subtle. I'd smelt it before but couldn't put my finger on it. And then the odour disappeared.

The room we stepped into was nothing like the arcade outside. This room was sleek and modern with a dozen high-end monitors and screens on walls, on desks, everywhere.

Standing in the middle of the room was Sandra Burton, looking relaxed and almost casual. Behind her were four men sitting at monitors, hands resting expectantly on keyboards and headsets on their head. Beside her stood Frank. He nodded to me, a frown on his face, while Sandra turned and smiled at me, then turned to Jimmy.

"Thanks Jimmy," she said. "You can go back to your work now."

Jimmy nodded and smiled. "See you later, Mr Curtis," he nodded to Frank, "Mr Fitzroy," he added. He turned towards the door humming a song I recognised as an INXS tune. Something about us all having wings to fly. He grinned at me one last time and shut the door softly behind him.

Sandra was no fool. She could see by the expression on my face that I had something dreadful to tell her, something that was about to shock her. She turned and walked over to the four men sitting at the screens and tapped each of them in turn on a shoulder. One by one, they took their headsets off and turned around.

"Take a break gentlemen, please," she said, glancing up at the clock above them. "Is half an hour all you need, Jack?" she asked, turning back to me.

"That'll be fine," I replied.

She turned back to the men. "See you at 4.30 men."

One by one they stood, their chairs scraping on the floor, and left the room.

"Take a seat, gentlemen," Sandra said, pointing to a small table in the corner of the room with four chairs arranged around it. "Do you want some coffee?"

We both shook our heads.

"Okay. What is it, Jack?"

"Yeah, Jack. Wassup?" Frank asked, still frowning.

I sighed deeply before starting to fill them in on the events of my day.

Both had liked Christine and both regarded her as a friend. That she was brutally murdered would come as a terrible shock to them both, especially Sandra, since Christine would have been murdered in the course of her work for Sandra.

I started with the visit from Cavanaugh and the trip to the morgue to identify a body which eventually turned out to be Christine. I left out the part about being unable to identify her body without the autopsy report stating the victim had a scar on her left cheek. They didn't need to know the gruesome details of the torture. That Christine was murdered would be enough for them both.

As I spoke, Sandra fingered a wooden cross around her neck gently, rubbing her thumb back and forth along its length. I could see that at one time, it had been ornately carved but now it had been rubbed smooth by the action of her hand. Beside her, Frank simply stared at me, his eyes blazing.

I told them it was the night I'd been sitting here in the same chair with Sandra on the other side of this table discussing our next job. I was with Sandra when the call came in from Christine telling me the client hadn't turned up and that she was heading home. I left soon after that, calling Sam in the hope I could see her at her home. She said she'd see me in a couple of days since she had an early start at work the next day, so I went straight home. Sandra was my alibi for the that night but that was something I couldn't tell the police.

When Sandra spoke, her voice sounded thick with emotion. "All she wanted to do was help find these animals," she said. She rested her elbows on the table and dug her index fingers into the corners of her eyes as she blinked back tears. Frank on the other hand was coiled, ready to lash out at however had killed Christine.

The world around me seemed to grow silent as I shut out the distant noise of the machines outside the door to think.

"Do you have any idea of who it was she was meeting?" I finally asked.

Sandra shook her head. Tears were brimming in her eyes and had begun coursing down her cheek. Brushing them angrily away with the back of her hand, she said, "He gave us a fictitious name like they always do. But this guy wasn't interested in her, Jack. As far as he knew, she was the pimp who would lead him to young boys." She glanced over to the monitors. "His name popped up a few days before the meeting and she volunteered to follow up."

She sniffled as she dug into the pocket of her oversized cardigan, looking for a tissue. She found one and dabbed at her eyes as she spoke. "It was random. Purely random that she went to meet him at all. It can't be anything to do with the job."

As much as Sandra was denying the connection, we all had the terrible suspicion that if Christine hadn't turned up to meet the client that night, she would still be with us now.

I had to break into Sandra's grief. There was more I needed to say. "As bad as this is, there could be more to this than Christine's murder."

I tried to put the facts in order, starting with my lunch with Martin Farrow. I told them about Peter Marshall, his job to write Simon Price's memoir and his subsequent fall and death from the Stradbroke ferry. Marshall's death had brought Martin Farrow into the limelight since he was assigned to take over writing Price's autobiography.

Both Frank and Sandra knew who Simon Price was since both were involved with the case where he was named as one of the paedophiles. Both raised sceptical eyebrows when I told them Price's book was meant to exonerate him.

As I talked, I tried to work out the time frame and connection.

"It was perhaps five days to a week after Marshall's death that Christine was murdered and I have this strange feeling they're related somehow. It's just too coincidental for me. But the only link I could see between both deaths is that Christine was instrumental in my discovering Simon Price's preference for prepubescent boys."

"But why murder her?" Frank asked. "Revenge?"

"That's the only thing I can think of at the moment. Christine is definitely one of the jig saw pieces that don't seem to fit at the moment."

I shook my head. "Maybe there's no connection at all. Maybe it's purely coincidental. But it bothers me that both died within such a short time of each other and the connection is Simon Price." I turned to look at Sandra. "Add to that Christine's work here uncovering paedophiles."

Frank was shaking his head. "It don't make no sense, mate."

Serpent

Sandra was still sniffling. "I need to process this. I think we have to step back and just wait to see if we hear from the police. At the moment, they have no idea she worked here and that's the way it has to stay. I don't want any hints going their way."

Sandra was right. Cavanaugh was smart and no matter how subtle I was, if I pushed him for information, he'd grow suspicious and he'd start digging deeper.

"Marshall's death may get ruled a suicide so we shouldn't go down any other path at this early stage," I agreed. "It's a waiting game right now. We wait to see what Cavanaugh comes up with."

"Wot? We jus' si' on our 'ands?" Frank asked, clearly annoyed. Sitting quietly and waiting was something Frank would not normally do.

"We do just that, Frank. I'll go and see Price on Monday and reacquaint myself." I smirked. "Just to see if I can extract some information out of him. I don't believe he's stupid enough to tell me anything but at least, I'll let him know I'm aware of his book and its contents, just to rattle his cage. If I find out anything, I'll get back to you both."

Sandra drew in a ragged breath. "What's sad is we can't even tell her father she's dead. Judge Buchanan has a right to know, even if they were estranged. I'm sure he'd be proud of what she was doing." She looked at me with desolate eyes. "But we can't do that. We have to keep quiet until the police put two and two together."

A knock on the door from the four men returning ended our conversation.

"Keep me informed please, Jack," Sandra said as she stood to open the door to the returning men. "And keep your head down. Do NOT get involved. Take a deep breath first and remember your purpose and mission. Don't let anyone know about the organisation."

"You can count on it," I replied.

11

JACK
SUNDAY 1ST SEPTEMBER

Jazz was in an unusually good mood when I picked her up the next day. Sally was not.

"I want her back home by 5 pm. It's a school day tomorrow."

Sometimes, well most times, it was easier to just agree with Sally. "I'll take care of it," I stated as I motioned Jazz towards my car.

"You'll take care of it?" she sneered at my back. "The last Christmas of our marriage comes to mind." Again she sneered. "Remember the tree?"

My chore had been to buy a tree. A thankless task because the only truly well-proportioned Christmas trees are the ones they use in advertisements. If you try to find one in real life you face inevitable disappointment. Your tree will lean to the left or the right, It will be too bushy at the base, or straggly at the top. It will have bald patches, or the branches on either side will be oddly spaced. Even if you do find a good one, by some miracle, it won't fit in the car and by the time you strap it to the roof rack and drive home the branches are broken or twisted out of shape. Then you have to wrestle it through the door, dragging pine needles behind you while sweating profusely, only to hear the maddening question that resonated down from countless Christmas' past. "Is that really the best one you could find?"

I bit back a nasty retort but thought better of it. She'd pull Jazz back inside in a heartbeat and I desperately wanted this day with her. Instead, I bit my tongue and said nothing.

We were almost ready to leave when there was a knock on the door and Jazz looked at it with annoyance.

"Can you get that please?" I called to her. "I'm just locking the back door."

"It's you," I heard her say.

"Yes, it is," replied a voice I recognised.

"Where's your badge?"

"Would you like to see it?"

"Maybe I should," came the curt reply.

Cavanaugh was reaching into his jacket pocket when I rescued him.

"She's been taught to be cautious," I explained, despite the fact she knew perfectly well who he was.

"Very wise," he said, smiling down at Jazz. For a brief moment I thought he was about to ruffle her hair. If he did, I'd have to rush him to the hospital for tetanus shots after the bite wounds.

Instead, he asked politely, "May I come in for a few minutes, please?"

Jazz harrumphed, good mood evaporating, and mumbled, "I knew this would happen. I'll be outside with the dog."

I led Cavanaugh through to the fourth bedroom that I'd converted into a study and offered him a seat, which he thankfully refused. It meant he wouldn't be staying long. He stood in the centre of the room with his hands buried in the pockets of his coat.

He noticed my notes on Elizabeth Delaney scattered on the desk. "Doing some homework?"

"Revising," I said, pushing the papers aside. "I can only spare five minutes, Cavanaugh. We're on our way out."

"Okay. Where has he been?"

"Pardon?"

"You said the murderer didn't start with Elizabeth Delaney, so where has he been?"

"Practicing, is my suspicion," I stated.

"You think he could have done something like this before?"

I nodded. "He may have. If he has killed before, it was done quietly and unobtrusively. For some reason however, with this one, he wanted to bring himself out into the open. He wanted to draw attention to his work. Perhaps his previous killings haven't been recognised."

Cavanaugh turned and wandered towards the window that looked out onto my withering garden beds. I wanted to ask if he'd found new information but he interrupted me.

"Is he going to kill again?"

I didn't want to answer because hypothetical questions are dangerous. Sandra's words echoed in my head. *Keep your head down. Do NOT get involved. Take a deep breath first and remember your purpose and mission. Don't let anyone know about the organisation.*

He sensed me pulling back and turned to face me. I had to say something.

"If I had to gamble, I'd say he's been planning his next move carefully. The next time, unless you catch him first, he's really going to make an impact."

"How can you be sure?"

"I can't. But his actions weren't out of control or consumed by anger or desire. He was calm when he killed her, going by the number of wounds before she died. Maybe I'm wrong," I shrugged. "Maybe he had a motive for killing Elizabeth. Maybe she knew something about him he wanted to hide."

Something in my brain was wriggling about, pushing its way forward. But as hard as I tried, I couldn't quite make out what it was.

"Where are the other victims?" he pushed. "Why haven't we found them? Why her?"

"Maybe you just haven't established a link yet."

He flinched, perhaps resenting the inference that he'd missed something important.

"You're looking for clues in the method," I added. "But they can only come from comparing crimes. Find another victim and you may find a pattern."

He ground his teeth in silence as though he was wearing them down.

"He knows the area," I continued. "It took opportunity and knowledge to dump Elizabeth's body where it was found. He knew there were no houses overlooking that part of Coomera and he knew when the area would be deserted."

"So he lives locally?"

"Either that or used to."

I could tell he was trying to see how the facts supported a theory he had, trying them out for size.

"But why choose such a public place?" he asked. "He could have hidden her in the middle of nowhere."

Again the wriggle in my brain. "I think it's because he wasn't hiding her. He let you have her."

"Why?" he frowned.

"Maybe he's giving you a sneak preview. Maybe he's proud of himself."

He nodded as he considered what I'd said. "Give me your take on the man who killed her," he asked finally.

I tried to look shocked. "Why ask me? You're the detective."

"Humour me," he said.

I nodded. "Okay." I glanced down at my notes and thought for a few seconds. "Okay. I'd say you're dealing with a sexual psychopath," I began. "Elizabeth's murder was an exhibition of corrupt lust, meant to shock us."

"But there was no signs of sexual assault," he reminded me.

"You can't think in terms of normal rape or sex crime. This is a far more extreme example of deviant sexuality. This man is consumed by a desire to dominate and inflict pain. He fantasises about taking, restraining, dominating, torturing and killing. At least some of these fantasies will mirror almost exactly what happened to her."

He snorted. "You make it sound like a bloody *Saw* movie."

"Think about it," I said. "Elizabeth was street wise. She relied on her instincts on who she could trust and who she should avoid. And yet, he managed to entice her to go with him. He didn't want a quick and violent session in a dark alley and then have the need to silence her so she couldn't identify him. Instead he chose to break her, to destroy her willpower until she became a compliant, terrified plaything. Even that wasn't enough for him. He wanted the ultimate in control, to bend her completely to his will."

The wall clock ticked loudly in the silence as I thought. "I think he knew who she was and he wanted something. Information, more than likely, and he almost succeeded."

"What do you mean almost?" Cavanaugh asked.

"He almost succeeded but Elizabeth wasn't entirely broken. She still had a spark of defiance left. He stabbed her multiple times to make her talk, wounds that were just deep enough to cause intense pain, but I don't think she talked. That last cut to her carotid artery in her neck was his final cut made in anger. It's what caused the embolism. She was dead within minutes."

He shook his head, a quizzical look on his face. "How can you know all that?"

"After twelve years in the force I've come across every type of scum there is." I pushed the notes further away. "This man you're looking for is socially inept and sexually immature."

"Sounds like your basic teenager."

"No. He isn't a teenager. He's older. A lot of young men start out like this but every so often one emerges who blames someone else for his loneliness and sexual frustration. This bitterness and anger grows with each rejection. Sometimes he'll blame a particular person. Other times he will hate an entire group of people."

"Does he hate women?"

"Possibly. But I think it's more likely he hates a particular sort of woman. He fantasises about punishing her and it gives him pleasure. A person doesn't suddenly become a fully-fledged sadist overnight. And certainly not one this skilful. This comes with experience. I don't think he started with Elizabeth."

"What's his motivation for killing her?"

"I'd say more revenge and control."

Cavanaugh was staring hard at me. "So who am I looking for?"

"I'd say he is above average intelligence, physically strong, but mentally stronger. He has managed to keep his emotions and deviances in check and has successfully been able to separate areas of his life without his friends, colleagues and family knowing what's going on in his head. His self-assurance amazes me. There was no sign of anxiety or first-time nerves with this crime. He took his time. Once again, I think Elizabeth may have known something and he wanted to know how much she knew."

Cavanaugh crossed his arms and jammed them under his armpits. Something I'd never seen him do before. It looked sloppy somehow. Nervous.

"There's something you're not telling me," I stated, watching his face contort and his lips compress.

Seconds ticked while he breathed in and out, watching my face.

"What?" I asked eventually.

"You asked if there were other victims." He stared at me without continuing.

I waited.

"We have another body."

My eyes flew open.

He put his hands up in the air to silence me before I spoke. "Not a woman," he quickly added. "A man." He shrugged. "It may not even be related. He died about a week before Elizabeth died but discovering Elizabeth Delaney's body so soon afterwards makes me think they could be somehow related."

Again I waited. It was like pulling teeth waiting for him to work out what he could tell me.

"And?" I urged. "Is there a connection?"

He bit his lip. "I don't know," he admitted reluctantly.

I snorted. "Then why are you here? What's the point of this visit, Cavanaugh? Your time is almost up."

He walked to the empty chair on the opposite side of my desk and sat down heavily, his shoulders dropping. "Apparently this man was writing a book for a well-known politician. A tell-all autobiography. His body was found washed up near Southport after he apparently jumped from a ferry coming back from Stradbroke."

This is probably where I should have told him about Martin and the book. I should have *'spilled the beans'* as James Cagney once said. I should have, but I didn't. I wanted to hear more. I wanted to hear what he knew. I wanted Cavanaugh to spill his own beans.

"And you don't think it was suicide?" I prodded.

"He was being paid $1,000,000 to write this book. And he was almost finished apparently. The money was almost in his bank account. But instead, he jumped. There was no note and no reason to jump." He shrugged. "He had a load of alcohol in his system but I don't think that was the cause for him to fall overboard."

"So where's the connection?" I asked.

"The guy who paid him was Samuel Price."

I feigned surprise as he grinned his wolf smile again. "That's right. Price was one of the paedophiles named in your last case. Apparently he intends this book to exonerate himself and possibly implicate others. From where I'm standing, that makes everyone in the book a suspect."

"And where's this book now?" I asked. I knew full well it was in the satchel Martin carried around like a bible but I wanted to know if Cavanaugh knew.

"It was claimed by Samuel Price's lawyer. It was hidden in Price's car making it his property. We tried to claim it as evidence but his lawyer is smart. A judge signed a release form and Price now has it in his possession."

"And being the prostitute who uncovered the paedophile ring, it connects Elizabeth to his murder," I stated unnecessarily.

He nodded. "If this gets out, I'll have hyenas all over me asking questions and shoving cameras in my face. It'll be a media circus."

"And Grayson will take over."

"And Grayson will definitely take over."

"And take the credit."

"Oh, he'll let me assist him, have no doubt about that. But yes, he'll take the credit."

"If he takes over," I began, playing along with him, "he'll probably get a promotion and you'll be left counting paper clips at the station."

"Now we're on the same page," he growled.

"So where does Sam fit in?"

The thought had been running through my head with his string of 'I's' and the 'me's'. There had been no mention of Sam and as far as I knew, she was still his partner.

Serpent

He stopped fiddling with his jacket. "Pardon?"

He was stalling. I watched his eyes roam around the room as he buttoned up his jacket, wondering how much to tell me.

"Your partner? Remember Sam? Have you mentioned all this to her yet?"

Then it occurred to me. Sam hadn't said a word to me. I know she shouldn't anyway, but you can always tell when someone is keeping something back and is itching to say something. Being her ex-partner, I knew her better than anyone. And with our new relationship, I had stepped further up on the ladder. But there was nothing. No itching. No hiding.

"Have you even told her about this visit to me today? And on a weekend?"

"There are things I am not at liberty to tell you."

"Bullshit! You haven't told her."

I couldn't believe this. Here he was complaining about Grayson taking the credit for uncovering the identity of the body and he was doing the exact same thing to Sam. She should have been in on all this information from the very beginning.

"Where is she now, Cavanaugh? Why isn't she here?"

"She's following up on other leads."

That was bullshit and he knew it. "You want all the credit," I stated.

Cavanaugh's iceberg demeanour was in place as he stood and walked towards the door.

"I'm right aren't I?" I called to him. "Answer me."

The wolf grin was back when he turned to look at me. "When did you last see Elizabeth Delaney?" he asked.

I hesitated. He'd already asked me this yesterday so I had to be careful. "You know as well as I do. She led us to the paedophile who was holding those three boys. You were there. That was the last time."

He pulled out his notebook and began writing something down.

Prickles of apprehension ran down my spine.

"Why are you writing that down?"

He looked up. "I'm not making anything of it. It's just information. You and I both collect information until two or three things fit together."

Turning the pages of his notebook, he smiled benignly. "It's amazing what you can find out about people these days. Married. One child. No religious affiliation. Educated in Hobart. Twice caught speeding on the M1 and one outstanding parking ticket. Father was a soldier, as was his father before him. Elder brother killed in Afghanistan. Ex-wife's father died in 1994. Aunt died in a house fire. You have private insurance and your car registration is due on Wednesday." He grinned. "I haven't bothered with your tax returns but I'd say you went into private practice because you have no other means of income to afford this house of yours in Coomera." He stopped. "Not too far from where Elizabeth's body was found."

He was getting to the point now. The whole spiel was a message to me. He wants me to know what he is capable of.

His voice grew quiet. "If I find you've withheld information from my murder investigation, I'll send you to jail."

He closed the notebook and slid it into his pocket.

"Thank you for your patience, Mr Curtis." He pulled his jacket closed as he stood in the doorway. "And thank you for your help. I'll be in touch."

Then he was gone, leaving me with Jazz standing in the hallway clutching a small, carved wooden cat.

"What's that?" I asked.

"My lucky cat."

"It's a lovely piece. Where'd you get it?"

"Mum's getting some work done in the garden at home. The guy who's doing it gave it to me." She tucked it into her hip pocket. "Can we go now?"

"You bet," I smiled, determined to put Cavanaugh's visit to the back of my mind. "Get your backpack and we're off."

12

MONDAY 2ND SEPTEMBER

There were some big homes overlooking the waterways 1 kilometre inland from Broadbeach, all with gardens sloping down to private moorings. I parked on the road in front of the house I knew to be Simon Price's and looked at the row after row of twisted, dwarfish, ash-coloured trees. A few curled, brown leaves were the only evidence they were still alive. There is nothing more depressing than deciduous trees in winter, I decided.

I walked up to the closed, ornate gate overlooking the road and glanced up at a CCTV camera attached to a post just as a man carrying a clipboard materialised through the front door. He took his time walking towards me, giving me the once over as he sauntered along. The scowl he gave me made him look like he had been assigned to guard one of the Queen's grandchildren in the Caribbean only to find himself here at the last minute instead. As he walked, I could hear the surf pounding on the beach in the distance.

"Can I help you?" he asked from behind the gate.

"I'd like to see Mr Price please."

"Do you have an appointment?"

"No. But I'm sure he'll see me. Please tell him Jack Curtis is here to see him. Detective Jack Curtis," I lied.

He reached behind his back and took a walkie-talkie from a pocket. He showed me his back for a while as he spoke.

Seconds later, he turned back to me and took a remote from his inside pocket of his jacket and immediately the gate whirred open.

"You'll be met at the front door," he grunted.

From somewhere inside, a woman appeared at the front door. She was in her early twenties and slim, her face so caked with makeup that the floor of the Amazon jungle probably saw more natural light. Her deep blue eyes were so made up, they looked like sapphires, making her olive skin and dyed blond hair stand out. She stood blinking nervously, her back ramrod straight.

As I reached her, she smiled up at me with a bright smile, "I'm Amelia Jensen. Mr Price's personal assistant. Can I help you?"

"I'd like to see Mr Price, please," I repeated.

Amelia expanded her smile a fraction further, creating tiny fissure in her smooth cheeks. "Do you have an appointment?"

"No. Just tell him Jack Curtis is here to see him. He'll see me."

Her smile faltered a little at the intensity of my voice. "Mr Price is too busy to take walk-ins," she murmured.

I turned and made a point of slowly looking around the empty parking area before turning my attention back to her. "Looks like the perfect time to call on Mr Price, by the look of it," I smiled.

Amelia's smile hardened a little. "Just because the parking area is empty doesn't mean…"

"Please just let him know I'll wait here until he is able to see me," I interrupted. "This will only take a minute and I am sure he'll want to hear what I have to tell him."

Her nostrils flared briefly before she turned abruptly and closed the door behind her.

I stood for a minute glancing around at the building and the gardens surrounding it. It was two storeys high with a long, sloping roof I knew would hold enough solar panels to light up the entire Gold Coast. A pair of square brick chimneys of the sort you'd see in a crematorium dominated the roof line and I wondered why someone would need a fire place, let alone two of them, in the sub-tropical climate of Queensland, even in

Serpent

winter. The building was rendered in a pale grey with windows that would have been floor to ceiling inside and the front door was made of solid wood with ornate brass fittings that Henry VIII would have admired. With the sentry at the gate, the greyness of the building and the desolate look of the trees, it somehow resembled something from a Grimm fairy tale. A wolf's lair perhaps.

I turned back to the door and stepped forward to knock just as it opened, causing Amelia Jensen to start a little and step backwards. Her face had paled slightly and her smile had faded after speaking to Price but she held herself together remarkably well, all things considered.

"He is too busy to see you at the moment but he can spare you five minutes later in the week."

"Is that what he really said?"

She blushed slightly. "Not quite."

"Are you new here?"

"I've been here a month."

"Did Price select you personally?"

She looked puzzled. "Ye-es."

"If I were you I'd get another job. He's a deviant."

I pushed my way past her, forcing her to press her back against the door.

"You can't come in here," she squeaked. Behind me I could hear swishing nylons against her thighs as she tried to catch up with me.

The house, I assumed, was arranged so that all the bedrooms were on the first floor, with an open area on the ground floor that would include the kitchen, dining room, living room and games room. Maybe even a library. As I turned a corner, the back wall made entirely of glass, appeared to be facing the back yard and an enormous swimming pool. A path led down to the pontoon where a yacht the size of my house sat waiting. To my left was a closed door. My bet was Price was in that room.

"Please, you can't..." Amelia Jensen pleaded as I opened the door, her voice going up an octave.

The study was huge with a ceiling at least five metres high. Through another doorway was an adjoining sitting room with a similar view. Along one wall, shelves full of books were lined up with the spines facing outwards. A few of the books I recognised as autobiographies of politicians and I'm sure the urge for his own book to be included in the wall of fame must have been immense. I stood in the doorway for a few seconds running my eyes over them. No pictures of Mrs Price or little Prices anywhere.

There were two desks, a little one in the corner where Amelia could sit in front of a computer, and a larger one, entirely clear except for a photograph of him on a yacht.

Behind the large desk sat Simon Price, living proof that you can't be too thin or too rich. He had not changed much in the year since I last saw his face in the newspapers, except now his beard could use a trimming and his Armani shirt didn't quite fit his frame as it once had. He didn't look happy to see me as he eyed me with contempt.

"I'm surprised you have the gall to show your face here after what you put me through," he growled. "Get out! You lied to security. You're not a policeman anymore and the force is probably better for your absence."

He reached for the intercom button but Amelia had already entered behind me.

"I told him he couldn't..." she started before Price put the palm of his hand in the air, silencing her.

"I didn't put you through anything," I stated. "The police did that."

"But it was you who opened the way for them."

With the high ceiling, his words echoed slightly as if his voice was the voice of God.

I stared at him for a second. "And you think exposing animals who abuse children was a mistake?"

"That's not what I'm saying. What I *am* saying is that I am not one of those animals, as you put it."

I smiled. "Hence the book."

He knew he was wondering what to say without giving anything away. His eyes squinted at me as he struggled for words. Eventually he said, "What book?"

"Come on, Price. I know about your autobiography," I smiled wider, enjoying his discomfort. "And I know you want to clear your name because I've spoken to Martin Farrow."

I watched as his anger rose and his face lost colour. "YOU WHAT?!" he shouted.

I shrugged.

Now he was apoplectic. "You are NOT allowed to do that!"

"Do what?"

"Talk to Martin!"

"What? I can't talk to a journalist? I didn't say he told me anything. Just that I spoke to him. But going by your reaction here, Martin just may have a few stories to tell me. Maybe we should have a few more drinks to compare notes."

I'd just cracked my halo. Once again my bad angel had won and the holy ground I was standing on was burning my feet.

"I'll sue!" he spluttered some more.

Why does everyone say that?

Amelia Jensen shuffled her feet nervously and pressed her back further against the closed door. She was probably wondering if she still had a job after my visit.

"Calm down," I said, my hands in the air. "I'm not here to discuss the book. Whatever is in it is your business and Martin's. I'm only here as a courtesy."

He spluttered a little but visibly calmed.

"I know Martin is the second writer you've employed to write your book and I know the first writer died."

When he didn't say anything, I continued. "What you don't know is that the prostitute who opened that particular Pandora's box a year ago has been found murdered. The police are investigating but as of today, they have no suspects."

"Are you suggesting..." he spluttered.

"I am not," I sighed. "What I'm doing here is asking you a simple question. Do you have any idea who may be desperate enough to kill the young woman, since you seem to be the connecting link."

"I have no idea what you mean. There is nothing in the book that would incriminate anyone. Including this young woman you say was found murdered."

For a few seconds no one spoke. In the silence, we both glared at each other.

"Before I say anything else to you," Price finally said, "I need you to sign a form."

He kept his eyes on me as clicked his fingers and stretched his hand out towards the Amelia Jensen still standing near the door. "Ms Jensen. The confidentiality contract please."

She stepped forward and took a sheaf of papers from the top of her desk and handed them nervously to Price.

"This is a standard confidentiality agreement drawn up by my advisers," he said, pushed the papers towards me with one hand while clicking a pen simultaneously with the other. "It is an undertaking on your behalf to keep all communication relating to this matter in hand between me and you." He used the pen to point to the relevant sections on the agreement, like an insurance salesman trying to slip a dodgy contract pass you. "I want you to sign here and here before we proceed any further."

I looked down at the papers he'd pushed towards me, then back up at him. "I don't think so," I stated.

He sat back in his chair, his elbows resting on the arm rests of the oversized leather chair. "And why is that?"

I smiled. "Because I know you're lying."

His eyes widened. "How...how dare you! About what?" he spluttered.

"I think you know perfectly well who would have motive to kill the woman. And I think Marshall may have just been collateral damage." I didn't think that at all but I said it to see what reaction I'd get from him.

At his sharp intake of breath, a shiver of uneasiness ran down my spine. His reaction meant I'd touched a nerve. Could I possibly be on the right track?

His eyes narrowed. "Marshall's death was an accident. Nothing more."

I had to keep pushing. "And yet it would seem someone wanted to stop him from writing that book and I think you know who that person is and why."

His face reddened. "I have no idea who that person is."

With that one sentence, I knew he was considering Marshall's death to be more than an accident as well.

My smile would have come across as self-satisfied and I knew it would anger him further.

"Of course, you do," I grinned.

"Why are you asking me all these questions? I don't have to answer any of them. You're not a policeman any more. You're a nobody," he snarled.

If there's one thing I've learnt over the years is to never trust a politician. When cornered, they will always turn into a bully and try to turn the focus of attention away from themselves.

"I'm simply asking for a few names," I replied with a shrug. "If you have nothing to hide, why not give me some?"

A slow grin spread across his face. He had beautiful white teeth. He saw my hesitation and the grin broadened. "You knew the murdered woman," he stated.

I stood silently not saying anything. Sometimes it's best to let people like him, people who like to hear the sound of their own voices, have the stage. Let them talk and nine times out of ten, they let something slip. I was hoping this time was the one time out of ten.

He nodded slowly. "She meant something to you, didn't she?"

"Just a few names. That's all," I repeated.

He snorted. "Well, sorry to disappoint you but I have no idea who this woman was or how she is connected to my memoir. I am simply publishing a book to clear my name of a crime I had no hand in." He glared at me. "The name you besmirched."

Besmirched?

"I doubt there is a connection at all," he said, standing up. He took his time straightening his Armani shirt before continuing, "You are simply worming your way into the investigation because you have become a nobody and you don't like it."

He turned to Amelia Jensen cowering at the door. "Ms Jensen. Please show Mr Curtis to the front door. And please do not allow him to return."

He turned to me. "Now leave or I'll be forced to call the police."

13

A blue Mazda was cruising along the Gold Coast Highway behind me. It slowed down when it came close and I saw Cavanaugh behind the wheel, looking like a man who would follow me all the way home at four miles an hour if he had to.

I pulled over to the side of the road, leaving space for him to pull over behind me. He took his time getting out of his car and walked slowly towards me then leant over to open my passenger side door. "Let's take a ride in my car," he said.

"Where are we going?"

"To the scene of the crime."

"What about my car?"

"I'll have someone pick it up later and bring to the station."

I didn't ask why. Everything about his demeanour said I didn't have a choice.

His car smelt of sweat and apple scented air freshener and I'd barely had time to buckle my seat belt when he did a U turn and headed north.

We drove along the Esplanade in silence and turned onto the Smith Street exit. Less than fifteen minutes later, the street merged with the M1 and we were headed north towards Coomera.

This stretch of the M1, between Labrador and my house in Coomera,

Serpent

is one of the ugliest pieces of land on the coast. It is treeless and flat with a brown stubble in the meridian strip interrupted only by light poles. I knew the area well. I drove this way every day of my life from my office in Surfers to my house. The council have plans to spend $2 million on lights and artwork to brighten up this stretch of the highway but I doubt that will be enough.

Half an hour later, Dreamworld came into sight and Cavanaugh took the exit, turning onto the service road beside the main highway and driving for another five minutes. I watched Dreamworld slip by until Cavanaugh suddenly hit the brakes, pulled over and killed his engine. Without a word, he got out and walked away, heading towards a wooden bridge over a sludgy stream. Even though he hadn't spoken to me since I first sat down in his car, anger had made his shoulders tense and his back ramrod straight. It rippled off his shoulders, making him look like an animal poised to jump.

I knew he was expecting me to follow so I opened my door and went after him through the loose dirt.

He stopped at a wire fence, then swung himself upwards on to a stone wall flanking the bridge. Using the same post, he let himself down on the other side then turned and waited for me to arrive.

The silence was unearthly. No birds, no rushing water. Only stillness. As the trees swayed gently in the breeze, a smell I didn't like was disturbed. A dank and almost mouldy odour, like someone's rotting shed in the backyard full of gardening tools, wafted towards us. The place bothered me a little in a way I can't explain.

Even though I was walking behind him, my shoes crunching on dead leaves, I could feel his pent up rage as he walked with his hands in his pockets and his head down. Without any warning, a train roared past, echoing in the silence.

Cavanaugh suddenly stopped on the path and I almost ran into him. "Recognise anything?" he asked.

I knew exactly where we were. Instead of feeling sadness, I felt anger. It was getting late and it was cold and he'd taken me into the middle of nowhere. I was tired of his snide glances and raised eyebrows.

"I know where we are. I saw the photographs."

He raised his arm and pointed. "Look over there."

I traced the path of his outstretched arm and saw a wall with a darker strip in the foreground that could only be a ditch. I knew this would be where they found Christine's body. Every time I close my eyes, I see her blue lips and mutilated body. Questions and doubts run around in my head like a needle stuck in the groove of a vinyl record.

"Why am I here?" I wanted to know why he had brought me here.

"Use your imagination," he smirked. "You're good at that."

For some reason he was angry. I used to know kids at school like him. Kids who were so ferociously determined to prove they were tough and never stopped fighting.

"Why am I here," I repeated in a whisper.

"Because I have some questions for you." He didn't look at me as he spoke. His gaze was held on the ditch in the distance.

"Do you know what I've been doing these past two days? I've been searching this area and dredging the ponds around here." He waved his arms to encompass the area up to the bridge. "It was a lousy job. There is three feet of putrid mud and slime around here. We found a couple of shopping trolleys. A couple of stolen bikes. A car chassis. Hubcaps, car tyres, a condom and about a thousand used syringes. But do you know what else we found?"

I shook my head, waiting for the punch line.

"Elizabeth Delaney's clothes, her mobile phone and her diary." He waited and wiggled his eyebrows. "It took us a while to dry everything out. Then we had to check her phone records. That's when we discovered that the very last call she made was to you. At 8.57 pm on Friday, 24th August, she called you from the Star Casino in Broadbeach. Perhaps you had arranged to meet her and you didn't turn up? My guess is she called you to find out why."

"Oh come on! What are you implying?"

He smiled, ignoring my question. "We also found a diary. It had been in the muck for so long the pages were stuck together and the ink had almost washed away. The crime scene guys had to dry it carefully and pull the pages apart. Then they used an electron microscope to find the faint traces of ink. It's amazing what they can do nowadays." He grinned his shark smile. "Truly CSI stuff."

While he was talking, he had walked up to me, his eyes inches away from mine. This was his Agatha Christie moment.

"What we discovered was a note in her diary under Friday 24th August. Meeting at 8.30 pm, Star Casino." His voice was thick with sarcasm. "You *do* know where that is, don't you?"

"Of course, I know where it is. Get to the point." I was trying to sound more confident than I felt. I could feel sweat trickling down my back, inching its way to the waistband of my jeans.

"The Star Casino is only a mile or two from that office of yours in Surfers, isn't it?"

I waited, saying nothing. He was leading up to something.

He nodded at my silence, then continued. "At the bottom of the page she wrote a name. I think she planned to meet that person. Do you know whose name it was?"

I shook my head.

"Care to hazard a guess?" he smiled.

I could feel the tightness in my chest. "Mine?"

A touch of fear passed across my conscientiousness. I knew someone was setting me up because none of us who worked for Sandra would leave a team member's name written down anywhere. It was an unwritten law between us all. Leave no trace. Christine would never have done that, especially not in her diary. She knew better.

Cavanaugh didn't allow himself a final flourish or triumphant gesture. This was just the beginning. I could see the glint of handcuffs as they emerged from his pocket. My first impulse was to laugh, but then the coldness clutched my heart.

"Jack Curtis, I'm arresting you on suspicion of murder. You have the right to remain silent, but it is my duty to warn you that anything you say will be taken down and may be used in evidence against you."

"You're joking!" I spluttered.

"Does it look like I'm joking?"

The steel manacles closed around my wrists. In one swift movement,

Cavanaugh forced my legs apart and searched me, starting at my ankles and working his way up.

"Do you have anything to say?" he asked.

It's strange the things that occur to you at times like this. But in the end, silence is always the best alternative. I let him shove me towards his car.

14

I have been staring at the square of light filtering in from a high window for I don't know how long. If I close my eyes, it's still there imprinted on my eyelids. There was no graffiti on the walls of the cell and it didn't smell of disinfectant, urine and misery. Yet. It featured a new solid metal door with a small hatch at eye level and in one corner, the red light of a video camera flickered.

I remember the old cells reeking of vomit: the marinated aftermath of revellers trolling the Surfers Paradise bars. There were no cameras in the cells three years ago. Just steel bars behind a corridor beyond. The mayor's budget must have stretched a little for the upgrade. I'd locked a few teenagers up after a night of drunkenness and tomfoolery but never had the misfortune to spend time in one myself. I was wishing that was the case now. On the bright side, it gave me time to think.

Occasionally I heard footsteps in the corridor and then an observation flap would open and eyes would peer at me. After several seconds, it would close again and I would go back to staring at the window. The only sound was a dripping tap in the cistern in the corner.

I had no idea what time it was because I was forced to hand over my phone, wallet, watch, belt and shoelaces in exchange for a threadbare grey blanket that feels more like hessian than wool. I know it's late, or rather early, because all the newly-arrived drunks are quiet now, so it must be after closing time. It took hours to fingerprint me and process me.

I have no idea where Cavanaugh is. He's probably tucked up in bed dreaming that he's keeping the world safe with me behind bars. When I was being arrested, I told him I wanted a lawyer, he advised me, "Get a bloody good one."

I knew I should call Sam to let her know where I was but I had one phone call and I needed a lawyer.

Most of the lawyers I know don't make house calls in the middle of the night. I asked for my phone back to make a call and the guard grudgingly agreed. He handed me my phone and stood watching me with his arms folded across his chest while I dialled Karen Sawyer's number.

I had no idea if Karen would represent me. There'd been no contact with her since my last case and I very much doubted that things would return to the same camaraderie we once shared.

When she answered, I could hear a male voice complaining in the background.

"What do you want, Jack?" No hello. No 'lovely to hear from you'.

"I need a lawyer, Karen."

"Where are you?"

"Surfers Police Station."

I knew she hadn't hung up because I could hear her breathing. "Find someone else, Jack."

"I've been arrested, Karen."

"Wow. What a surprise."

"Sarcasm at a time like this is not funny. Will you represent me?"

"What have you done?"

"Hey! Innocent until proven guilty!"

She sighed. "What is it you're *supposed* to have done?"

"Murder."

She gasped. "Holy shit! Who?"

I sighed. "It's a long story, Karen. Will you represent me?"

"Stupid question, Jack. Of course I will. You may be a pompous ass but you're not a murderer."

I felt a lump form in my throat but swallowed it down. "I need you to do something else for me. I want you to call Frank and ask him to go to my house and take the dog and cat home with him. They haven't been fed tonight and the way things are looking, I'm not sure what the next few days are going to hold."

The cat was not the problem. Sherlock was a rescue from the RSPCA and from day one, he's been pretty well self-sufficient when it comes to food. If he didn't like what I served him, he hunted for his own food outside. The dog was another matter. He'd been treated badly in his short life before I rescued him and as such, he was terrified of just about everything.

I found him at a crime scene where he'd been locked inside the house without food or water for over two days but even before that, his life had been hard. He looked like a concoction slapped together by a blind Frankenstein. He was the size of a Labrador with a mottled, wiry coat of a terrier and the large floppy ears of a spaniel. He had a hairless tail that looked like he'd chewed it off himself. With his owner dead, he was headed for the RSPCA but as I watched him shaking and whimpering in a corner, I decided to take him home with me where his prospects were far better than with them. He took to me instantly but it quickly became obvious he also included Frank in his inner circle.

"Frank's the best you can come up with?" Karen asked.

"Just do it Karen," I sighed, ignoring her slur against Frank. A little belatedly, I added, "Please."

Another sigh. "I'll be there in an hour." Then she hung up.

While I waited, I paced the cell. I stood. I sat. I walked. I sat on the toilet. I stood again. My nerves were raw.

Cavanaugh thinks I've been holding things back or being economical with the truth. He's right. Hindsight is a wonderful thing. Right now my mistakes kept colliding inside my head, fighting for space with all the questions I have.

I honestly hadn't recognised Elizabeth in the morgue at first. I was unsure because the body in the morgue seemed more like a vandalised shopfront mannequin than a real human being. It was the report stating she had a scar that had made me sure.

I lay on the narrow cot, feeling the springs press into my back and waited for Karen to arrive. Cavanaugh was right. I was in a shit-load of trouble.

True to her word, Karen arrived an hour later. There was no small talk about 'long time no see'. She pulled up a chair on the other side of the table in the interrogation room where I'd been handcuffed and sat down. This was all business.

The holding cells were on the floor below us. I could smell coffee and hear the tapping of computer keyboards so not everyone was home tucked up in bed.

Karen opened her briefcase and took out a blue folder and a large legal notebook. I was surprised how she could combine a Claudia Schiffer appearance with the demeanour of a crime lawyer at this hour of the night. Morning.

"We need to make some decisions," she began. "They want to start the interviews as soon as possible. Tomorrow." She looked at the watch on her wrist. "Today. 9 am." She glanced back at me. "Is there something you'd like to tell me?"

I blinked. "Like what? Confess, you mean?"

"Anything," she said, leaning her elbows on the table and clenching her fists under her chin.

"I want you to get me out of here," I said abruptly.

She began explaining that the police can hold me for forty-eight hours in which time they either have to charge me or let me go.

"I bloody know that! But I want you to get me out tomorrow morning."

"That's a tad ridiculous, Jack. You know the rules."

"Then do something!" The anger and panic mingled together to make me sound like a whining child.

"Did you know the girl?"

"Yes."

"Did you arrange to meet her on the night she died?"

"No."

Karen was making notes, leaning over and scribbling and underlining words.

"This is a no brainer, Jack. All you have to do is provide an alibi for the night of Friday 24th August. And they have to let you out."

I hesitated. "I can't do that."

She gave me a weary look like a teacher who hasn't received the answer she expected. She stood up and gathered her notes then knocked twice on the door to signal she was finished.

I was stunned. "Is that it?"

"Yep," she replied.

"Aren't you going to ask if I killed her?"

She turned and looked at me. "Did you?"

"No!"

"Okay then. Save your plea for the jury and hope it doesn't come to that. I'll be at the interview. In the meantime, think about an alibi."

The door shut behind her leaving me full of disappointment. What had I expected?

Five minutes later, I was taken back to my cell.

15

TUESDAY, 3RD SEPTEMBER

The wooden table in the interrogation room was pitted and worn and stained by thousands of coffee cups. At the left-hand side of the table, near the corner, someone had carved a broken heart into the wood. The last time I sat in this room, I was on the other side.

Cavanaugh walked in, followed by a younger detective with a long face and crooked teeth who tried hard not to look at me as he placed a tape recorder on the table and plugged it in. Karen followed them in and sat down in the chair next to me.

She leant over and whispered in my ear. "If I touch your elbow, I want you to be quiet."

As I nodded in agreement, I saw her blink quickly. I hadn't showered or changed since yesterday morning and the odour from my armpits almost stopped my own breath.

Cavanaugh sat opposite me not bothering to remove his jacket. He rubbed a hand across the whiskers on his chin. Maybe he hadn't been tucked up in bed after all. The thought made me feel uneasy.

The young detective checked the tape recorder was working, nodded to Cavanaugh, and stepped away, his back against the wall. He ran his fingers through his receding auburn hair every few seconds awkwardly as if to reassure himself that there was still some there.

"The interview of the suspect, Jack Curtis, has commenced at," Cavanaugh looked down at his wrist watch, "9.14 am. Detective Cavanaugh is conducting the interview."

Cavanaugh placed both hands on the table, fingers entwined, and settled his eyes on me. The seconds ticked away as he watched me saying nothing. I had to admit it was a very eloquent pause.

"Where were you on the evening of Friday, 24th August?"

I heard voices outside the interrogation room suddenly raised. I recognised one of them as Sam's but I didn't recognise the other one. The voices became subdued but I knew they were talking about me. Soon enough, Sam would enter the room.

Cavanaugh picked at something on the sleeve of his jacket as he listened to the voices. As I expected, seconds later, Sam burst into the room.

Her eyes rose instantly to the blinking light in the corner of the room, indicating a tape of the interview was in progress. She knew she would have to be careful what she said. I almost felt sorry for Cavanaugh because I knew at the end of the interview, he would be on the receiving end of an Irish tirade.

She glared at Cavanaugh as she dragged the chair next to him away from the table. A screech filled the room followed by a thump as she dropped it heavily on the floor. Cavanaugh smiled sweetly up at her.

"Detective Samantha Neil has entered the room at," he looked down at his wrist watch, "9.21 am."

Her eyes turned and bored into mine as she sat down beside Cavanaugh.

"Now, Mr Curtis, in your own words," Cavanaugh continued, keeping his face smooth and expressionless for the camera, "can you fill me in on your whereabouts on the night of the Friday, 24th August when Elizabeth Delaney was murdered."

I watched Sam's head lift at the mention of Elizabeth's name but Cavanaugh either missed it or chose to ignore her. Since Cavanaugh missed nothing, my guess was he didn't want anything to interrupt his chain of thought.

If he'd bothered to look, he'd have seen Sam's reaction. Sam knew

Elizabeth Delaney was Christine Buchanan's alias, something Cavanaugh did not know, but what neither of them knew was that Christine had worked for Sandra Burton with me.

As Cavanaugh's eyes stared into mine, Sam remained silent. I knew there'd be questions later, but I was grateful for her faith in me at the moment. Even if it was temporary.

I cleared my throat, feeling uncomfortable, while Sam's eyes held mine.

What Cavanaugh wanted to know I couldn't tell him because a big part of the story included my association with Sandra Burton. I also had to be careful about names. To Cavanaugh, the victim's name was Elizabeth Delaney. To Sandra and me, she went by her real name of Christine Buchanan.

Not knowing the exact time Christine had been murdered, I ran through the night in my mind. At around 7 pm, I was sitting with Sandra Burton in her office going over events of the past week. At about 8 pm, we had a bite to eat at a small Italian restaurant a couple of blocks down until about 9 pm. I had to keep this piece of information to myself because well, Sandra would not be considered an upstanding member of society if they knew what she was doing. But she played a major part in my story.

I received a quick phone call from Christine at about 8.30 pm telling me she had arrived at the rendezvous and was waiting. Almost half an hour later, she rang me again to say the client had not turned up or contacted her and she was leaving to go home. I told her I'd give her a call in about half an hour. When I tried, she didn't answer.

I had an uneasy feeling Cavanaugh had the footage of her waiting at the hotel and the times she phoned me. I also had a feeling the whole basis of my arrest was that no one phones someone out of the blue for no reason at all. If he'd managed to get a warrant for my phone calls that evening, he would find that after trying to ring Christine back, there was my phone call to Sam to see if she wanted some company, which was why she was staring at her lap right now, praying I'd keep my mouth shut.

All in all, there was nothing I could tell Cavanaugh. Dilemma.

"I don't recall," was all I could say.

Serpent

"Did you work that day?"

"Yes."

"What case were you working on?"

"That's confidential."

"Who hired you?"

"Confidential." I was tempted to put on a sing-song voice but I didn't think Cavanaugh was in the right frame of mind.

"What time did you leave the office?"

"I had an appointment at 7 pm so I left the office at around 4.30 pm to go home and feed my animals. From there I went to keep my appointment."

Cavanaugh was trying to pin me down. He knew as well as I did that lying was a lot harder than telling the truth. The more you weave into a story, the harder it is to maintain. It becomes a straitjacket, tying you down and giving you no room to move.

"Did you know Elizabeth Delaney?" he asked, his eyes burning into mine.

I glanced at Karen who said nothing. She hadn't said a word since the interview started.

"Yes."

"Where did you first meet her?"

I told him the whole story. He already knew most of this but it was theatrics for the tape that was rolling. I told him how she'd contacted me a year ago and how she helped us solve the last crime. Beside Cavanaugh, Sam was still looking at her lap, her lips pressed together, and nodding. When I was finished, I opened the palms of my hands, signally I was finished. Cavanaugh watched me in silence, expecting more.

"When was the last time you spoke to her?" he finally asked.

We were at the crux of the matter. The part I had to lie about.

"A year ago."

"Your name was in her diary."

"I can't explain that."

"You met her that night."

"I did not."

"Then you lured her away from the hotel."

"I did not."

"You tortured her."

"I damned well did not." More adamant now.

"This is horseshit!" Cavanaugh exploded, throwing his pen on the table. It bounced around for a few seconds and settled in the corner of the room. Gone was the Kumbaya moment.

"You are deliberately withholding information and you've spent the two days covering your arse. You are trying to misdirect the investigation and you are the trying to steer the police away from yourself."

I watched his chest rise and fall as Karen touched my elbow. She wanted me to be quiet. I ignored her.

"How am I doing that?" My own voice was rising. "How am I steering you away? I'm telling you the truth. I did not see her that night."

"I want to speak to my client," Karen said insistently.

"To hell with that," I shouted. "I've done nothing wrong. You have my name in a diary which I have explained and a call to me that I didn't answer. That's it. You have no motive."

Karen touched my elbow again. "Jack. I advise you to be quiet."

I clamped my mouth shut and stared at the wall, my nostrils flaring as I breathed deeply.

"Why did she phone you if you've had no contact with her?"

"A mistake?"

"Where were you on the night of the Friday, 24th August?"

"At home."

"Who were you with?"

I glanced at Sam. Her eyes had lifted from her lap and rested on mine.

"I was alone. I went home and went to bed. Alone."

The statement hung in the air like a torn cobweb looking for something to cling to. I was telling the truth. I *had* called Sam to see if she wanted company. She said she had an early start the next day and would have to pass. It had been a few days since we'd been together and I was missing her. After the rejection, I went home, had a few too many drinks and went to bed.

As his eyes held mine, he gave me a sceptical look I deserved. I had an unsettling feeling he could see the workings of my mind.

What I was certain of was Cavanaugh wanted me to be nervous enough to open up and tell them everything I'd discovered. On the record. And he wanted me to panic.

None of that was going to happen although the inference was clear. Cavanaugh was trying his hardest to implicate me.

"Don't be stupid, Cavanaugh. Check the CCTV footage at the hotel and you'll see I wasn't there." I was hoping the gleam in my eye would unsettle him.

"Gee," he said, his voice full of sarcasm as he palm-smacked his forehead, "Why didn't *I* think of that?" His Viking blue eyes simmered with anger. He had picked up another pen and was slapping it onto the palm of his hand as he grit his teeth.

"I did NOT kill Elizabeth Delaney," I stated. "But it's always nice for the seals at the zoo to have a new ball to play with."

Again Karen touched my elbow. Again I ignored her.

My patience suddenly evaporated. "Okay, Cavanaugh. Let's pretend I was a trained police officer for twelve years." My eyes flicked from Sam to Cavanaugh as I spoke. "Let's pretend I know that certain *other* laws come into play when a citizen talks to police," I said, ignoring Sam now and glaring at Cavanaugh. I was in full rant. "Mostly the ones about saving your breath by skipping the bullshit."

For a moment, no one spoke. Sam shot me a squinty-eyed look that was meant as a warning at the same time Cavanaugh's pen stopped moving. His jaw did the clampy thing while the look he shot me could have frozen peas.

"Jack, Jack, Jack," he smirked. "Twelve years of going through the motions and now look at yourself. A private investigator with barely enough clients to make ends meet. Three years ago, you were trying to prove how good you were. Now look at yourself."

The horror of my past few years was something I did not need to be reminded of and I couldn't believe he was talking about the charred remains of my career during a professional interview. I tried not to let him see my anger but it was hard to do that when I knew my face was red.

"Watch it, Cavanaugh. You're crossing a boundary here," I warned, looking up at the blinking light of the camera.

His nostrils flared. "You think you're so smart. But you're as simple as duck soup." He nodded slowly, a knowing look on his face.

I opened my mouth to speak but Karen jumped in and said, "That's quite enough."

My stomach began to settle down now that I felt like I was on top of the situation again.

"It's my turn now, Detective Cavanaugh, before it gets any more personal than it already has." Karen's voice was a smooth as silk. "What evidence do you actually have? By now you would have seen CCTV footage of the night Elizabeth Delaney was killed so you know that my client did not meet her at the hotel."

She let that sink in. "You know she called my client before she left and he has stated he never answered the call. He also has no idea why his name was in her diary except to say that he knew her a year ago so it is highly likely that it has been in the book since then."

Again she let the silence hang before continuing. "He has been upfront and told you where he was on the night of the murder and without any timeframe of *when* the murder actually took place, that should be sufficient for you at the moment."

I leant back and rested both arms on the armrests, my hands knitted together over my stomach as I listened.

Karen stared hard at Cavanaugh. "That is hardly a motive for murder, Detective. If it was, half my clients would be hoping I did not have a serious accident."

She smiled as Cavanaugh grit his teeth some more.

"My client is not hiding any information from you. In fact, he has been totally upfront with you from the beginning. It would seem you are intent on pinning this murder on him without motive, means or proof."

I leant forward. "You've had your fun, Cavanaugh. You dragged me in here to grill me like this knowing full well I had nothing to do with this."

A ghost of a smile crept across his face. He shook his head and snorted. "You're just going to walk out of here and forget all about Elizabeth Delaney? Is that what you're saying?"

Karen touched my elbow. "I would strongly suggest you release my client until you have more evidence, Detective. I can go to a judge with what you have here and I'll have him out within an hour. But it will go down on your record that you have arrested an innocent man on nothing but supposition," her head tilted to the side, "and a personal grudge. That is harassment. The backlash on your career will be devastating."

Sam leant forward and spoke into the recorder. "Interview concluded with Jack Curtis by Detective Samantha Neil and Detective Cavanaugh at," she glanced at the clock on the wall, "10.33 pm." The light of the video camera flickered off.

Cavanaugh inhaled angrily, about to object no doubt, but Sam held her hand up to stop him, as if gesturing to a dog to stay.

"Enough of the theatrics," she growled at him. "What the hell is going on?"

He glared at Sam. "I'm doing my job. I'm investigating a murder. This man is hiding something, which is, in fact, hindering my investigation." He hesitated, his head cocked to one side as he squinted at her. "And my instinct tells me *you* shouldn't be here in this room during this investigation."

Sam ignored the barbed remark and turned to me. "Just tell us what you know, Jack."

"I already have, Sam. I had no idea Elizabeth Delaney had been murdered until Cavanaugh asked me to view Elizabeth's body in the morgue on Saturday afternoon. Then he turned up at my house on Sunday to ask me questions."

Sam's eyes widened as she turned to Cavanaugh. "You what?"

Somewhere deep inside anger fizzed. "You involved me from the very start and now you have to wear that mistake," I said to Cavanaugh. "I'm going to prove my innocence with or without your help."

I fought to keep the anger down. *You're jealous* my good angel said. *Punch him* said my bad one. I much preferred the second option.

"You're negotiating with us? Seriously? Is that what you're doing?" Cavanaugh asked, almost spluttering.

"Then suggest an alternative approach." I pointed my index finger at the ceiling.

"Oh wait. There isn't one." I did a little wiggle of my head to show how smart I was.

Sam's face darkened as Cavanaugh's eyes bulged.

"You were always a failure waiting to happen," he spat at me, ignoring Sam's look. "And now you're looking for a case to bring you back into the limelight." His Adam's apple bobbed in his neck as he chuckled. "That's the definition of narcissism."

The insult hit home. I didn't like the things he said but I couldn't fault the logic. I *had* been a loose cannon. I *was* headstrong. And I pay the price of those faults every single day of my life.

I eased air into my lungs through clenched teeth as a sudden rush of heat flushed through my body, a raw edge exposed.

"Ouch." I faked a cringe but the anger was building.

The mocking sneer on his face finally did it. I lost it.

"Let me tell you something, *Detective* Cavanaugh. I'm not an idiot. I know how things go," I snapped as anger knotted my gut. "You think I'm looking for some drama to bring me back into the fold?"

He gave a knowing nod as I struggled to keep the emotion out of my voice.

"Well you've failed brilliantly because it was you who involved me in this in the first place."

Karen stood up. "Is my client free to leave right now or do I have to visit my friend the judge to have him released within the hour?"

I could hear his teeth grinding from across the table. "Pick up your things at the front desk," he muttered. "But as of now, your car is impounded. We're going over it with a fine toothed comb."

"And why is that, Detective?" Karen asked.

"Because we have no idea where Elizabeth Delaney was murdered but we know where she ended up. That would require a vehicle to transport her and I want to know if that vehicle was yours. We will be searching extensively for hair, traces of blood and DNA."

I was about to protest when Karen touched my elbow. "He's in his rights to do this, Jack. Let him. It can only go in your favour when it comes back clean."

Sam leant over the table and agreed with Karen. "Just do it, Jack."

I knew they were right. It just irked me. I simply nodded.

Cavanaugh slid his chair backwards. He put both hands flat on the table and levered himself upwards. He didn't look at me as he picked his folder up. "I wanted you charged with murder but Inspector Grayson said there isn't enough evidence." He looked up at me. "Yet," he finished. "But I'm going to keep looking until we find more. It's just a matter of time."

"You don't like me, do you?" I asked.

He shrugged. "Not particularly."

"Why?"

"Because you think I'm a dumb clothes-horse who doesn't read books and thinks the theory of relativity has something to do with inbreeding."

I frowned. "That's not true. I know you're a smart cop."

He shrugged and reached for the door handle.

"How much of this is personal?" I asked.

His answer rumbled through the closing door as he left. "Don't flatter yourself."

I turned back to look at Sam. Her normally dark, sultry eyes stared back at me with flashing Irish sparks of anger.

"I want to talk to you," she mouthed silently.

Six frightening words.

16

The same constable who had taken my belongings when I arrived handed me the parcel with my watch, phone, wallet and shoelaces. I had to count my money and sign for it.

"Inspector Grayson wants to see you in his office." His voice sounded flat and before I could reply, he said, "Apparently you know where that is."

He sounded as tired as I was. I'd only had a few hours sleep on the thin mattress in the cell and if I was right, he was at the end of a graveyard shift, working through the night.

I put my possessions in my coat pocket and looked up at him. "A tough night?" I asked.

His eye twitched. "Aren't they all?"

He looked like he was fresh out of the academy, all spit and polish. My guess was his enthusiasm was slowly being eroded with the realisation that you can't stop the worst coming out in some people. It happened to a lot of recruits. They join the police force eager to make a difference but within a couple of years you see a slow change beginning. They see break and entries, kids stealing cars, drunks driving home after a night at the pub and killing some poor pedestrian and they see drug pushers selling drugs to small children in schools. Eventually, their enthusiasm wanes and is replaced with disheartenment. Even worse, they burn out. Not every recruit loses momentum, but the odds are high. It takes a certain type of person to turn up day after day and manage the dregs of society.

I made my way down to Grayson's office and stopped to look around. Telephones rang, computer keys clicked and policemen stood in the corridors shouting back and forth to each other. I didn't recognise half of them.

Someone's voice from the back of the squad room said, "Good to see you again, Jack."

As usual, Pete Bridgman was sitting at his desk still looking like a five-year-old on his first day of school. His trousers were always pressed. His shirt was always clean but his clothes always seemed a little too small for him with his tree trunk legs and broad shoulders.

No one else spoke to me as I nodded to Pete and kept walking towards Grayson's office.

If I'm honest with myself, I missed working with Inspector Grayson. He's a veteran of twenty-five years standing at six feet tall, closer to sixty than fifty years old and solid looking – well, fat really. The last time I'd seen him his head was devoid of any hair and his eyebrows hovered over his eyes like giant grey caterpillars. Despite the bags under his eyes, there was a sharp perceptiveness about him and I felt an ornery kind of kinship to him. He was tough, emotionless and harsh but he knew his business.

Inspector Grayson was sitting at his desk on the phone saying, 'uh-huh, uh-huh, uh-huh,' and looking bored. His feet were on the desk and while he spoke, he held up a finger and crooked it to indicate he wanted me in his office. What I noticed first was that he'd aged more than the four years that had actually passed. Maybe it was the hard work that had etched deep grooves around his mouth and eyes but I suspected it was the fact his wife had left him a year ago when their youngest child reached eighteen.

As the light from the overhead light shone on his bald head, he sat eyeing me in silence for a few moments as he tapped his pencil idly until something was said on the other end of the phone that caught his attention.

"Hey. Don't tell me about your budget! I've got my own to worry about. Let me do my job and you do yours."

He dropped the phone down from a height, not exactly slamming it but making his point. He dropped his feet to the floor and said, "Shut the damn door!"

He leant back in his chair, his fingers tented across his round belly, and a scowl already in place. I could hear the air-conditioner droning away in the background but it wasn't enough to take away the thick odour of cigarette smoke.

I shut the door and stared silently at him.

"You've made an enemy of Cavanaugh," he stated. "He doesn't like you and he thinks you're smarmy."

My eyes widened. "Smarmy? Me?"

"Smarmy and definitely hiding something. I don't like what you're doing either and frankly, considering your past career, I'm surprised by your behaviour. I think you're manipulating the case and if you continue, you'll end up in a screaming heap."

"Now I'm scared." I said the words with a massive amount of sarcasm and I saw it put colour into his cheeks. The colour of anger.

"He has some valid points," he growled, pointing to a chair on the other side of his desk. He didn't look happy, but then again, he seldom did.

He watched me settle before continuing. "Have you seen a psychologist yet?"

His voice was still deep and husky, and I always said he was weeks away from throat cancer. So far, he has managed to dodge that bullet.

"Have you given up smoking yet?" I replied, my eyes dropping to the overflowing ashtray on his desk.

He shook a cigarette out of a bent packet and lit it up, pointedly watching me the whole time, then breathed the smoke in then out deeply. His colour subsided and his mouth stretched into a semblance of a smile. "I've missed that sense of humour of yours, Jack."

He pulled a file towards him, turned a few pages then looked up at me.

"I've seen the file Cavanaugh has on you." He tapped the file with his index finger.

"He's been in here this morning trying to force me to keep you in jail for another twenty-four hours. You want to use a life line or call a friend or can you work it out all by yourself what it was about?"

"If you didn't know it was all circumstantial, I wouldn't be sitting opposite you right now watching your blood pressure soar."

He punched the stub of his cigarette out in the ashtray already resembling a volcano. "It's circumstantial at the moment, but he's not finished yet. Not by a long shot. Can I expect any nasty surprises coming from you?" he asked, putting a foot on the wastebasket and leaning back in the chair.

I took a deep breath. He'd done me a favour by not keeping me in jail another day. The least I could do was try to explain my side.

"What he has at the moment is a phone call to me from Elizabeth Delaney's phone which I can't explain," I lied. "I'm sure he's checked the CCTV footage and he knows I wasn't at the hotel before or after she left. He also has a diary found at the crime scene with my name in it which could have been from a year ago." I stared hard at him. "You know the case I'm talking about. It was that paedophile case last year. Again I don't know any other reason. But I'd have to be pretty stupid to take her phone and diary out of her handbag and then simply throw them in the bush so the police could find them, knowing that my name was in the diary. That's all he has so far. Smoke and mirrors and coincidences."

"Coincidences we leave to the astrologists. I like to deal with facts."

"I'm not going to argue with you about that."

He took his foot off the wastebasket, and leaned forward, smoke floating in a cloud behind him as if his coat were alight.

"He says you can't provide an alibi."

"I told him I was with a client until 9 pm and went home afterwards. And I can't tell him who because of client confidentiality."

I must be getting better at lying because all Grayson did was sigh as he stared hard at me for a few moments. "Cavanaugh likes to show off his feathers. I told him to let you go because I thought it was premature to charge you with anything. But if he comes up with anything more solid than what he has now, I won't be able to repeat that bit of flexibility. Ex-policeman or not. You'll be on your own in the big world."

"I understand that."

He glanced towards the glass partition overlooking the squad room for a few seconds then looked back at me. If I didn't know better, I'd say Grayson's hesitation was because he was trying to find the right words. A first for me.

"At Cavanaugh's request, I'm taking Sam off the case."

My heart did a double flip but I kept quiet. That was a serious request to make. It meant a lack of confidence in your partner and I could count on one hand the number of times partners were separated at the request of one of them.

He tapped his pen on the desk abstractedly. "There's another case she can work on now," he added, holding my gaze. "He believes this case would be compromised if she remains on it." He raised his eyebrows and stared hard at me. "Do you know anything about that?"

Cavanaugh had told Grayson his suspicions about our relationship. Of that I was sure. But instead of confronting Sam with the accusation, Grayson had given her leeway and taken her off the case without asking for an explanation from her. Our private relationship was supposition on Cavanaugh's part right now, but he was a smart cop who never missed anything and Grayson couldn't disregard the allegation he'd made. If anything happened to compromise the case, Cavanaugh would not hesitate to make a formal complaint against Grayson and he'd have a lot of explaining to do.

I could see in Grayson's eyes he was disappointed that Sam hadn't been the one to come forward with the admission. Despite Grayson's regard for Sam, what I couldn't do was tell Grayson about Sam and me. She wanted a little time before exposing her private life to the people she worked with at the station and I had to respect that. All I could do was shrug.

"I didn't do this," I stated simply.

He tossed the pen on the table. "Then find out who did."

"That's what I intend to do."

"Okay then. I don't want to see you on the opposite side of my desk again. If I do, I won't be this genial guy you're looking at right now." He shook another cigarette from the pack in front of him. "Don't say you weren't warned."

17

The clock on the wall said it was 11.35 am as I walked out into the warm sunshine, tired and dirty and smelling of stale sweat. I immediately started to look for a cab because I didn't want to face Sam just yet. I had to think and having her asking all kinds of questions wasn't going to help me. I have never loved anyone as much as I love her but I needed to be alone right now to think.

Karen appeared through the door of the station and told me she was heading to her office in Surfers Paradise so she could give me a lift back to my office if I needed one. Since I was now without a car, I accepted the ride and thanked her. I sublet a good-sized office with a view over the street with a private door leading directly out to the corridor from her law firm, Barclay and Davidson, on the 13th floor of the Regis Building in Cavill Avenue. It's convenient and sometimes I even get a surveillance job or two from her law firm.

I felt tired after my sleepless night in jail and frayed at the edges. The case seemed to be fragmenting, the pieces spinning away from me and glittering in the distance. There were too many elements involved to be merely coincidental.

The first thing I did when I entered my office was to call Frank. He answered after two rings with, "Guv. Wanna tell me wots 'appening?"

I spent the next few minutes going over the events of yesterday, starting with Cavanaugh taking me to the crime scene and arresting me.

"Cavanaugh found Christine's diary and phone at the crime scene and not surprisingly, my name was in the diary and on the call list of her phone. That was the basis for the arrest. What he's trying to do is scare me and he's furious it's not working. It's all circumstantial evidence and Karen shot him down in flames. But I have to watch my back. I can't believe he even thinks I had something to do with it. He doesn't like me but he sure as hell knows I'm not a killer."

"I'd like to get me 'ands on 'im, though."

In the background, I could hear the ping of the video games so I knew Frank was at Adventureland. "I can hear the noise in the background so I know where you are. Can you fill Sandra in of what's happened while you're there. Tell her I'll try to find out as much as I can but it's going to be difficult from now on because Sam has been excluded from the investigation. She and Cavanaugh are no longer partners."

"Wot? Whenid vat change?"

"Grayson called me into his office this morning and hinted that Cavanaugh has seen a connection between Sam and me. Cavanaugh knew we were friends but maybe he's seen something to make him think we're more than that now. If that's the case, he doesn't want Sam passing on information to me that could breach the investigation."

It didn't bother me who knew about us. I wanted to tell the world. But at the moment, at this early stage in our relationship, and with every police officer at the station knowing me and everything about me, it was wise to keep it to ourselves and out of gossip circles.

In the back of my mind was Simon Price's book. Everything pointed towards the book he commissioned Martin to finish as the connection to Christine. But how? I made a note to call Martin for the names of the people mentioned in the book.

"How's the dog?" I asked. "And Sherlock?"

"When are you gunna give that dog a name? E's fine. That cat though." I heard a puff of air as he exhaled. "Cheeky bugger. Funny fing is, he won't leave the dog's side. Sticks to 'im like shit to a blanket."

I heard a noise like Frank was coughing up a fur ball himself and realised he was laughing.

"So wots ya plan, mate?" he asked.

"I had a lot of time to think about that last night while I was in the cell. All I can think is I have to go to her apartment to see if there's anything there that can help me with my investigation. It won't take long for Cavanaugh to work out that Elizabeth Delaney was actually Christine Buchanan so I have to act fast before he searches her flat. I want to be one step ahead of him since he's not about to give me any insights."

"Okay, mate. Call me if ya need anyfing."

I checked my calendar to see if I had any appointments booked and I was grateful there was nothing pressing in it because my eyes felt gritty from lack of sleep. I was about to shut the office and catch a cab home when my mobile rang.

"Hello, Mr Curtis," a man's voice said. The voice was obviously altered with clicks between words as if they were assembled from different conversations.

"Who is this?"

"We have mutual friends." The voice alternated between high, then low, first male, then female. At one point, there appeared to be three voices speaking simultaneously, then they fell away to a single male voice again.

The office seemed to drop in temperature as I breathed and listened for a clue to who was calling. "I'm taping this," I lied.

The voice chuckled. "I stabbed her many times, Mr Curtis. I broke her nose and smashed her teeth. Believe me, I am the one the police are looking for." The last words were all spoken in a child's voice, high-pitched and happy.

I felt a stabbing pain behind my eyes and my blood sounded loud in my ears like waves crashing against a headland. There was no saliva in my mouth, just a dry, dusty sensation. When I eventually swallowed, it was as if swallowing a mouth full of dirt. It was painful and I struggled to find my voice.

"Mr Curtis? Are you all right?" The words were calm, almost tender, but spoken by what sounded like four different voices.

"I'll find you."

He laughed. The synthesised nature of the sound was more obvious now. "But I found *you*," the voice laughed again. "Just like I found *her*. And because of you, I have flamed into being and bought you out of mediocrity. The least you can do is show some gratitude."

Because of me?

"You're sick. But that isn't going to save you," I said with more confidence than I felt.

"In her final moments, in those bright red minutes before she died, I lusted for her but that would have been a weakness. And Mr Curtis, I am not weak. I chose her and loved her in my own way."

The voice was now deep and throaty. It boomed in my ear like the voice of God.

"Fuck you," I croaked.

Bile was rising in my throat as I felt sweat pop out on my forehead.

"Don't go yet." A tiny child's voice pleaded.

"I'll find you," was all I could say before hanging up.

I was tired and the phone call had unsettled me. What I needed was a shower and a change my clothes, to eat some food and get some sleep. All in that order.

I caught a cab and kept my eyes open for anyone following me.

18

I weighed up my options for a meal while I sat in the back seat of the cab on the way home. I could either have the cab driver stop off at McDonalds on the way home and watch the fare tick away on the meter while I waited for my food to arrive or I could take the time to defrost something from the freezer. I had no idea what was in the freezer so that left a third option. Pizza delivery.

I paid the cab driver and stepped out to the comforting smell of an early BBQ cooking somewhere in the neighbourhood. The next-door neighbour was out rearranging his sprinkler and when he saw me, he waved for me to wait.

"Hey, Jack," he called out. "Wait up."

I held up my hand in a tentative greeting. Gary was always long-winded and in my present state of weariness, I couldn't guarantee I'd keep this smile on my face for long.

"Hey Gary," I said, watching him stand up and dust the grassy wet patches circling his knees before stepping over the sprinkler. While I waited I rotated my stiff shoulders trying to relieve the sharp pain running up my neck.

"Hey," he smiled. "Just wanted to fill you in on some neighbourhood stuff." He pushed his hands into his jean pockets while he spoke. "You

Serpent

know I'm the Chairman of the Neighbourhood Watch Committee. Right?"

I nodded and smiled. "Yep. I saw the notice in my mail box. Congratulations."

"Well, it's just lucky I'm retired now so I have the time to watch out."

I'd heard a few rumours that Gary was the local busy body but I'd never say that to his face.

"We're lucky to have you," I said. See I can be nice.

He looked pleased with the praise. "Thanks. Appreciate that," he grinned as he puffed out his chest. "What I wanted to tell you is that we've had a couple of minor burglaries in our local area. Nothing much, so don't worry. Just some kids breaking in to see if they can find anything to take to Cash Converters, I'd say. One guy down the road is a carpenter and he had a wood planer taken from the back of his ute a while back."

"Maybe you should put in a report at the police station," I suggested.

"I told your friend that but he said they wouldn't be able to do much about it. If they turned up at Cash Converters, then they'll have to give a name and the police can start a search. Even then, they'll probably give a false name. He told me to save my time since it was such a petty crime but to keep my eyes open."

I frowned. "My friend?"

"The policeman."

"When was this?"

He pursed his lips as he thought. "Last Saturday, I think. Did he find you?"

That had to be Cavanaugh. Gary had to be the nosy neighbour Cavanaugh had spoken to when he was looking for me.

I nodded. "Yes, he did. Thanks."

"No problem. I saw a white van I didn't recognise at the end of the street," he continued, ignoring my glance at my watch, "but by the time I went inside to get my phone to take a picture of the registration plate, it had gone. I must have scared him off." He puffed his chest out again. "That's my job. I thought it might belong to the guy whose been stealing things."

I grinned. "Well, he won't find much to steal from my yard."

I let my eyes wander over my front yard. A few straggly trees and a dry patch of grass that was starting to come back thanks to the recent rain we'd had.

He took a moment to glance at my yard before his eyes darted to his own lush lawn and garden beds full of flowering scrubs. He nodded as if he could only agree with me before turning back.

"Bronwyn has another music recital on the weekend," he smiled. "You missed the last one but you want to come to this one?" he asked.

Bronwyn was Gary's niece he'd been trying to set me up with for over a year. Up until now, I'd managed to come up with an excuse every time. The last time I saw her, she was chasing two dogs at breakneck speed down the street in a blue, glittery maxi halter dress perfect for when she was nominated for a Logie performance. I imagined that normally it would have swept the ground but this day she was hitching it high above her knees with both hands, giving me a full view of the glittering thongs on her feet.

"I'd love to Gary but sorry, I have to work again."

He nodded as if he had expected my answer. "I'll let you know when the next one is on, then."

"Great," I replied waving goodbye. I unlocked the front door just as my stomach rumbled noisily.

19

I knew where Christine lived but I asked the Uber driver to drop me off a couple of streets away from her house. The last thing I needed was a neighbour seeing a man dressed in dark clothing sneaking up to her front door in the middle of the night. There would be no good outcome from that.

In the darkness outside her house, I stood hidden behind a tree looking at the front door as the wind whipped around me and flattened my sweatshirt and pants against my body.

For a brief moment, I closed my eyes because I had a foreboding feeling that everything was about to change once I entered her house. The police knew that where they found Christine's body was not where she was killed and because her torture and murder had taken time to complete, the logical place for the murder was in her home.

I pulled the hoodie over my head and shoved my hands in the front pockets and moved out of the shadows towards where I knew her spare key was hidden. With two swift turns, I heard the lock click and the door opened. My footsteps echoed on the polished floorboards leading into the lounge room.

The room looked nothing like mine. Mine looked like someone was either moving in or moving out. This one looked like something from

Better Homes and Gardens. There were brightly coloured embroidered throw pillows on a white leather lounge and a matching oriental rug placed in the middle of the designated lounge area with a wooden coffee table in the middle. The vase on the table was empty of water but had held what I thought were the remains of red roses. High in the corner, a television had been attached to a bracket that in turn had been attached to the wall. A tall Tiffany lead-light lamp stood near a window decorated with fine lace curtains. On a normal night, the suffused light from the lamp would have given the room a warm, cosy feel. On the entrance table, a light flashed on her answering machine saying the tape was full. Her coat was still on a hook, her car keys on the entrance table and attached to them by a metal ring was a small, wooden carved lizard.

On the lounge floor I saw a large, dark stain that could only be old blood pooled around an overturned chair. I puffed air through my mouth trying hard to contain my emotions.

I stumbled from room to room looking for evidence of forced entry.

On the kitchen bench was one mug with the remains of coffee coagulated like dark sludge in the base. Sitting beside it were two opened envelopes and a phone bill. The kettle was lying on its side and one of the dining chairs had toppled over. On the bench, a wooden holder held a set of kitchen knives. The largest knife space was empty.

With my hand still in my pocket, I opened a kitchen drawer so as not to leave prints. It contained neatly folded tea towels, a roll of bin liners, a pen and a notepad. I put my foot on the pedal of the kitchen tidy and noted it was empty except for a tissue and a tea towel. I was about to turn away when a smell wafted up from the bin. I bent over and smelt chloroform.

I checked her bedroom. Her clothes were hanging undisturbed on racks and her jewellery was still in a drawer in the vanity. Anyone looking would have easily found them.

She had been far too careful to open the door to a stranger. Either she knew her killer or he was already inside. But where and how? The patio doors were locked and led to an enclosed small brick courtyard and I knew a sensor triggered the security lights.

The office was cluttered but tidy and nothing obvious seemed to be taken. Her laptop was still sitting on a single desk. I was about to move on when I noticed a dusting of dark powder on the carpet. I touched it with my finger and raised it to my nose. Lavender and roses. That would indicate a bowl of potpourri on the windowsill. But where was the bowl and its contents now? Perhaps she accidentally broke it but she would have swept it up and emptied it into the pedestal bin in the kitchen. There was nothing except the tea towel and tissue in the bin. I looked closer at the window and saw splinters of wood at the edges where paint chips had been disturbed. I peered outside. On the ground, the remains of the potpourri was spread on the pavers.

I closed my eyes to try and visualise what had happened. I saw someone jemmying the window, not to steal or vandalise, but something far worse. He knocked over the potpourri as he squeezed through the opening and had to clean it up. Then he waited.

Christine arrived home. In her hand were her keys which she put on the table. She draped her coat over the hook along with her handbag and walked into the kitchen taking the mail and her phone with her. She filled the kettle and spooned coffee into a mug. One mug. He attacked her from behind as she drank the coffee, holding the chloroform filled tea towel over her face. When she lost consciousness, he dragged her into the lounge, leaving faint tracks against the grain of the carpet. He bound her feet and hands to a chair and waited for her to wake up. Hours later, she was dead.

A jolt of rage forced my eyes open. I saw my reflection in a mirror, a despairing face full of confusion and fear.

I let my eyes travel around the room, looking for anything out of place. The side table still held her keys and I walked over to pick them up. On the key ring, the small wooden lizard dangled between her car key and a collection of unknown keys. I took the spare front door key from my pocket to see if one of the assorted keys on the key ring was Christine's front door key, painstakingly matching the teeth from the one in my hand to the others on her key ring. The front door key was missing.

I stood in the lounge room staring at the keys trying to make sense in the absence. The front door was locked from the outside when I arrived so the killer must have taken her door key with him when he left. The question was, why did he do that? He had no need for the key since he was already in the home.

I went over in my mind again, step by step, what I thought the sequence of events must have been when Christine arrived home. I was assuming the killer was already inside the apartment because of the potpourri outside the window. That had to be his entry point. She opened the door and placed her keys on the side table. Then she would have draped her coat over the hook along with her handbag before walking into the kitchen with her mail and phone. I let my eyes travel to the kitchen. That seemed logical.

Think!

I ran through it in my mind again. She definitely walked into the kitchen. The coffee cup was still sitting on the bench with coffee grounds in the bottom of the cup. I told her I'd call her back after the meeting with Sandra so she would have planned on opening her mail while drinking her coffee and waiting for my phone call.

I ran my eyes around the kitchen, then slowly turned towards the hook behind the door. Her coat was there but he had taken the diary from it, her handbag along with her phone from the kitchen, before taking her body to the dump site. Why would he do that? Was his number was one of the numbers she'd called?

Then Cavanaugh's words at the crime scene came back to me. '*We found her clothes, the diary and her phone.*' If she was killed here, and by the amount of blood soaked into the carpet I knew she was, why had he taken her clothes with him? I'd read the autopsy report. Her body was found in just a bra and knickers. It just didn't make sense.

I turned my gaze towards the study. And why didn't he want it to look like a break in? What difference would it have made if she had been killed during a simple break and enter. Except this wasn't a simple break and enter. He was waiting for her to arrive and then killed her before taking her body to a site he had planned.

I stood running things through my head. Nothing was adding up.

Just then the phone rang. My heart almost leapt out of my chest. I couldn't risk answering it even though nobody knew I was here. I waited, listening to it ring until the answering machine clicked in. Full.

That's when my mobile started to ring. I fumbled through my jacket pocket and needed two hands to hold it steady. I didn't recognise the number.

"Is this Jack Curtis?"

My heart almost stopped. "Who is this?"

"It's the Surfers Paradise Police Station. Someone called us about an intruder at an address in Ashmore. The informant gave this mobile number as a contact number. Is that correct?"

My throat closed and I could hardly get the words out. I started to say I was nowhere near that address. *No, that's not good enough!*

"I'm sorry I can't hear you," I mumbled instead.

I turned off the phone and stared at the blank screen in horror. I couldn't hear myself thinking over the roar in my head. The volume had been steadily building until it now rattled inside my skull like a train entering a tunnel.

I have to get out and run! Had I touched anything? The kitchen bench? I was pretty sure I only touched surfaces with my hand in my windbreaker pocket.

I grabbed the car keys from the side table. All I could think of was escape.

Above the thrashing palms outside, I heard a baleful cry of a crow. It stopped then rose again: a chilling sound carried high on the wind.

20

It was after midnight when I left Christine's house in her car. The roads were varnished with rain and patches of fog disappeared into the drizzle. I put the wipers on and one screeched halfway across the windscreen, stopping with a thunk, then screeched back, coming to rest. Panic was still surging through me and making a quick exit was my only thought. I moved my head from side to side, trying to see through the windscreen, while the one wiper stuttered up and down as I planted my foot on the accelerator. I imagined roaring off into the night away from her house but instead there was no surge of power at all. The speedometer slowly inched upwards.

Stealing Christine's wreck of a car was the least of my worries. Staying awake behind the wheel and not crashing was uppermost on my mind. My foggy brain told me I needed to see Sandra Burton and tell her what had happened. Maybe even stay the night at the game parlour because I couldn't go home. That would be the first place they'd look for me. I took the exit towards Oxenford, a road that leads to Tamborine Mountain where I knew there were acres of bushland for me to hide. Periodically, the headlights swept across hedges.

"Worry about your alibi," Karen had said to me before she turned and entered her office. Now I had two things to worry about. Even if I could prove I didn't kill Christine, which I couldn't, they were definitely going to blame me for her murder now that I'd entered her home. Isn't that what I'd told Cavanaugh? A lot of murderers visit the scene of the crime to relive the kill? There was no doubt in my mind they'd be coming for me now.

Somewhere along the way, I pulled over into a muddy track while thoughts crashed around inside my head. At some stage I fell into an exhausted asleep and dreamt. Cavanaugh was crossing fields in front of a long line of policemen holding snarling German Shepherds on leashes, hunting me down. Undergrowth tore at my clothes as I ran, clawing my way up embankments. The dogs were getting closer. And then out of nowhere, Cavanaugh's face appeared, smiling and waving.

There was a tap, tap, tapping sound. I woke to find a bright light shining through the window. My eyes felt full of grit and my body stiff as I fumbled for the button to open the window. When it didn't work, I realised it was because the engine wasn't on. Instead, I cracked the door open a fraction.

A grizzled head peered at me from under a woollen cap. A dog was barking at his heels and I could hear the throb of a tractor engine.

"You're blocking my path, mister."

"Sorry," I mumbled as I shut the door and started the engine.

Light grey clouds, stunted trees and grassy fields lay ahead while the sun was beginning to rise but struggling to warm the morning. I reversed out of the track and watched the tractor pass through a wooden gate and bounce over puddles towards a barn that looked like it would fall over at the next breath of wind.

As the engine idled, I turned on the heater to full blast and glanced at my watch. 6.30 am. I had to call Sam.

"Where the hell are you!" she yelled without a greeting.

I had to shout to be heard over the roar of the heater. "Sam. I need your help."

"Jesus, Jack. What now?" I could hear exasperation in her voice.

"I went to Elizabeth's apartment last night and there's blood everywhere."

Even in my foggy brain, I knew to refer to Christine as Elizabeth. I shook my head to try and clear it. I had to tell Sam. Soon. "It's where she was killed," I told her.

Sam went quiet. "You went to her house?" There was disbelief in her voice. "Why would you do that?"

"I didn't do this Sam. But Cavanaugh's going to pin it on me." I sounded like a stranger even to my own ears. Panicked and out of control. "The phone rang when I was there but I didn't answer it. Then my mobile rang. It was a call from the station to say that someone had reported a break in and my number was the contact number for an emergency."

I heard her mumble a profanity.

"Listen to me, Sam. Someone reported a break in. But I was quiet, Sam. Real quiet. It had to be someone who was watching me who reported it. He's been watching me all along."

"Jack. Can you hear yourself? You're sounding paranoid and delusional."

"Listen to me, Sam," I almost yelled. I glanced at my face in the rear vision mirror. Bloodshot eyes stared back at me and a tic jerked at one eye. I did look delusional.

I turned away from the mirror quickly. "I may have left prints there. I don't know but maybe I did."

I could hear her breathing in the silence. Finally she said, "You have to report this, Jack."

"And tell them what? I broke into a murder victim's house? Listen to me. Someone is trying to frame me."

"But why, Jack? Who?"

My breathing was becoming ragged. "I don't know. That's what I'm trying to work out."

Sam has always been the emotional one. Always the first to explode. Now it was me and I know I sounded crazy.

"He called me, Sam. The killer called me yesterday after Karen dropped me back at the office. Only one hour after I got to my office, he called. He knew I was there. He was watching me all the time."

"He called you? What did he say?"

"He gloated to me about killing her, like he enjoyed it. I've seen all manner of evil, Sam, but this guy," I shook my head, even though she couldn't see me do it, "this guy is the worst. And he's been watching me Sam. I know it. I need your help."

"To do what, Jack? I'm a police officer and you're putting me in a terrible spot. Grayson is already watching me. There are procedures for this kind of thing. You need to come in to the station."

"Please, Sam. One favour."

She sighed deeply. "Okay, Jack. Then you come in to the station and explain."

I almost laughed. Explain what? I had no idea what was going on.

"I want you to meet with me. I have some things I have to tell you."

I knew I couldn't put this off any longer. I had to tell Sam about Sandra Burton's organisation and my part in it at some time and I had to tell her about Christine. It wasn't something I could keep to myself forever. If Sam was to be a part of my life, I needed to be honest with her. Whatever the consequences.

There was silence on the line for a few seconds and I knew she was thinking.

"You certainly do," she muttered eventually. I heard keys jingling on the other end of the line. "I'm just about to head into the station. I'll find out what I can about last night first. Cavanaugh and I aren't partners anymore so I'll have to get the information from the duty officer somehow." She paused. "You're putting me in an awkward position here, Jack."

"I didn't do this Sam," was all I could say.

When Sam spoke, her voice was soft. "I know that, Jack. But nothing is adding up." There was a moment of silence. "I want you to remember I'm on your side."

My heart lurched at the tenderness in her voice. Maybe we had a chance after all.

"Okay." Her voice was brusque again, all business. "Let me see what I can get and then we'll meet. And I want to know what the hell's going on." She paused again. "I want to know everything. Do you understand?"

"I understand."

My next call was to Frank.

21

Willie Vanko's auto shop looked run-down and unreliable, if not blatantly dishonest, from the outside. Inside wasn't a whole lot better. But Willie, a Pole whose surname I couldn't pronounce and had been shortened to Vanko by a generation of customers, was just about the best mechanic I knew.

I have never liked this area of Surfers despite being only a short walk from the constant roar of Surfers Parade. Willie's shop had been a good source of information for me over the years since every deadbeat friend of Willie's tended to congregate there at some time or other. He was constantly up front with me but I always felt uneasy there.

Willie's garage was situated in a block that was fighting the council tooth and nail for redevelopment. Willie's block had been bought by the owner of a Japanese noodle house next door who wanted to extend his reach further on down to the next block and Willie was heavily involved in a partially legal battle to ensure that he wasn't shut down. The Japanese businessman responded by sending fish smells through the vents into Willie's garage.

Inside the workshop, the air was thick with the smell of fish and noodles as Arnold, small and wiry, worked under the hood of a Nissan. The sound of loud swearing came from inside Willie's office. The door flew open and Willie stormed out, grease on his bald head and his blue mechanic's uniform open to the waist to show a dirty white T-shirt straining over a huge belly. He climbed arduously up onto a set of boxes placed beneath the air vent and put his mouth to the grille.

"You slant-eyed sons of bitches!" he shrieked. "Quit stinking up my garage with fish or I'm gonna get nuclear." There was the sound of something shouted back in Japanese from the other end of the vent and then a burst of Oriental laughter. Willie thumped the grille with the heel of his hand and climbed down.

He squinted at me in the semi-darkness. "Detective Curtis. How you doin'? You wanna cup a coffee?"

"Not today Willie. What I need is for Arnold to look at this car here," I pointed to Christine's Mazda, "and see if there's anything he can do. Maybe it needs a service but it's running badly. I can leave it here for a few hours and come back."

He smiled at me, a look like a cat would give to a mouse. "Sure, Jack. We'll be happy to look at it."

Something in the smile made me pause. "If it's going to be pricey, ring me first. Don't just go ahead and fix it. I don't need it to run like new, I just need it to run better than it does right now. Even for just a few days."

He gave me a thumbs up. "See you in a couple of hours, detective."

∼

Sam, Frank and I were sitting in a quiet corner of Charlie's on Surfers Boulevard, in deference to Sam's wishes. I'd insisted because if anyone was watching us, it would be obvious, since this coffee shop was in the hub of Surfers. If it turned out the police were looking for me, we'd see them coming and be able to make an easy escape through the maze of alleyways.

Sam was wearing dark trousers and a black jacket with a scowl on her face, Frank was wearing torn jeans and a Guns and Roses t-shirt and a smirk. I was wearing the same clothes I'd been in for two days because I'd fallen asleep on the couch after eating the pizza.

The coffee shop was busy, which I liked. There was lots of noise which meant no one could overhear our conversation. I was being paranoid, but a lot had happened in the past few days and if I've learnt anything from my years as a cop, it's that you can't be too careful.

Frank said he was starving and ordered buffalo wings and a coke while Sam and I sipped cups of coffee. I didn't think I could hold down anything since my stomach was churning. As Frank ate noisily, I explained everything to Sam about Christine, Sandra Burton and the organisation where Frank and I worked. I left out Sandra's headquarters and Sam was smart enough not to ask. Then I told her about Christine's involvement which had probably caused her murder.

Sam remained silent, scowling from time to time for much of our conversation, interjecting occasionally to clarify things while scribbling notes in a small notebook. At one point, her hand brushed my arm lightly and she left it there for an instant, her skin warm through my shirt. I'd kept the secret of my new job from Sam, not just because she was a policewoman but because I thought she would react badly. I was wrong.

Her eyes were slightly distant and she was playing over in her mind what I'd told her, even asking Frank questions which she would normally avoid.

I finished up with my visit to Christine's apartment last night and the phone call from the station to my mobile phone regarding a break-in. After only four hours sleep last night and even less the night before, my mind felt foggy. The strong coffee was beginning to help but I had no idea what was going on and I was far from a 'ta da' moment.

"Baffle me with your brilliance, Frank," I sighed when I'd finished talking.

"Sumfing don' feel righ'. I don't like i'," he stated, looking up at me with squinting eyes. As he talked, he picked up another buffalo wing as his eyes flicked around the room, never resting in one place.

"Wha' I fink is," he mumbled as bits of chicken dropped from his mouth, "it 'as to be someone ya know." He made a small, exploding gesture with his hands, like a magician making a rabbit disappear in a puff of smoke. Sauce flew above his hand and fell onto the floor beside him. He ignored it and reached for a napkin.

Serpent

"It 'as to be someone you wouldn' suspect," he said, wiping sauce from his face with a tissue. "Someone ya come in contac' wif regular-like 'oo blends in the background. But this someone knows you and everyfing bou' you."

He swallowed noisily then began eating again. I saw Sam wince as sauce dripped off his chin onto the table. He smiled at me through gappy teeth. "You go' any enemies, guv?"

I snorted. "Where do I start?"

He shook his head and tittered lightly. It was a strange sound coming from a face that looked like a mad scientist had put it together. I was silent because I didn't want to alter Frank's chain of thought. I had a feeling we were close to the finish line.

A waitress came over and asked if we wanted more drinks.

Frank awarded her with a toothy smile. "Nah darlin', fanks anyway."

I noticed her eyes widen as he beamed up at her before she turned and walked quickly away.

"So," he continued. "Bes' guess? Someone's tryin' to frame you." He picked up a fresh napkin, wiped his fingers on it then threw it on the table.

I was trying to get my head around this. Something was buzzing loudly in my head.

Someone I knew who knew everything about me. Someone who blended into the background. Someone I see regularly. The list was small.

There's a moment in film and television when a particular shot or word signifies that moment when the penny drops. Sometimes, it's something little that goes 'click' and everything seems to fall into place. Then when comprehension dawns, the camera zooms towards the face of the hero and the music reaches a crescendo as the light of realisation grows in their eyes. Real life is not like that. It's deathly quiet. But suddenly you know. I had this bad feeling in the pit of my stomach like there were ten snakes in there and all of them were fighting to get out.

"Wow," I whispered. "You're a genius, Frank."

I stared at him and he stared right back, wiggling his eyebrows and burping before looking around the room. "You should watch yaself a little more in public, Jack. People will be finkin' we're a couple of ravin' poofs 'aving a momen'."

Sam sat up straight and stared at me. "What is it, Jack? What am I missing?"

I took Christine's car keys out of my pocket and stared at them lying in the palm of my hand. The lizard attached to them felt smooth and beautifully carved and I felt the warmth of it in my hand. I'd noticed the same craftsmanship on the cross that Sandra Burton wore around her neck.

"I need to make a call," I stated.

"Who?" Sam asked, sitting up straight with her eyes wide.

I had no time to answer. She'd know soon enough.

I pulled out my phone and found Sandra Burton's name. I scrolled down to the number listed under 'mobile' then pushed the blue shaded number. The screen changed and the phone rang on the other end. Two rings later, Sandra answered.

"Hello, Jack," she answered in a weary voice. "This number is for emergencies only. This had better be good."

"It is an emergency, Sandra."

I quickly filled her in on what had happened last night at Christine's house, explaining the call from the police station and finishing with me taking Christine's car. She listened in silence until I finished.

"That's just crazy, Jack. What do you need? And please don't say an alibi. That is the one thing I will have to refuse."

Her voice had saddened but I could hear the steely quality that meant she wouldn't change her mind.

"That's not why I called, Sandra. What I want to know is where you got the cross from around your neck?"

I put the phone on speaker as Sam sat back in her chair and blinked in confusion. Frank on the other hand, leant forward, forearms resting on the table as he listened. His eyes were like dark pieces of granite.

"My cross?" she asked in a perplexed voice.

"The wooden one you always wear."

"Uh. Jimmy gave it to me. He said he made it especially for me to protect me. I love it. Why?"

"I told you I took Christine's car because the police have impounded mine. Her key ring has a carved wooden lizard attached to it."

Sam inhaled sharply and Frank muttered some profanity.

"You went through Jimmy's background before hiring him, didn't you?" I asked.

"You shouldn't have to ask me that. Of course I did." She sounded affronted, as if I was questioning her ability.

I ignored the tone and asked, "And you were satisfied with your search?"

"I hired him, Jack."

"Tell me about him, Sandra. It's important."

The hesitation only lasted a few seconds. She knew she could trust me but even so it was an odd request to make.

"O-kay." She drew the word out as she thought. "Well, to start with, Jimmy has a complicated history. He told me that at the age of nine, he was picked up at his school, St Mary's, and taken from his family before being put into foster care where he was eventually adopted officially. He said his father was away in the Army a lot. He thought he was a mechanic or something like that. He never saw him again. He told me he left school at fifteen and ran away from his adoptive parents, doing odds jobs and working at various organisations like the Salvation Army and The Smith Family over the years."

"Did you try to get any more information about him?"

"I don't take this job lightly, Jack. Of course I did. Everything we do here depends on my diligence and thoroughness."

"I'm not doubting you. I'm just trying to put things together. A lot of things have been happening Sandra, and I'm trying to work out what's going on. What else did you find out?"

"I tried to uncover more about his family background but brick walls kept popping up." Her voice had softened which meant she was appeased. "I contacted a woman from Children's Services who wouldn't give me much information because all files are locked to protect the children, she told me. What she did tell me was that his mother walked into a police station one day and accused her husband of sexually abusing their nine-year-old son. That started the ball rolling. He was picked up from his school and examined and bruises were discovered on his thighs and upper legs. Jimmy kept refusing to admit his father had abused him but the damage was already done. Social workers stepped in and within a few months, his mother had disappeared and Jimmy was in foster care. No names were released and the files are meant to remain permanently closed."

I listened in silence, my chin resting on chest as I concentrated and took it all in.

"I was satisfied, Jack. Jimmy is a product of the very people I try to uncover on a daily basis. After a year on the job, he has proved his trustworthiness. As you know, we have used him quite successfully for surveillance."

She was right. Despite his size at six foot two, Jimmy has proven to be someone who could blend and not be noticed.

"Is Jimmy in the parlour at the moment?"

"No. He had a day off yesterday and is not due back until this afternoon. What's going on, Jack?"

"I'm not sure. I just don't know. If he turns up today, call Frank immediately." I hesitated. "On second thoughts," I glanced over to Frank, "I'll send Frank over now so he can keep an eye on things. I'll keep you updated when I know more."

Beside Sam, I saw Frank's eyes as I hung up. He blinked first, then a slow smile came to his face before he nodded and sat back in his chair. "Little weasel. I never liked 'im," he muttered.

I shook my head. "We don't know yet for sure, Frank. Did he even give the carved lizard to Christine? Maybe she got it from somewhere else. We live in one of the biggest touristy areas in the world. The shops are full of souvenirs like that." I chewed my lip for a moment. "The questions keep piling up though." I jiggled my head from side to side. "The big question is why would he kill Christine? Sandra once told me he was smitten with her."

In the back of my mind was the phone call I'd received at my office. The caller said, *'I loved her in my own way.'*

I searched hard in my memory for answers. "How would he even know where she lived? That sort of information is kept in a file that

Sandra would absolutely lock away from prying eyes." I shook my head. "We have to be wrong. It can't be Jimmy. Even if it was, why would he want to frame me for her murder? I've never done or said anything out of place to him."

What was it that Sandra said about Jimmy? Fostered at nine and finally adopted years later. Usually, when a child is adopted, the child takes on the name of the adoptive parents. That would mean Croft was his adopted name. So what was his name before being adopted and why hadn't he given it to Sandra when she was doing the search? At nine years old, he would have remembered it. Sandra said there was very little information available before the age of nine, except for the school he was picked up from. But she also said he dropped out of school around the age of fifteen and lived on the streets for a while, doing volunteer work for various organisations.

"What I need is more information on Jimmy to eliminate him." I was thinking out loud, lost in thought. "I need past information that up to now has been restricted to Sandra when she did her initial search for background on him. There has to be something we don't know. What I need is the name of the Social Worker who signed off on Jimmy as a nine-year-old. I know he was adopted at approximately twelve years old and at that time, his name changed. What I need is his birth name and why he was taken away from his family. His father may have been in the army but his mother apparently disappeared which is why he was taken into the Care system. If it is him, maybe this is all about what happened to him before he was adopted." I shook my head trying to shake the weariness away. "Maybe I'm wrong and Jimmy has nothing to do with this. It seems so totally ridiculous. But it's all I can think of."

I looked up at Sam. "I need your help with this, Sam. I need that information."

"That will leave footprints in the system," Sam said. "You know that, Jack. They'll find out it was me eventually."

She was right. I couldn't compromise her. It meant her job and I didn't want to be responsible for her losing it on something so flimsy as intuition.

I stared into my empty coffee cup. I needed to be sure before I went any further. The wooden carvings were just a hunch and far from conclusive. No judge in the world would sign a warrant for someone's arrest based on that alone. Getting the Social Worker's name was a good start but that still didn't prove anything. It only gave me Jimmy's background. What I needed was something solid that only Jimmy knew. The problem with that was I'd had very little to do with him. I'd seen him a few times at the game parlour when visiting Sandra but that was it. I could count on one hand the number of conversations I'd had with him.

And then it hit me.

Sometimes all it takes is a few words to be uttered for the penny to drop. Sometimes, it's something little that goes 'click' and everything seems to fall into place. For some people, it triggers something in your memory and we remember where we left our car keys or the name of that someone or that song we've been wracking our brains to think of. It's the instant that signifies the break in a case. That's when comprehension dawns.

My mother used to tell me there were no monsters in our world, no real ones. They only existed in the movies. She was wrong. They're all around us and if we give them the opportunity, they'll crawl out from under their rocks. Even as I felt my stomach contract, even as I felt my heart turn to ice, I somehow managed to detach. I felt something in me harden and I felt that old familiar surge of adrenaline rushing through my veins when pieces start to join up. It was like looking through a fog and suddenly coming through into brilliant sunshine.

When most people think of a murderer they think of a glassy-eyed lunatic. Someone who looks the part and acts the part. Actually, the typical murderer is something completely different. They look ordinary. The kind of person you wouldn't look twice at. Not a monster working in a game parlour.

I remembered talking to Jimmy on the day I identified Christine's body at the morgue. And then I remembered the faint odour on his clothes.

I could feel Frank and Sam staring at me and I could feel the colour draining from my face as I suddenly placed the odour. Chloroform. At the time, I'd thought it was a faint odour of bleach but it could very well have been chloroform.

Thoughts collided in my brain. When had I smelt it? It was the day I'd identified Christine's body. But she'd been dead for a week by then. And then I smelt it in the kitchen bin in Christine's house.

Was I making a big mistake and trying to make things fit a clumsy suspicion?

I knew for a fact that the smell of chloroform can stay on clothes for weeks if clothing comes into direct contact with it.

And then, like a lightning bolt, I knew. He'd laughingly talked about adding a roulette wheel to the parlour. He told me 21 was his lucky number and red was his lucky colour.

My heart almost stopped. "I have to call Cavanaugh, Sam," I mumbled.

For seconds, no one said a word. Then she reached for her phone, pushed buttons, then held the phone to me. On the screen was Cavanaugh's mobile number.

Frank stared silently at me as I punched the numbers into my phone and dialled.

"Are you sure 'bout this, mate?" he asked sceptically.

As I nodded, Cavanaugh answered.

"Cavanaugh."

"It's Jack Curtis, Cavanaugh."

"Well, well, well." I could hear the sneer in his voice. "I was wondering when you'd contact me. Good. Because I need you to hand yourself in."

"I will, but not yet. I need to ask you some questions."

He snorted. "You want to ask *me* some questions?" he chuckled. "That's rich."

"Drop the sarcasm, Cavanaugh. I'm trying to help with this investigation."

"You're bargaining with me again?" he chuckled.

I ignored the barb in his voice. "How many stab wounds did Elizabeth sustain?"

He snorted down the line. "You read the report, Curtis. Twenty-one."

"And was chloroform on her dress?"

He hesitated. "Yes."

"And was red the colour of her dress?"

He said nothing for a moment, then he bellowed down the line. "Now how the HELL did you know that?"

His breathing had gone ragged and I knew I had the proof I needed. Now I had to convince him.

"You bloody-well come into the station!" he bellowed. "You do it NOW, willingly, or I'll have a warrant for your arrest out with every car available."

"I will. But while I contact my lawyer, I need you to pull a file on someone. This is the person you're looking for. His name is James Croft and he is approximately nineteen or twenty years old. All I know is he was picked up from St Mary's school and taken from his parents before being placed into the Foster Care system at about the age of nine. He was adopted at approximately twelve years old and at that time, his name changed. What we need is his birth name. That's the only part of his life no one knows about. His father may have been in the army but his mother apparently disappeared which is why he was taken into the Care system. Maybe this is all about what happened to him when he was adopted."

He snorted. "Okay. I'll play along. Who is this guy?"

"He's your killer. He once told me red was his lucky colour and twenty-one was his lucky number. I have also smelt chloroform on his clothes. It's too difficult to explain over the phone, but I believe he is somehow involved in the case of the guy who fell off the ferry from Stradbroke as well. I'm not sure how or why, but trust me, he is. Everything is too coincidental. This guy is a cold-blooded murderer and you need to dig up that information before I come in."

"You're lying to cover yourself, Curtis."

"Think, Cavanaugh. I'm coming in but not until you do this." I hesitated. "His father was in the army, a mechanic perhaps. I don't know anything about his mother. He was on the streets from about fifteen, volunteering for the Salvos, or some organisation like that."

Think!

"His motive for doing this is in that information. I'm sure!" I added.

"Okay, Curtis. What say I do find the name? Let's just pretend it's that easy. What then? How do I get them to release the information?"

There was one name that came to mind. "Go to Judge Buchanan."

"Judge Buchanan? Why the hell would I go to him specifically?"

I took a deep breath before continuing. "Because he was Elizabeth's father. Elizabeth Delaney was an alias. Her real name was Christine Buchanan."

In the silence over the phone, I could imagine the anger building before he spoke. "You knew this all along and didn't say anything?!" His voice was dangerously quiet.

Sam dropped her chin to her chest. I knew she could hear Cavanaugh's voice from across the table and she knew I was in serious trouble.

"You're withholding information from me?" he yelled. "Are you actually telling me that? You *do* know that's a criminal...."

"I don't know if he's aware his daughter was murdered," I interrupted. "I'm betting he'll be more than happy to sign a warrant if it means finding out who killed her."

I knew Cavanaugh was trying to calm himself. I could almost hear his teeth grinding together. "You get your lawyer up and running with this, Curtis. You do it today. What I'll do is give you twenty-four hours to get in here. But that's it." He waited a few seconds. "In that time, I'll chase up the information and believe me, I'll look into this James Croft. But you be in this station by 10 am tomorrow morning with your lawyer or there'll be a warrant out for your arrest. You're lucky I'm such a nice guy."

I pressed the 'end call' button and dropped the phone on the table before looking up at Sam.

"Okay, Jack," she said. I hated hearing the sadness in her voice. "You have twenty-four hours before you turn yourself in. I suggest you use every minute of that."

She was right. I had to turn myself in but I had one day before I had to do that. First I had to dig up as much information I could to give to Cavanaugh as a trade-off for his information on Jimmy. If I was right, the rest of the balls will fall into place.

22

A bell tinkled above my head as I entered the shop. The aroma of scented oils, perfumed candles and herbal poultices curled up to my nostrils. Shelves made of white melamine stretched from the floor to the ceiling, crammed with soaps, oils and jars full of everything from pumice stones to seaweed.

A large woman emerged through a back door wearing a brightly coloured kaftan that started at her throat and billowed outwards over her large breasts. Strings of beads clacked as she walked towards me.

"Come in. Come in," she said, waving me towards her.

This was Lois Chapman. I recognised her voice from the phone call I'd made at Charlie's as Frank and I had sat drinking another cup of coffee and working out my next move while Sam returned to the station.

I'd called St Mary's and was told Lois Chapman had been the Grade 3 teacher during the dates I gave her but I was told she had since retired and had bought a shop in the touristy area of Cavill Avenue.

Things were finally beginning to go my way. Her shop was only a street away from Charlie's, barely a five minute walk away. Before I called Karen to organise for her to be at the station the next morning, I told Frank to head over to Adventureland to keep an eye out for Jimmy while I went to see Lois. Karen suggested meeting at her office a couple of hours beforehand so I could fill her in on any updates from this afternoon. She wanted to be prepared and updated so there'd be no nasty surprises.

"Oh my," Lois gasped, placing her hands on either side of her face. "Look at those eyes. Dull and dry. And you haven't been sleeping well, have you? Toxins in the blood. Too much red meat. Maybe a wheat allergy."

I smiled. "We spoke on the phone," I explained. "I'm Jack Curtis. I'm a Private Detective."

"Ah. That explains it. Doctors and policemen make the worst patients. Doctors never take their own advice and policemen, well, most of them think they know everything." She looked shamefaced. "Present company excepted."

She pirouetted with remarkable agility and bustled deeper into the shop, talking at the same time. "Come on. Follow me."

Behind the door was a small back room with just enough space for a table, two chairs and a bench containing a small sink. On a bench against the wall, an electric kettle and a computer were pressed against the wall and plugged into the wall socket. A melamine shelf above the bench held a dozen jars, all filled with what looked like different coloured tea leaves, none of which were labelled. In the centre of the table was a woman's magazine opened at the crossword.

"Herbal tea?"

"Do you have coffee?"

"No," she scowled.

"Tea is fine."

She flicked the electric kettle on then stood, hands on hips, facing the shelf holding the jars. As her head moved from left to right, she rattled off the different blends but by the time she finished, I'd forgotten the first few.

"Camomile, I think," she spoke over her shoulder. "It's good for relieving stress and tension."

Glancing over her shoulder as she reached for one of the jars, she smiled, "You're not a believer, are you?"

"I've never been able to understand why something so bland can be good for you."

She laughed, her whole body jiggling. "It works in harmony with the body. Smell is the most immediate of all our senses and is hot-wired directly into our brains."

She set two small china cups on saucers on the table and filled a ceramic teapot with steaming water. The tea leaves were filtered twice through a silver sieve before she pushed the cup towards me.

"How do you read tea leaves like this?" I asked.

"I think you're making fun of me, Detective Curtis," she smiled.

She sat down and took a deep whiff of the aromatic tea. "How can I help you?"

"Eight years ago you were a teacher at St Mary's," I began.

"I was," she said, blowing gently on the tea.

"This is a long shot but I'm hoping you can help me. Do you remember a boy by the name of Jimmy who would have been in Grade 3 at the time," I hesitated while doing my math, "about ten years ago. He was picked up by the police during school hours. He may not have returned after that."

She placed her cup on the saucer and looked up at me. "Of course, I do."

I was stunned. Why hadn't I thought of this before? I was definitely losing my touch. Maybe it was just weariness but I had to be more alert that this if I expected to solve this mystery.

"Do you remember his name?"

She answered instantly. "James Lachlan."

A shiver ran down my spine as the name swam around in my brain.

Lachlan? Another connection to Simon Price and his book? I took a deep breath, trying to calm myself, as I sloshed the tea around in my cup.

"Do you remember much about him?" I asked, sounding casual.

"He was quite bright, although a little self-conscious about his size. Some of the other boys used to tease him and call him Frankenstein. He had a stillness about him that you don't see in most children." She stared into her teacup, tiling it gently back and forth. "A lot of the teachers found it very unnerving. He was never any good at sports, too clumsy, but he had a lovely singing voice."

"You taught the choir?"

Serpent

"Yes, I did. I suggested singing lessons but his mother wasn't the most approachable of women. I only saw her once at the school. She came to complain about Jimmy stealing money from her purse to pay for an excursion to Natural Arch."

"What about the father? Do you remember him?"

She looked at me quizzically. Clearly I was expected to know something and she was wondering if she should continue.

"Jimmy's father was not allowed at the school," she said. "He had a court order taken out against him at the beginning of the year when Jimmy was in third grade. Didn't Jimmy tell you any of this?"

"No." I didn't want to go into any details at the moment in case she decided to stop talking.

She shook her head and the beads around her neck clanged from side to side. "It was me who raised the alarm. Jimmy had wet himself in class twice in a few weeks. Then he soiled his pants and spent most of the afternoon hiding in the boys' toilets. He was very upset, as you can imagine. When I asked him what was wrong, he wouldn't say so I took him to the school nurse. She found him another pair of trousers and that's when she saw the welts on his legs. It looked as though he had been beaten."

She took a sip of the tea before continuing. I'd wished I'd been able to tape this but I had no idea she would be able to give me so much information.

"The school nurse followed the normal procedure and informed the headmistress who, in turn, notified the Department of Children's Services." She glanced up at me. "I know the process, Detective Curtis. A duty social worker would have taken the referral and discussed it with a duty manager."

She sighed and sipped some more before continuing. "He was picked up by the police that afternoon and the dominoes would then have fallen. Medical examinations, parent interviews, allegations, denials, case conference, 'at risk' findings, interim care orders, appeals, each tumbling into the next."

"Can you tell me about the court order?" I asked.

"I only heard about it second-hand since I was the one who started this ball rolling. There were allegations of sexual abuse, which the father denied. Then came a restraining order. The police investigated but I don't know the outcome. The headmistress dealt with the social workers and kept me out of the loop."

"Do you know what happened to Jimmy?"

"All I heard was that after his father died, he became even more reserved. That was when he was taken into the Foster Care System."

I blinked. "His father died?"

"Committed suicide, I heard. Before they could prosecute him for child abuse."

In the silence, a clock ticked somewhere. I felt like the wretched senator in Godfather 2 who went to bed with a beautiful girl and woke up with the head of a horse in his bed. I felt heat on the back of my neck as I took a deep breath. The hairs on my arms were standing erect but I couldn't interpret my emotions. Fear? Excitement?

I said nothing for a moment while I collected my thoughts. "Do you think that was the case? That Jimmy was abused by his father?"

"In some households, Detective Curtis, just waking up in the morning is a form of abuse."

The front door bell tinkled and Lois stood up. "I have to go, Detective. I hope I've helped and I hope he's happier now than when he was that poor boy."

She led the way through the door, greeting the new customer with a happy welcome. As I left, I glanced behind me. Despite the chirpy behaviour, I saw a deep sadness in her eyes.

23

I stood on the busy street, lost in thought. There was low grade buzz in my brain and I tried to sort everything into some semblance of order.

I couldn't wait for Cavanaugh now, nor could I trust him to give me any information he discovered. I now knew Jimmy's birth name. I also knew Social Services kept files on children who were sexually abused. I once had full access to them but not anymore. What I needed was help from someone I hadn't seen in almost four years. Her name was Melissa Stark.

When I first met her, she was a duty social worker but I knew she still worked in Child Protection. Not many people last ten years in this field, but she had. They either burn out or blow up.

Mel was your original hippy with beads and bangles, distressed leather jackets and torn denim jeans. She was always challenging opinions because she liked people who stood up for what they believed in, whether she agreed with them or not.

Growing up in Byron Bay, she had listened to her father, a local fisherman, talk about 'men's work' and 'women's work'. Almost predictably, she became an ardent feminist with a doctorate thesis in 'When Women Wear the Pants'. Mel's husband, Ben, was tall and thin and went grey at nineteen but kept his hair long and tied back in a ponytail. I only ever saw it loose once when he was swimming in the ocean. His hair floated behind him like a mass of dead seaweed.

When I was a policeman, I'd had dinner a few times with them, having visited Mel many times in the course of work. We got on straight away. We ate vegetarian meals, drank too much wine and the hangovers lasted until Monday and the flatulence until Tuesday.

I knew her office was in Broadbeach so I decided to call her and ask her to have lunch with me.

Half an hour later, Mel made a face at me through the window of the small restaurant. Her hair was straight and pinned back from her face and instead of the distressed denim, she was wearing black trousers and a tailored beige jacket.

I waved her in to the seat opposite me. As I passed the menu across to her, I asked, "Is this the management look?"

"No. It's middle age," she laughed, looking grateful to sit down. "These shoes are killing me." She kicked them off and sighed with relief.

"You weren't at your office," I asked.

"Nope. I came straight here from an appointment in the children's court. An emergency care order."

"A good result?"

"I've seen worse."

We glanced through the menu and placed our orders with the waiter before settling down to talk.

"Is Sally still being hard to get along with?" she asked.

"We have bad days and good days," I said, jiggling my head from side to side. "Jazz is good though, most times. She's almost fifteen." I pulled a face. "That says everything."

She shook her head and smiled. "Teenagers."

"How's Ben?" I asked.

I pictured him an ageing hippy, still wearing Punjabi pants I laughingly called 'poopy pants'.

She turned her face away, but not before I saw the pain drift across her eyes like a cloud.

"Ben is dead."

Sitting very still, I let the silence grow while I blinked in shock.

"When?" I finally asked.

"A year ago. One of those SUV with bull bars went through a stop sign and ran him down as he crossed the street."

Our coffee arrived and we sat in silence while I watched her lick the milk froth from her spoon.

"They say the first year is the worst. I tell you, it's like being beaten. I still can't get my head around the fact that he's gone. I was so angry with him for not paying more attention as he crossed the damn street, I felt like he'd abandoned me. To spite him, I sold his record collection." She smiled sadly. "It cost me twice as much to buy it back again." She laughed as she stirred her coffee.

I tried to keep the hurt from my voice. "You should have gotten in touch with me."

She reached over and put her hand briefly on mine. "You'd left the police force by then and I'd lost your number and address. I know I could have found you," she smiled apologetically, "but I just didn't want to see anyone for a while. It would just remind me of the good old days."

"Where is he now?"

"In a silver pot in my filing cabinet." She made it sound like he was pottering around in the garden. "I can't put him in the ground. I might just go out someday in the ocean and throw them on the water." She shrugged. "Just not yet. I'm not ready to part with him."

Our food arrived, toasted BLT's with fries, and we took a few minutes arranging napkins and downing the fries.

"So. Why the call after such a long time?" she asked waving a chip at me.

"I need to get hold of a child protection file."

"Ah. And you can't get hold of it because you don't have any authority now."

"Correct."

She lifted the sandwich carefully, bit into it and chewed while she thought.

"What's the name?" she finally asked.

"James Lachlan."

Mel had made the connection immediately. "Is this David Lachlan's son?"

I put my sandwich back down on the plate and shook my head. "That name keeps popping up. At the moment, it's all supposition but you're the second person today whose made the connection."

She nodded. "I remember the case because of the name," she said, wiping her mouth with a napkin. "Nine, maybe ten ago. I had to drag a magistrate out of bed at two in the morning to sign interim care orders. The referral came from a schoolteacher," she explained as she pushed her own plate aside. "The mother didn't want to say anything at first. When she saw the medical evidence, she broke down and told us she suspected her husband."

"Can you get me the file to look at?"

Closed childcare files have been stored in the basement of her office building for a hundred years and can only be viewed by an appropriate member of the staff or an authorised agency with a court order. It was a big request because all access has to be made part of the record.

I could see she wanted to ask me why but probably thought it best not to. She stared at her reflection in her teaspoon while she pressed her lips together in thought.

She glanced at her watch. "I'll make a few phone calls. Come to my office at one-thirty."

We ate the rest of our lunch, talking and laughing about Ben. Fifteen minutes later, she kissed me on the cheek and left.

24

Mel's desk was clear except for a computer monitor and two piles of files on either side of the desk. Her computer was decorated with stickers, and cartoons, one of which showed an armed robber pointing a gun and saying, 'Your money or your life.' The victim replied, "I have no money and no life. I'm a social worker.'

Her office was on the third floor of the Social Services Department and most of the offices were empty. Behind her desk through the expanse of window, a half-built office building loomed.

She told me I had an hour before she got back from doing her shopping and in that time I could look through the three files in my hand, held together by a thick red rubber band.

I don't know what I was expecting to find. I don't even know why it felt so important to read the files. Maybe I was hoping that by reading them, they would give me an idea of why he had set out to murder Christine. I was hoping for *something*, I just didn't know what that something was. If Jimmy spent time in a children's home or a psych ward, this would have been recorded. There would be names, dates and places as well as interviews, family assessments and both medical and psych reports. With any luck I could cross-reference and find a link to why he chose Christine.

The first page of the first file was a record of the phone call from St Mary's School. I recognised Mel's handwriting. *'Jimmy displayed a number of recent behavioural changes'*, she wrote. Apart from wetting himself and soiling his pants, apparently he displayed inappropriate sexual behaviour by dropping his pats in front of a seven-year-old girl.

Mel sent the information and the file on to the Area Manager and started a new file.

This new file had the 'red edge', marking it closed to everyone except those with a court order. It recorded Jimmy's name, date of birth, address and details of his parents, his school and any known health problems.

Mel had organised a full medical examination. Dr Graham Burton found *'two or three marks about six inches long across both buttocks'*. He described the injuries as being consistent with *'two or three successive blows with a hard item such as a studded belt'*.

Dr Burton stated Jimmy had been distressed throughout the examination and had refused to answer any questions. He also noted what appeared to be old scar tissue around the anus. *'Whether the injury was caused accidentally or deliberate penetration is not clear,'* he wrote. In a later report, he hardened his report and described the scarring as being *'consistent with abuse'*.

Bridget Lachlan was interviewed and while hostile at first, she accused social services of being busybodies. When told of her son's injuries and behaviour, she began to adjust her answers, eventually making excuses for her husband. When asked about any inappropriate sexual behaviour, she categorically denied her husband could have done such a thing. She became tearful and asked to see Jimmy. She was told all allegations of sexual abuse have to be reported to the police and after being told this, she grew even more anxious. Clearly distressed, she admitted to having concerns about her husband's relationship with Jimmy. She wouldn't elaborate.

Jimmy and his mother were taken to the police station and formally interviewed where a strategy meeting was held. Leafing through Bridget's police statement, I tried to pick out the crux of her allegations. Two years earlier she claimed to have seen Jimmy sitting on her husband's lap, not wearing any underwear. Her husband, she said, only had a towel around

Serpent

his waist. During the previous year, she had often found that Jimmy had no underwear when he undressed to have a bath. When asked why, he said *'Daddy doesn't like me wearing underpants.'*

Although not a strong statement, in the hands of a good prosecutor it could be damning. I expected the next statement to be from Jimmy. It wasn't there. I turned several pages but it wasn't there. There wasn't even a mention of a formal statement having been made, which would explain why David Lachlan was never charged.

A child's evidence is crucial. Unless he or she admits to being molested, the chances of success are slim. The abuser would have to admit to the crime or medical evidence would have to be incontrovertible. In Jimmy's case, it wasn't.

I kept flipping through the file, piecing together the history of what happened next. Mel recommended that Jimmy be placed on the Child Protection Register – a list of all children who were considered to be at risk. She applied for an interim custody order – getting a magistrate out of bed at two in the morning. David Lachlan was arrested, his house searched along with his car. He maintained his innocence throughout and described himself as a loving father who had never done anything wrong or been in trouble with the police and he was a respectable businessman who had dealings with the local councilman, Simon Price, who would undoubtedly vouch for him.

I stopped when I read this part. There it was. The definite connection to Simon Price. And a possible connection to the suicide victim at last. I continued, hoping for more.

David Lachlan claimed to have no knowledge of Jimmy's injuries but admitted to *'giving him a whack'* when he dismantled and broke a perfectly good alarm clock. The police didn't have enough evidence to charge David Lachlan but the criminal investigation continued. Based on the physical evidence and Bridget Lachlan's statement, Mel recommended that Jimmy be removed from his family and placed in foster care unless his father agreed to voluntarily stay away. Jimmy spent five days in foster care before David agreed to leave the family home and live separately until the allegations were fully investigated.

I flipped over to read more. Next came the psychologist's report. Dr

John Compton, described Jimmy as *'anxious, fidgety and temporarily fragile'* and displaying *'symptoms of post-traumatic stress order'*. He also seemed to be *'defensive'* as if he was *'trying to hide something'*. Of Bridget Lachlan, he wrote *'Her first concern is always for her son. She is particularly reluctant to allow any further interviews with Jimmy because of the anxiety these create.'* Jimmy had apparently been wetting his bed and was having problems sleeping.

Her concern was understandable. At a rough count, I estimated Jimmy had been interviewed more than a dozen times by therapists, psychologist and social workers. Questions were repeated and rephrased for any inconsistencies. Because of this, the police file was suspended but the file was left open and because Mel considered Jimmy to be at risk, Social Services had applied for a permanent care order and the lawyers were set loose.

I moved to the end of the page and read the name of the magistrate who signed the care order. The name jumped out at me. Judge Buchanan. Christine's father.

I don't know how long I sat staring at the name. It couldn't be a coincidence. It just couldn't. First the connection to Simon Price by David Lachlan and now, the judge who signed the care order, Judge Buchanan. It was the connection I had hoped for but I had no idea what that connection would lead me to or what it meant.

"What are you mumbling about?" Mel was back from her shopping, balancing two cups of coffee." She placed my coffee in front of me. "Are they any help?"

My hands were trembling when I looked up at Mel. "What did you make of David Lachlan?" I asked.

She sat down and kicked her shoes off again. "I thought he was a pig."

"Why do you say that?"

"He confronted me outside the court when I went to use my phone. He asked me why I was doing this, as if it was personal. When I tried to get past him, he pushed me against the wall and put his hand on my throat. He had this look in his eyes..." She shuddered.

"You didn't press charges?"

"No. But I noted it in that third file." She pointed to the one I had opened yet.

"What happened with the care order?"

"One magistrate, Judge Buchanan, agreed with the application but two others claimed there was insufficient evidence to sustain the argument."

"So you tried to get Jimmy made a ward of the court?"

"I certainly did. I wasn't letting the father anywhere near him. The judge and I went straight to the court and got a hearing that afternoon. The papers should all be there." She motioned towards the file.

"Who gave evidence?"

"I did."

"What about John Compton?"

"I used his report."

I could see Mel was getting annoyed and defensive with my questions. "Any social worker would have done what I did. If you can't get the magistrates to see sense, you go to a judge. I did and I won." She sat down heavily in her chair. "Two weeks later, his father committed suicide and left a suicide note saying *'Sorry'*. A week after that, his mother gave him up to the courts."

"A one word apology? But for what?"

Mel's voice has gone cold as she shrugged. "This is ancient history, Jack. Leave it alone."

I shook my head. "But why did his mother give him up?"

"She had no means of support for Jimmy, she said, and no income. There was no other option for her but to hand him over to foster care."

"But his brother Andrew Lachlan is a very rich man. Surely he would help support her and his nephew? He may have been a violent man but he was all about family."

She shook her head. "I'm just repeating what she said."

From the moment Jimmy became a ward of the state, every major decision on his welfare was made by a court instead of his family. Turning the pages of the file, I came across the judgement. It bore a court seal and was signed by Judge Buchanan.

Mel was watching me. "Did you find what you were looking for?" she asked.

I looked up. "Did you ever have much to do with Judge Buchanan?"

"Funny you ask that."

"Why?"

"I had someone else ask me almost the same question. That's two interesting calls in one day."

"Who asked to see the file?"

"A homicide detective by the name of Cavanaugh. He wants to know if your name crops up in any of them."

Her eyes were piercing as she looked at me and I could see she was angry with me for holding something back. Social Workers don't confide in people easily. They learn early on not to trust, especially when they deal with abused children, beaten wives, drug addicts, alcoholics and parents fighting for custody.

"This detective says you're a person of interest in a murder, Jack." Her eyes hardened. "He says you have had contact with Jimmy and wants to know if a complaint has been made against you. I've been wondering why you kept that a secret."

This was Mel's territory. She has nothing against me but now she doubted me and my motives. Our past history will mean nothing to her now if it looks like I have abused our friendship to gain access to a file for my own personal use.

"It's all fiction, Mel. A fishing expedition." I couldn't hide the anger from surfacing in my voice. Turning the other cheek is for people who want to look the other way. I was sick of being accused of something I hadn't done.

"So what is it you've done?" she asked with a barb in her voice.

"Alleged, Mel. Innocent until proven guilty."

She pursed her lips and puffed a little air through then. "Okay. Alleged, then."

"Cavanaugh thinks I killed a friend of mine by the name of Christine Buchanan."

Her eyes popped open. "Would that be Judge Buchanan's daughter?"

"I didn't do anything wrong, Mel. Unless being trusting is a crime."

Serpent

She glanced down at her phone as she spoke. "Then why are you running?" she asked.

"Because someone wants to frame me for her murder and I think that someone is Jimmy. I have no idea why."

She raised her hand. "I don't want to know any more. I'm in enough trouble for showing you the files."

Again with the glance to the phone on the table.

"What happened to Compton's notes?" I asked. "They're not in the file."

She hesitated. "Um. He may have asked to have them excluded."

I blinked. "Why would he do that?"

"Perhaps Jimmy asked to see his file." I could tell she was hedging but for the life of me I couldn't say why.

"Come on, Mel. Did he see the file or not?"

She avoided the question. "He's allowed to do that. When a ward reaches eighteen years of age, he is allowed to see the write-ups by the duty social worker and some of the minutes of the meetings. Doctor's notes and psych reports are different. We need to get permission from the specialist before we release them."

I closed my eyes for a few seconds and tried to clear my mind while I listened to a hundred thoughts milling like elusive fish at the edge of my subconscious. "Are you saying that Jimmy saw his file?"

"Maybe." In the same breath, she dismissed the idea with a shrug. "It's an old file. Things get misplaced."

"Could Jimmy have removed the notes?"

She glanced at the phone again and whispered angrily. "You can't be serious, Jack! Worry about yourself."

She shook her head, refusing to say anything more. Without her help, my frail improbable theory that Jimmy was framing me went south. Talking quickly, in case she stopped me, I told her about the chloroform, the carved cross and how Jimmy had probably been stalking me for months, infiltrating the lives of everyone around me.

"That's why I need to find Compton's notes. Or Compton himself. Maybe he remembers something."

"I can't help you anymore. I've done enough. I think you should leave,

Jack," she muttered as she reached over and took the files from my hands. Again the glance at the phone.

"Are you expecting a call?" I finally asked.

"No."

"Why the glances at the phone?"

She sighed heavily. "I left instructions with my secretary. If I didn't call her in half an hour, she was to contact the police."

I glanced at my own phone, counting backwards. "Christ, Mel!"

"I'm sorry. I have my career to think about."

I stood up quickly. According to my calculations, I had five minutes before the secretary notified Cavanaugh.

"John Compton," she blurted out, "retired five years ago."

I turned to her, my hand on the doorknob. "Tell me where I can find him, Mel."

She scribbled something down on a scrap of paper. "Last I heard he was living near Varsity Lakes." She held the address out to me as she picked up her phone. "Now go. You'd better move quickly."

25

I moved quickly to the Willie's garage to pick up the car, expecting Cavanaugh to round a corner at any moment. He said he'd give me twenty-four hours but I didn't trust him as far as I could kick him and knowing I was a step ahead of him would make him furious.

As I walked, I tried to put the pieces together while wondering where else to go from here. Jimmy was five years younger than Jazz was now when he lost his father and I can only imagine that a tragedy like that can take a terrible toll on a child. A child is made a ward of the court. His father commits suicide and the mother hands him over to foster care. A sad story, but it wasn't a unique one. Every instinct I had told me there had to be more to this.

Children aren't made wards of the state as much anymore. The old system was too open to abuse. Precious little evidence was required for eligibility to become a foster parent and no checks were required. Mostly, being a church-going Catholic was all the qualifications you needed. The procedure was rife with corruption with most of the kids going from one bad situation to another far worse one. Nowadays, they go straight into safe houses until an adoption is arranged.

Jimmy had shown all the signs of being sexually abused and most victims of child abuse find ways to protect themselves. Some bury their pain deep in their subconscious minds and suffer from traumatic amnesia while others refuse to reflect on what has happened at all. Thankfully, not many go down the track of being a murderer.

I remembered reading a case file once written by a researcher in America. The case involved a three-year-old girl and was presented to a panel of experts including eight clinical psychologists, twenty social workers and fifty graduate students. The researchers knew from the outset that the child had *not* been sexually abused.

The mother alleged abuse based on her discovery of a bruise on her daughter's leg and a single pubic hair (that she thought looked like her husband's) in the girl's nappy. Four medical experts examined her and nothing showed as evidence of abuse. Two lie detectors tests and a joint police and Child Protection Service investigation cleared the father. Despite this, three quarters of the experts recommended that the father's contact with his daughter be either highly supervised or stopped altogether.

I couldn't ignore the similarities between that one and Jimmy's case. Everything that had happened at the onset was based on the mother's hint of sexual abuse. Even though she denied it later, the damage was already done. The report had been made and examinations had commenced. From then on, there was no going back.

Where had the mother gone after she handed Jimmy over? David's brother, Andrew, had money behind him, why didn't she appeal to him for help? And where was she now? Being nine years ago, she would be roughly forty now. I was missing something important.

I stopped outside a pearl exhibition and took my mobile phone out of my pocket. The only person I knew who could help me was Sam.

The phone rang once before she picked up. "Where are you?"

"Still in Surfers."

I filled her in on my conversation with Lois Chapman and how I'd learnt about her shop in Surfers. I told her I knew Jimmy's birth name now and how I'd contacted Mel and how she'd allowed me to read the file on Jimmy.

"I won't get any more help from Mel, Sam. Cavanaugh contacted her while I was reading the files and told her I was a suspect in a murder.

She's angry with me for not trusting her with why I needed to see Jimmy's files. She thinks I used her. Which I guess I did in a way."

"You can patch things up with her after you clear yourself," she stated. "The good news is you now have his name and can make more progress before you need to hand yourself in tomorrow."

Sam was right. I couldn't run for ever but in the little time I had, I needed to find out why Jimmy wanted to destroy me. I knew he didn't want me dead because he could have killed me a dozen times over by now, so for some reason he wanted me alive so I could see what he was doing and *know* that it was him. The big question was why.

Weariness was clogging my brain. I needed to concentrate and focus on what I needed to do next. As far as I could see, I had two options. I needed to talk to John Compton and I wanted to talk to Jimmy's mother. She held the clue to everything.

"Sam. I need to know where Jimmy's mother is now. Bridget Lachlan disappeared after the father committed suicide but where is she now? She's the only one now who knows what happened to Jimmy all those years ago."

I could hear voices in the background, one voice in particular.

"Is that shithead in the background I can hear?" I asked.

I didn't have to explain who I was referring to. She knew.

"Yes. Stay put," she muttered. "I'll call you back. When he's gone I'll do a search for her."

With that she hung up.

I walked into Willie's garage and saw Willie slouched over Christine's car and Arnold's legs poking out from under the chassis. The good news was I hadn't heard from Willie so I was hoping all it needed was a service.

"How's the car, Willie?"

"Arnold, what's the story on Detective Curtis' car?" Willie yelled at the car.

"It's shit," Arnold yelled back. "Tell him you'll give him $500 to scrap it."

"Arnold says to give you $500 to scrap it," Willie repeated.

"I heard him, Willie. Tell Arnold I'll burn his house down if he doesn't fix the car today."

"Day after tomorrow is the best I can do," came the voice from under the chassis.

"I need the car this afternoon, Arnold."

Willie nudged a cylindrical piece of metal with the toe of his boot. If I didn't know better, I'd say he was being coy.

He clapped me on the shoulder with a greasy hand. "Is this your piece of shit, detective?"

"This piece of shit belonged to a friend who doesn't need it anymore. But sadly, I do. I can't leave it with you, Willie. I need it today, as is."

"How the mighty have fallen," Willie muttered as he shook his head.

Arnold pushed himself out from underneath the car. I hadn't seen Arnold for three years and I was surprised at how he'd aged. Unlike some, with age came added hair. Hair sprouted from his ears, nose and armpits. Hair even sprouted like coarse, grey spirals from the dirty singlet he was wearing. I had to focus on not taking a step back.

"Tell him," Arnold said.

Willie sighed. "Detective." He hesitated. I'd never seen Willie lost for words but I can only assume this was the one and only time he was. "Do you know this person well?"

His question took me by surprise. "What do you mean?"

He took hold of my arm. "Does this friend have enemies?"

I looked from Arnold to Willie. It was as if they were synchronised. Both frowning. Both with arms crossed. Both with heads cocked to the side.

"What?" is all I could say.

"Tell him," Arnold repeated.

Willie took my arm. "Your friend's car here. Arnold found something underneath."

Willie looked like he was urging me on. As if I knew what he was talking about.

I shook my head. "I have no idea what you're talking about, Willie. Just spit it out."

Willie looked furtively around his dirty workshop, James Bond style. "We found a tracking device," he whispered. He leant towards me and spoke softly in my ear. "Arnold disabled it."

Serpent

My mind raced as it searched for answers. Was that how Christine's killer knew where she lived? He planted the device under her car and followed her home. It could have been done at any time and at anyplace, even while she was in the Star Casino. In the parking lot behind Sandra's lair. At the shops. It meant that anyone could have done it and that chasing Jimmy could be a massive mistake and a major waste of time. I was doing what I'd always said not to do, making my suspicions fit the facts. Finding this tracking device meant I was back to square one.

Even though Willie stood in front of me watching my every move, all I could see was Cavanaugh's face. The throbbing vein in his neck, the clenched teeth and his mouth curling in dislike.

Maybe it was my ego but I had learnt many years ago to go with my hunches, no matter how absurd they may seem.

And that's what I was going to do. I was going to continue chasing Jimmy.

26

Samuel Price stares at me as I stand in his lounge room with the gun pointed at his chest. I can see the questions come to his face. How did I get in? Who was I? He has never seen me before and he is wondering what I want and which of his brilliant lines will work for him. Because life has always worked for him.

I smile. I love this part.

"Take my watch," he said.

He's rattled, for sure, but not as much as I'd hoped. I love to see the fear in their eyes to sweeten the moment. He's showing faux bravado of a soft man who has never had a tough moment in his life. He thinks this is a small problem he can pay his way out of. He'll get out of it for sure, he thinks. He always has. For him, things just seem to go right with minimal effort. Just bravado. He believes he has charisma and charm that separates him from the rest of us mere mortals.

"It's a Rolex timepiece," he says. "Do you have any idea how much this costs?"

I shouldn't be enjoying this as much as I am. "Tell me," I smile.

"Probably forty-five thousand."

I give a soft impressed whistle. Then I say, "I'm not here for that."

"Why are you here then?"

"I'm here to clear my father's name."

I watch for a reaction. This will be my favourite part. He doesn't let me down. There's bafflement. Confusion. "I don't know what you mean."

"Sure you do." *I smile.*

I let him think for a bit. How much should he tell me?

I am still pointing the gun at his chest as he thinks. It's his gun. While he was enjoying his last meal, I disabled the alarm and entered his house and took the gun from a locked desk drawer in his office. I knew it was there. I watched him place it there several night ago. And I knew where he put the key to the drawer. I've planned for this.

He shook his head. "I don't know who you mean."

"David Lachlan."

"David Lachlan?" *He frowns.* "But Lachlan killed himself ten years ago."

I grip the gun tighter. Patience.

"Yes, he did."

"So why?"

Price never even knew the man whose reputation he was going to ruin.

"Look," *he said.* "Whoever you are, we can make his right. I have lots of money..."

I pull the trigger.

I anticipate the recoil. The bullet blows a hole in the rich man's chest. Money does a lot for a man but it doesn't stop a bullet to the chest. He is dead before he hits the ground.

I don't worry about DNA this time. The threat and visit should be enough. The man might have an alibi, I can't cover all the bases what with the rush to get this done, but I know that's unlikely to sway anyone. He has motive. I don't.

He might get lucky. He might have an alibi and get a lawyer who gives a shit. He may not end up spending the rest of his life in prison. In short, I'm giving him a fighting chance.

That's something I've never given to anyone else. Let the game begin.

27

Real estate agents call Varsity Lakes 'a varied collection of modern gems by the lakes' but from what I could see, there was very little difference from one house to the next. I stopped at a white house and asked an elderly woman directions to the address Mel had given me since Christine's car didn't have GPS and I was unfamiliar with this area. She eyed me suspiciously, glanced at the number plate, then pointed to the end of the road.

I parked in the street and walked up a path, stepping over toy cars as I made my way towards the front door. Hanging parallel to the path was a stained sheet with two ends tied to a tree. A small red-haired boy sat underneath it with a plastic ice cream bucket on his head.

He pointed a wooden stick at me and asked, "Are you a Slytherin?"

The word was vaguely familiar but I couldn't place from where. "Do I have to be one to enter?" I smiled.

"You can only come in here if you're from Gryffindor." The freckles on his nose were the colour of milky coffee.

A young woman appeared at the door. Her blonde hair was tied back in a ponytail and by the looks of her, she was fighting a cold. A baby was perched on her hip, sucking on a piece of bread while she sniffled into a tissue.

Serpent

"Leave the man alone, Brendan," she said tiredly. She smiled at me. "He thinks he's Harry Potter."

I stepped around a push bike with trainer wheels attached and walked towards her. Behind her in the lounge room, I could see an ironing board standing erect beside a basket of clothes.

"Can I help you," she asked, rocking the baby backwards and forwards.

"Hopefully, yes. I was given this address for John Compton."

A shadow crossed her face. "He doesn't live here anymore."

Hiding my disappointment, I asked, "Do you know where I can find him? It's important that I do."

"I'm sorry. You're too late," she said as she swapped the baby to the other hip. "He died."

Probably realising how blunt the statement was, she added, "I'm sorry if you knew him."

Without thinking about it, I turned and sat down heavily on the step.

She glanced up and down the street before asking tentatively, "Would you like to come in for a glass of water?"

"Thank you. That would be nice."

I followed her to a kitchen that smelt of sterilised bottles and porridge. Crayons and pieces of paper littered a dining table beside a play pen full of stuffed animals.

Still balancing the baby, she filled a glass of water from the tap and handed it to me.

I thanked her and asked, "Do you know what happened to him?"

"I only know what the neighbours told me. Everyone in the street was pretty shook up by what happened. You don't expect that sort of thing, Not around here, anyway."

I frowned. "What sort of thing?"

"They said he must have come across someone trying to rob the place but I don't see how that explains anything. What sort of burglar ties an old man to a chair and tapes his mouth shut? He lived for four days that way without anyone knowing. Folks say he had a heart attack but I heard he died of dehydration. It was the hottest week of the year…"

"When was this?" I interrupted abruptly.

"August just gone. So about twelve months ago. We bought the house a month later. A bargain," she smiled wryly. "I reckon some folks are feeling guilty because nobody noticed him missing. They said he was always pottering in the garden and taking walks by the lake. During those four days, someone from the church choir knocked on the door and a man came to read the water meter. The front door was unlocked but no one thought to go inside and check on him."

I could see her lips moving but I wasn't really listening. The ground had dropped away beneath me like a plunging lift. All I could think was *another accident.*

"He was a really nice old man, people say. A widower. You probably know that already, though. I don't think he had any other family. I don't think he…"

She stopped talking mid-sentence and stared at me. "Are you alright? You don't look so good," she asked as the baby squirmed irritably in her arms.

"Excuse me," I muttered. "I have to use my phone."

I unlocked the phone and found the number for Lois Chapman. I had to stop my voice from sounding panicky.

"Lois. It's Jack Curtis here. The headmistress at St Mary's, you said she resigned for family reasons?"

"Oh hello, Mr Curtis. Yes. She was a friend of mine. Her name was Alison O'Reilly."

"When did she resign?"

"About nine months ago. It was all very sad. Her mother died of smoke inhalation in a house fire and her father was badly burned. She moved to Springwood to nurse him. I think he's in a wheelchair now."

I could feel my heart pounding. *Nine months ago.*

"How did the fire start, do you know?"

"They think it was a case of mistaken identity. Someone put a parcel outside the door and when her mother opened it inside, it blew up and caused the fire. It was all over the news. I'm surprised you didn't see it on the news."

A rush of fear became liquid on my skin. My eyes were fixed on the young woman swaying with her baby, watching me anxiously from beside the stove. She looked frightened, as if I'd bought something sinister in to her house.

I thanked Lois then made another call. Mel picked up immediately but I didn't give her time to speak.

"The car that hit Ben, Mel. What happened to the driver?" My voice sounded shrill and thin.

"The police have been here, Jack. A detective by the name of Cavanaugh…"

"Just answer me." I knew I sounded panicky so I took a deep breath and tried to calm my voice. She was already guarded with me. I didn't need to make things worse. "Tell me about the driver. Please."

The silence lasted a few seconds before she answered. "It was a hit and run. They found the stolen four-wheel drive a few blocks away."

"And the driver?"

"They think it was probably a teenager joyriding. There was a thumbprint on the steering wheel but it matched nothing on file."

"Tell me exactly what happened."

"What? Why?"

"Please, Mel."

She stumbled over the first part of the story, trying to remember whether it was 7.30 or 8.30 that evening when Ben went out on his motor-bike. I could hear the sadness in her voice. She said he was going out to the local liquor shop wearing a fluorescent vest, a yellow helmet with his grey hair tied back in a ponytail hanging down his back. Eyewitnesses said he parked on the opposite side of the road near the intersection and began to walk across the road. He paused and turned at the last moment when he heard the car heading towards him. He disappeared beneath the bumper bar and his body was dragged for a hundred meters beneath the chassis.

"Jack, what's going on?" I imagined her wide mouth and timid eyes squinting in confusion.

I ignored her question again. "What about your boss, Andrew Booth? Where is he now?"

I was trying to keep my voice calm but the more I delved the more I was sure Jimmy had begun killing at least twelve months ago.

Mel answered in a quivering voice. "He works for some government advisory body on teenage drug use."

I remembered Andrew. He dyed his hair, played golf off a low handicap and loved a glass of Scotch most nights. His wife was a drama teacher and every summer holidays, they took off with their twin girls....

"How are the twins?"

"You're scaring me Jack."

"Did something happen to them?" My voice was getting louder and I had to calm myself. The young mother was inching towards her phone.

"One of them died last Easter of a drug overdose."

I remembered the twins. Kim was a good swimmer with a beautiful stroke, in the pool or in the sea. I had been invited to a barbecue one weekend when she must have been about nine. She announced that she was going to swim the English Channel one day. I remember joking with her and saying, 'It'll be much quicker to take the tunnel'. Everyone had laughed and Kim just rolled her eyes. I don't think she talked to me after that.

Her twin sister, Charlotte, was the bookish one, with steel-framed glasses and a lazy eye who had shown odd behaviour patterns when very young. Although she had a high IQ, she hated large groups and was clearly distressed when her routine changed. As such, she was taken to see a psychologist who diagnosed her with slight autism. She spent most of the barbecue in her room, complaining that she couldn't hear the TV because everyone outside were laughing too loudly.

I wondered which one had gone off the track and taken the drug overdose. I couldn't imagine either of them doing something like that.

I was going over the list in my head. Judge Buchanan. Mel. John Compton. Andrew Booth. Alison O'Reilly. All were involved in the same child protection case. Compton was dead but the others had all lost someone close to them.

"What was the name of the doctor who did the initial examination? You told me but I can't remember the name."

She took a sharp intake of breath. "Why, Jack? Tell me why."

"I will. But please, Mel. I'm running out of time. What was his name?"

"Doctor Graham Burton."

"Is he alive?"

"Yes."

Her voice sounded evasive and I was sure Cavanaugh's visit had something to do with that. She once trusted me, both she and Ben, but this new Mel was purely because of something Cavanaugh had told her.

"You've been listening to Cavanaugh, Mel." I heard a tsk over the line. "Don't bother denying it. I know, okay? But before I hang up, please tell me if any of his family have died recently. Do it because we were once friends. Because you and Ben once trusted me." I let that sink in. "I'm still that person, Mel. It's just that someone has put me in this difficult position and I'm trying to work it all out."

But what has this to do with me?

Mel was mumbling about hanging up on me but I couldn't let her go yet.

"Mel, please."

"Okay," she said in a strained voice. "His wife has been dead for about a year. Someone ran her off the road. She was on her way to pick up her kids from school when someone ran a red light. She swerved to avoid them and ran into a street light by the side of the road. She was killed instantly."

"Did they find the driver of the other car?"

"No. There was minimal damage to his car, onlookers said. He just grazed her but she overcorrected and hit the pole head on. He drove away and they never found him." I heard a sob. "You're really scaring me, Jack."

"Just a few more questions, Mel. Who put together the legal submission for the care order?"

"I did, of course."

"And which police officer signed the approval for it to go to the judge?"

She hesitated. I could tell she was about to lie. "I don't remember."

"Who signed the report, Mel?"

She hesitated again then muttered, "You did."

I was stunned. "Me? When did I do that? And why?"

"Inspector Grayson had just left to go on holidays and you were the only one still at the station. I put the form in front of you and you signed. You thought it was a foster parent authorisation."

I moaned inwardly. "My name was in the file?"

"Yes."

"And Jimmy probably saw that when he viewed his file."

Again, a hesitation. "Yes."

"You took it out of the folders before you showed them to me?"

"It was a long time ago. I thought it didn't matter."

There was my connection to Jimmy. *'Because of you.'* He blamed me for signing the papers that sent him into foster care. It didn't matter that I had no memory of signing them or any idea *what* I was signing. Mel had asked me to sign them and I trusted her.

"I need one more favour, Mel."

"Jesus, Jack. Haven't I done enough?"

"I need Andrew Booth's phone number."

"What? Why, Jack?"

Her voice sounded muffled. When Mel became agitated, her habit had always been to put her elbows on the table and rest her forehead in her hands while talking. I could hear the agitation in her voice now and I knew her voice sounded muffled because her head was in her hands right now.

"I need to see him. I have to make sure of my facts before taking them all to Cavanaugh. This will help clear me, Mel. But to do that, I need his number."

She sighed, an exhalation that came from deep in her lungs. Finally, she said, "I'll text it."

I hung up and looked at the young mother. Her eyes were wide as she clutched her baby tightly in her arms, jiggling him up and down to calm his cries.

I heard the ping from my phone which meant a message had come in. I glanced down and saw the message from Mel. Just a phone number. No wishes of good luck or let's chat soon. Just the number. It felt final somehow and a deep sadness filled my heart at the loss of yet another friend. I didn't have many to start with and my friend base was quickly shrinking.

Serpent

I dropped the phone in my pocket and turned to the young mother. "I'm sorry for the intrusion." I tried to keep my voice calm so as not to scare her any further than I already had. "Thank you for the water," I added.

As I walked down the front steps, I heard her panicked call telling her son to come inside the house.

I had almost reached the car when my mobile rang again. I glanced at the screen.

It was Sam.

28

Two police cars passed me on the road to the Sunshine Palm Hospice where Bridget Lachlan now lived. Sam had spoken to the senior oncologist at the hospice who told her that a year ago Bridget had been diagnosed with aggressive breast cancer and would now only have weeks to live. She told him I wanted to visit and he'd said he'd leave my name with reception.

The sun had begun to angle towards the horizon but I still had two hours of daylight left. I couldn't afford to waste either of them. Jimmy was probably looking for me and I was sure he wasn't going to wait for me to figure it all out.

The police cars spooked me. Mel's secretary must have called the police because Cavanaugh had high-tailed it over to her office. My only hope was that Mel was able to reassure Cavanaugh that I had not been a threat. I needed every scrap of time to try and piece this together.

With this uppermost on my mind, I kept glancing in the rear mirror on my way to the hospice, half expecting to see flashing blue lights behind me. If that happened, it would be the opposite of a high-speed police chase. They could overtake me on pushbikes unless I could magically find fourth gear in Christine's car. Maybe it would turn out to be one of the O.J. Simpson moments, a slow-motion motorcade, filmed from the news helicopters.

I remembered the final scene from *Butch Cassidy and the Sundance Kid* when Redford and Newman kept wisecracking as they ran out to face the Mexican army. Personally, I'm not quite as fearless about dying and I see nothing glorious about a hail of bullets and a closed coffin.

The driveway to the front of the Sunshine Palm Hospice curved around out-buildings lined with palm trees, finally emerging into a parking area. I followed the signs to the palliative care ward on the ocean-side inhaling the salty air that blended with the smell of fresh mulch in the gardens.

The corridors were empty except for a trolley laden with sheets and towels. A dark-haired nurse, her hair pulled back tightly in a bun on the top of her head, sat behind a glass partition staring at a computer screen, seemingly oblivious that I was standing on the other side of the partition watching her.

I cleared my throat noisily. "Excuse me. I'm here to see Bridget Lachlan."

Only her eyes moved. They flicked towards me as she asked, "Are you family?"

"No. I'm a detective," I lied. "Her oncologist has given permission for me to ask her a few questions. My name is Jack Curtis."

She reached for a book and flipped through the pages slowly. Apparently, the Sunshine Palm Hospice ran on a very easy schedule because her movements were relaxed and unhurried.

She nodded and stood, then walked through the door that led to the corridor where I stood waiting.

I followed her smooth, rolling walk and squeaking shoes along the corridor that turned left through double doors leading outside. A loose gravel pathway dissected the lawn where two bored-looking nurses shared a sandwich on a garden seat.

We entered a single-story annexe and emerged into a long, shared ward with maybe a dozen beds, half of which were empty. A skinny woman with a smooth skull was propped up on pillows watching two young children scribbling on drawing paper at the end of her bed. Beside them, smiling, their mother cooed encouragement.

At the far end of the ward, through two more doors, were the private rooms. The nurse entered the dimly lit room without knocking.

At first, I didn't notice anything except the machines but as my eyes adjusted to the dimness, I saw a middle-aged woman with a ghostly pallor and sunken cheeks lying at the centre of tubes and leads. A bag of solution dripped along tubing that snaked in and out of her body and a tube hung from her nose. Her blonde wig was slightly askew and her pendulous breasts lay flat on either side of her sunken chest that was covered by a pink chemise. A tattered red cardigan lay over her bony shoulders.

"Don't give her cigarettes," the nurse ordered. "Every time she coughs, it shakes the tubes loose."

"I don't smoke."

"Good for you."

She stood looking down at the woman for a few seconds. "She has good days and bad days. I have no idea which one today is." She walked towards the door. "You can find your own way out when you're finished."

Music was coming from somewhere and it took me a while to realise there was a portable radio playing softly on the bedside table next to an empty vase.

I'd wasted my time because she was either asleep or too heavily sedated with Morphine to answer any questions.

I leant my shoulder against the wall and rested my head wearily.

"This place gives me the creeps too," she said, without opening her eyes.

I pushed myself off the wall and walked towards the only chair in the room, positioned by the bed. "It is depressing," I agreed, moving the chair closer to the end of the bed so she didn't have to turn her head to see me.

Her eyes opened as if in slow motion and we stared at each other in the semi-darkness.

"Have you ever been to Maui?" she asked.

"It's in Hawaii."

"I bloody know where it is." She coughed and the bed rattled. "That's where I should be now. I should be lying on a beach in Hawaii with a Margherita in my hands. I should be watching the sunset and wondering where I'll be eating my evening meal and who is going to take me to dinner and sharing my bed later."

Her eyes were puffy and dribble had leaked from the corner of her mouth. "Are you another doctor or a priest?"

"I'm a detective."

She cackled. "No point getting to know me, handsome. Not unless you like funerals."

The cancer must have struck quickly. Her body hadn't had time to waste away. She was pale and thin, but you could still see she'd been beautiful in her youth.

"The problem with cancer is it doesn't feel like cancer," she said softly. "A head cold feels like a head cold. A broken arm feels like a broken arm. But with cancer, you don't know unless you have x-rays and scans. Except for the lump, of course. Who can forget the damned lump?" She breathed softly for a few seconds before adding, "Do you want to feel it?"

I shook my head. "I'm okay."

"Don't be a wuss. You're a big boy. Have a feel. You're probably wondering if they're real. Most men do."

I couldn't disguise the look of pity on my face and it infuriated her. She drew her cardigan around her chest tightly and turned away from me.

"Go away."

"I need to ask you a few questions."

"Ha," she laughed. "Forget it!"

"I'm here about Jimmy," I stated, hoping his name would get her attention.

Her head turned slowly towards me. "What about him?"

I wasn't sure where to start. I had dozens of questions to ask and I'd already irritated her. "When was the last time you saw him?" I countered.

"When he was eight. Maybe nine. He was always in trouble. Wouldn't listen to anyone. Not me, anyway. I gave that kid the best years of my life and he was always ungrateful."

Her sentences had become ragged and breathless. Her features suddenly softened. "You've talked to him, haven't you? How is he?" she asked.

"Angry I'd say. Definitely angry."

I didn't want to go into the story, especially in her condition and without some sort of proof, but to have killed both Christine and I now suspected the writer Marshall, not to mention my theory on Compton, Burton, Ben and Alison O'Reilly's parents, he'd have to be feeling pretty angry.

She sighed. "I used to think they gave me the wrong baby at the hospital. It didn't feel like mine. I suppose he looked like his father, which was a shame, but I couldn't see any of me in him, except the eyes. He had two left feet and a round loaf of face. He could never keep anything clean. He had to be touching everything to see how they worked. Always spilling things and making a mess. Just like his father."

She sighed. "I never felt what they say mothers are supposed to feel. I guess I'm not maternal, but that doesn't make me cold, does it? I didn't want to get pregnant in the first place. I was only twenty-one, for Christ's sake."

She raised her eyebrows. "You're itching to get inside my head, aren't you? Not many people are interested in what someone else is thinking or what they have to say. Sometimes people act like they're listening, when really they're waiting for their run or getting ready to jump in. What are you waiting for, then?"

"I'm just trying to understand."

"David was like that. Always asking questions, wanting to know where I was going and when I was coming home." She mimicked his pleading voice. "'*Who are you with?*' It was so pathetic. No wonder I got to thinking is this the best I can do? I wasn't going to lie next to his sweaty back for the rest of my life."

"He committed suicide," I reminded her.

She chuckled. "I didn't think he had it in him."

"Do you know why?"

She didn't seem to hear me. Instead she stared at the closed curtains. When she finally spoke, she didn't look at me. "He called himself an entrepreneur. What a joke! He barely made any money. His brother had the brains."

She turned to me with half-closed eyes. "I wanted a divorce. He said no. I told him to get himself a girlfriend. He wouldn't. People say I was cold but I knew how to find pleasure. I knew how to use what I had. Does that make me a slut?"

I had to change the subject and lead her to the answers I needed. I had a feeling the nurse would walk in at any time and I hadn't even begun my questioning.

"You accused your husband of sexually abusing Jimmy," I stated.

She shrugged. "I just loaded the gun. I didn't fire it. People like you do that. Doctors, social workers, cops, school teachers, do-gooders."

I stared at her in shock. "Are you saying you lied? Did we got it wrong?"

She cackled again. "The judge didn't think so. Neither did the social workers."

I had to know for sure. "But did you lie?" I repeated more firmly.

"I think sometimes people forget what the truth is if you hear a lie often enough."

She reached up and pushed the buzzer above her head.

She was calling for the nurse, I knew that, but I couldn't leave yet. "Do you think your son hates you?"

"Don't be an idiot. We all end up hating our parents."

I was astounded at her callousness. "Don't you feel guilty for what you've done?"

She clenched her face in pain and laughed hoarsely. A chrome stand holding a morphine drip swung back and forth. "I'm forty-one years old and I'm dying of cancer. I'm paying the price for what I've done."

The nurse arrived, looking pissed off at being summoned. One of the monitor leads had come loose and Bridget held up her arm to have it reconnected. In the same motion, she waved her hand at me dismissively. The conversation was over.

I took the same route back to the reception area and walked slowly to the car. By now, the sun was beginning to sink below the horizon. I sat in the quietness of the car for a few minutes, running through the conversation I'd just had with Bridget Lachlan and letting it sink in. She'd lied about her husband abusing their child, simply because she wanted a divorce from him. She'd also allowed her son to be taken from her and put into foster care and she'd been directly responsible for her husband committing suicide.

She was right. She was paying the price for what she'd done.

I'd done everything I could for one day. Exhaustion was taking over. What I needed now was to get something to eat and get a good night's sleep before meeting with Cavanaugh in the morning.

I indicated, pulled out into the afternoon traffic and headed home.

29

THURSDAY 5TH SEPTEMBER

Karen and I waited half an hour for Cavanaugh to arrive.

I'd spent the previous two hours in her office, filling her in on the events of the past two days, before we both headed over to the station. I wanted her to know everything but I wasn't about to do the same with Cavanaugh. There were still things I wasn't quite ready to share with him.

Beside me, Karen kept glancing at her watch and her phone as her foot tapped gently on the floor. Every now and then, she snorted softly when her phone buzzed.

Cavanaugh sauntered in with the same detective following him who immediately switched the tape recorder on.

"Once again, you're late. You said 10 am." I reminded him as I testily glanced at my watch.

"My apologies," he said genially as he sat down, dropping a folder onto the table.

He went through the formalities of stating who he was, who I was, who Karen was and the time before turning his attention to me.

"So, Mr Curtis," he began, crossing his arms in front of his chest and leaning backwards. "In your experience, would you say it's true that killers often return to the scene of the crime?"

Here it comes, I thought. He knew about the break in and he was setting the stage for himself. I glanced at Karen who nodded, indicating I could answer.

"Every killer has a behavioural imprint," I stated. "And yes, some do return to the crime scene."

"Why would you say they do that?"

"Lots of reasons. They may want to relive what they've done, or collect a souvenir. Some may just feel guilty and want to stay close."

"Which is why kidnappers often help with the search?"

"Yes."

"And arsonists help fight fire?"

I nodded. The detective with his back leaning against the wall was pretending to be an Easter Island statue, barely blinking.

"I have some questions for you, Mr Curtis. Let's start with Sunday 1st September. Where were you that day?"

I was surprised. It wasn't where I thought he would start and it threw me a little. It was the morning I was taking Jazz to Dreamworld. Cavanaugh knew that since he came to the house that morning.

"I was at home for the morning." I stared at him, a little confused where he was going with this line of questioning, "as you well know since you visited me at my home. After that, I took my daughter to Dreamworld for the day."

A spark of excitement ignited in his eyes as he leant forward. He was ready to deliver his next punch.

"We have CCTV pictures of your car in the parking area of Dreamworld on that day, barely a hundred metres from where Elizabeth Delaney's body," he put his hand up, palm outwards, "sorry, Christine Buchanan's body was found."

He slid the photograph across the desk. I was helping Jazz put her backpack on.

Karen held out her hand for the photo and I passed it on to her.

Cavanaugh pulled out another sheet of paper from the folder. "Do you remember how we discovered her body?"

"I think you said a dog disturbed it."

"We received a phone call but the caller didn't leave a name or contact number. He phoned from a burner phone near the entrance to Dreamworld."

I nodded. "Okay."

"Did you use that burner phone to call the police, Mr Curtis?"

I opened my mouth as Karen put her hand on my arm, silencing me.

Cavanaugh grinned. "You yourself said the killer knew the area intimately."

"Yes, I did."

"How would you describe your knowledge?"

I laughed. "I know where you're going with this. Even if I did kill Christine, which I didn't," I stressed the last part as I glanced up at the light blinking in the corner, "and buried her in the scrub near Dreamworld, do you really think I'd take my daughter along to the murder scene to have a look while I relived the moment of her death?"

Cavanaugh slammed the folder shut. "I'm asking the fucking questions. You worry about your answers."

Karen interrupted. "Perhaps we should all calm down."

It was his turn to glance up at the blinking red light in the corner as he tried to control his temper. He breathed deeply before continuing. "We had a call reporting a break-in to a house last night."

Now for the real punch he's been working towards, I thought.

"When our officers arrived, the house was empty. A thorough search was done." He smiled. *What big teeth you have grandma.* "We now know that this was the home of Christine Buchanan," he grinned some more as he looked up at the camera again, "also known as Elizabeth Delaney."

Karen's head turned towards me but she said nothing. It was a warning glance and I knew it. I let him talk without interrupting him. I needed to know where he was going with this.

"How do you explain your fingerprints found on a glass in the victim's kitchen? There was also your DNA on a tissue in the tidy bin in the same kitchen."

I froze. I didn't touch any glass. My mind went back to Christine's house. I remembered putting my foot on the treadle of the bin and seeing a tissue in it. But it certainly wasn't mine. I'd even opened a drawer with my hand inside my wind breaker so not to leave prints.

He pulled more photos from the folder and tossed them across the table to me. They scattered messily and I gathered them together. They were pictures of the kitchen and the lounge room as I had seen them that night. In a dish drainer sat an upturned glass.

Karen put her hand firmly on my arm again and gestured for me to hand the photos to her.

"When were you going to tell the police that you knew the true identity of the victim?" Cavanaugh asked.

I couldn't tell him because that would bring Sandra into the picture. So far, every question asked would lead to her, and I couldn't allow that. Which meant I had to think on my feet.

"In the course of my investigations to clear myself," I began, "I had only just been made aware of this information. I went to the house to make sure this information was correct before telling the police. I did not want to give them false information and therefore hinder their investigation."

If someone had said that to me when I was a detective, I'd have thrown the book at them. It sounded like a lie and by the look of disgust on Cavanaugh's face, he knew it too.

Karen had been looking through the photos one by one as I was speaking. At the derisive grunt from Cavanaugh, she looked up and began talking.

"Let me point out to you Detective Cavanaugh, my client has informed me of his visit to the victim's home. As he said, he has been very involved in his own investigation of the crime since you are so intent on falsely accusing him of it." She dipped her head to the side. "Which is why he was there. Investigating."

When Cavanaugh said nothing, she continued. "I'd like to add for the record," she glanced up into the corner and held up her phone to where the camera's red light blinked, "my investigators have done a door knock on Elizabeth's neighbours this morning, and no one has admitted to making the call to your station to report a break-in. When asked, the neighbours also informed them that no police have even spoken to them at all. *My* people are the only ones so far who have bothered to do a door knock and I am beginning to wonder why that is. I would also like to add that my bet is the call was made from another untraceable phone."

Her eyes stared into his with the ghost of a smile. "But my guess is you already know that." Her eyes almost sparkled. "So Detective Cavanaugh. Maybe it was the true killer who called the station because my client has constantly been watched and followed by him."

A rictus smile touched Cavanaugh's lips this time. "Okay, Mr Curtis. Tell me what *you* know about Jimmy Croft."

I felt cold inside. I was hoping he hadn't discovered something about Sandra's operation and that something was making him furious. I couldn't tell him anything so I remained silent, watching him.

"Okay. Don't answer. Just listen to me then."

He stood up, pushing his chair roughly away, and rocked from foot to foot as he spoke to me. "Take my word for it, you'll find it fascinating."

He walked two paces away then turned to face me. "Jimmy Croft has no girlfriend or partner. He lives in one of the four bedrooms of a boarding house with other people who are waiting to find a unit to rent. He hasn't put in a tax return for a year which would suggest he hasn't worked for that period of time or he's new to a place of employment. But he is working, because somehow he has regular money to pay his rent and put into a bank account. We're trying to trace where the money comes from but so far, there are so many different shell companies involved, I doubt we'll ever find out."

I held my breath and waited.

He chewed his lip for a moment as he thought. "His father was never in the army as you suggested, as a mechanic or anything else. So far we haven't been able to trace either of his parents. There's no information before he was fifteen but it would seem he dropped out of school around then and lived on the streets for a while, doing volunteer work for various organisations. The Salvos called him a 'big softie'. We haven't found any history of psychiatric illness or hospitalisation."

I tried to hide my surprise by glancing at Karen. That he hadn't discovered Jimmy's birth name or made the connection to the Lachlan brothers meant that Mel had withheld the information in the red edge file from him which in turn meant there was still hope for our friendship. It also meant she had believed my story and trusted me to a certain extent. The relief was immense. But without that information from her, Cavanaugh had also been unable to trace Bridget Lachlan.

Cavanaugh began pacing backwards and forwards as he talked.

"Everybody says nice things about Jimmy where he lives. The landlady and the other tenants. He's neat and tidy and he keeps to himself." He glanced across at me as he walked. "What I find really strange is nothing you said about him is true. I can understand you getting some things wrong, we all make mistakes, but it's as though we're talking about a completely different person. It's as if the Jimmy, this vicious killer you keep telling me about, has disappeared."

I couldn't tell him that the Jimmy who worked at the games parlour was the person he'd just described. Quiet and well liked. But the Jimmy I'd uncovered in the past twenty-four hours was a whole different person. A calculating, vengeful, sadistic killer with an agenda.

"You've got the wrong person," was all I could say.

"That's what I thought. So I checked. Tall guy. Brown curly hair. Six foot plus, on the thin side. That's our boy. Then I wondered why he'd tell all those lies to you. It doesn't make sense."

Karen touched my arm so I stayed silent.

"In any case," Cavanaugh continued. "I don't think he killed Elizabeth Delaney aka Christine Buchanan."

I frowned. "Why is that?"

He sighed like a man having a conversation with a two-year-old. "Because a dozen people at an evening class can verify his whereabouts on the night she disappeared and was supposedly murdered."

I would have laughed in his face if the situation wasn't so dire. "You can't actually be telling me you know the exact time of her death." I tried to make the words sound casual but they came out sounding tentative and hesitant. "All you know is the date she disappeared."

He opened his mouth to speak but I cut him off.

"Let me finish. I know all about larvae eggs and the time it takes for a fly to lay eggs in a body and for those eggs to turn into maggots. I know all about how the body decomposes and the rate that it does. I know all that. I also know you can't tell me the exact time she died or what times it was between. You can pinpoint the date and an approximate time because of the time stamp on the CCTV footage from the Star Casino and you can work backwards according to the decomposition rate, but nothing else is possible after a week. So by saying Jimmy has an iron-clad alibi from people who saw him at an evening class is simply crap."

Having said all that, things just weren't adding up. An evening class?

"Sometimes I'm pretty slow on the uptake," Cavanaugh said in a genial voice. "But I get there in the end. It just takes me a little longer than clever people like you."

He said the last sentence with bitterness rather than triumph. "You see, I asked myself why Jimmy Croft would make up all those lies. And then I thought, what if he didn't? What if *you're* the one telling all the lies? You could be making this up to divert my attention."

I almost gasped. "You can't be serious!"

"Why did you ask me if there was chloroform on her clothes?"

"I told you. I smelt it on his clothes."

"Mmm. Yes, you did, although you have never told me how you know Jimmy Croft. But I suppose that's client privilege too." He gave a wry smile. "That phrase comes in handy with you, doesn't it?"

He nodded slowly while I held my breath, waiting for the rest. He was zeroing in on chloroform for some reason, trying to discredit me. I knew I hadn't slipped up but in my weary state, I couldn't be sure.

"So I did some reading up on chloroform. Do you know that it takes a few drops of chloroform on a mask or a cloth to render a person unconscious? You have to know what you're doing when you play around with that stuff. A few drops too many and the victim's breathing is shut off and they suffocate. Are you suggesting Jimmy Croft has that knowledge?"

"Yes. Because he's done this before," I stated.

He nodded. "Ah. But of course."

His eyes roamed around the room as he talked but I could almost hear the cogs grinding. "Do you know what I find really hard to explain?" he asked. "Why you gave me a crock of shit about somebody called Jimmy Croft when we both know he's got nothing to do with this."

I harrumphed as he turned to me, all white teeth and dark angry eyes. "But two can play at that game."

He pulled his chair out and sat down, visibly angry. "Okay Ms Sawyer. Explain this to me then. We've processed your client's car. The GPS tracking in Mr Curtis' car? It shows he travelled from his house to the victim's house and back again on the night of the 24th August. The night of the murder."

This time I did let out a gasp and once again, Karen's hand tightened on my arm.

Cavanaugh nodded at my reaction. "And while we're at it, please explain the fingerprints on the glass found in the dish drainer of the victim's house and his DNA on a tissue in the bin."

"Oh come on!" Karen laughed. "That was nothing but overkill. Do you seriously believe my client, who has twelve years of policing experience, doesn't know about CCTV, GPS tracking, phone tracking and DNA? And how dumb would he have to be to drive his own car to the murder scene, have a drink from a glass in the victim's apartment and leave it on the dish drainer, then wipe his mouth with a tissue before putting it in the bin to be found by the police?"

She shook her head smugly then stopped suddenly. She held her right hand in the air to stop Cavanaugh from speaking. "Wait a minute," she said, pulling the photos towards her. At the tone in her voice, nothing changed in the room but everything went quiet as she searched through the photos.

Finally, she looked up. "Was there even a tissue box in the room? Because I can't see one in the photos. Are you actually suggesting my client had a drink of water, then walked from the kitchen to the bathroom to get a tissue," she laughed softly, "then walked back to the kitchen, wiped his mouth and threw the tissue in the bin? Are you seriously suggesting that?"

"It's your job, Ms Sawyer, to explain why your client's fingerprints and DNA were in the victim's house."

"No it isn't, Detective. It's *your* job to find out why they were there at all because my client is not that stupid."

Doubt filled his eyes as he turned his attention to me. "Okay. Let's pretend you had nothing to do with this. Let's pretend it wasn't you and you've been doing your own investigation." A steely look came into his eyes. "Let me remind you that withholding information is a punishable offence."

Karen sighed heavily. "Can we get to the question, please?"

I could almost hear his teeth grinding. His jaw tightened and his nostrils flared as he glared firstly at her, then at me. "If it wasn't you, then who do you think is trying to frame you?"

There it was. Out in the open and on tape. Jimmy was trying to frame me. But for the life of me, I didn't know why.

"Jimmy Croft," I muttered.

Cavanaugh exploded. "Oh for fuck's sake! Stop it with the…" he did speaky signs with his fingers, "Jimmy did it. We need more than your baseless accusations!"

He sat back and tipped his head back, looking at the ceiling as he tried to compose himself. Seconds ticked by before he looked back at me. The anger was still there but his voice had softened again. "Okay. Tell me why?"

"I'm working on that."

I couldn't tell him that Mel had withheld information from him, even if it meant taking the pressure off me. She had given me a glimmer of hope for our friendship and I wasn't about to jeopardise that. Even if I told him about the assumptions I'd made regarding the people in the red edge file, I doubted he'd believe me in his present frame of mind.

He grinned. "You're working on it," he repeated sarcastically.

"And I need more time," I stated.

A shadow of frustration crossed his face. "Okay. Let's assume you had nothing to do with the murder. At the moment, you should have nothing to hide if you're innocent. But maybe your lawyer can tell me how dead bodies have a tendency to stack up when you're around," he said, visibly trying to stay calm while the recording rolled on.

My heart did a little skip. Had he actually found out about the other connected deaths somehow? But if he didn't know that Jimmy's birth name was Lachlan, he didn't know about the red edge file and the list of people in it who had a connection to Jimmy as a child. Which also meant he didn't know about the deaths connected to Mel, Burton, Compton, Alison O'Reilly and Andrew Booth. It had to be something else.

I harrumphed smugly. "Dead bodies? What dead bodies? We're discussing Elizabeth Delaney."

He grinned his wolf grin. "We also have Samuel Price."

I watched him smile wider as shock registered on my face.

"Samuel Price?" I asked.

"That's correct. He's dead. He was killed yesterday in his home."

While I gaped at him in shock, he opened a folder on the desk and pretended to read the top sheet of paper. Beside him, Karen craned her neck to see the report.

"May I have a copy of that please?" she asked.

Cavanaugh smiled as he took a sheet of paper from under the one he was reading and passed it across to her. While she read, thoughts crashed around in my head.

Who could have killed Price? If it was Jimmy, it meant he had definitely killed Peter Marshall and the only motive for that was to stop the book with his father's name in it from being published. But what if it was someone else? My brain scrambled to come up with some names. David Lachlan's brother? Maybe he wanted his family's personal business kept personal and not published in Price's tell-all memoir. It made sense if he wanted the book to go missing. Samuel Price would have become a liability and would have had to be removed as well. Maybe Andrew Lachlan went straight to the source of the matter and made sure it all disappeared. He wasn't the kind of person who sat around in social clubs with their fingers curled around the handles of espresso cups dreaming about the day when everyone respected them. He was the sort who took matters into his own hands. But to kill Price, Andrew Lachlan would have to have known about the book in the first place, and yet again, according to Martin, the publication was being kept a secret. But then, to kill Marshall, Jimmy would have to have known about the book as well. Again, nothing made sense.

I made a mental note to call Martin.

Cavanaugh looked back down at his report. "It says here, he was shot point blank in the chest at 4 pm yesterday. Apparently he died instantly."

He looked up at me. "You wouldn't happen to know anything about that, would you Mr Curtis?"

I was seriously worried now. If he knew I'd visited Price, then he knew I'd been thrown out after a bout of mutual shouting. Amelia Jensen would have told him all about that.

"Of course not." My voice sounded angry but inside a voice screamed *What the hell?*

"Of course not," he repeated with a smirk. "So perhaps you can explain why you visited Mr Price on the afternoon before his death." He glanced down at his report. "Apparently there were heated words with Mr Price at the meeting."

Once again, I couldn't say why I had visited Price. I would have to mention Martin Farrow and the autobiography he was writing and if I did that, Cavanaugh would know I'd been withholding information from him on the Sunday he visited me at home. He had even said if that was the case, he'd throw me in jail. And here I was.

I was saved from answering by Karen. "My client agrees that he visited Mr Price on the day before his murder and there were heated words spoken. Mr Curtis does not argue with that. He went there in the course of his investigations." She glanced across to me with raised eyebrows. I nodded my head in agreement. "But apart from that, you have no proof whatsoever that my client killed Mr Price."

Cavanaugh sat forward. "Why did you visit Price?"

Karen nodded at me but gave me a warning squint.

"I went there in the hope to find a connection between the murder of Elizabeth Delaney and someone in his memoirs."

He pounced on my words. "So, Mr Curtis, you knew about the memoirs?"

"Of course I knew," I scoffed. "*You* told me about the memoirs on the day you came to my house, the same day I took my daughter to Dreamworld. You told me that a manuscript was found hidden in the car of a man who was found drowned after jumping off the Stradbroke ferry. You told me the manuscript was picked up by Simon Price's lawyers before you could read it."

He frowned. "I did?"

"You most certainly did," I stated.

Cavanaugh snorted. "So what connection to Simon Price were you looking for? And what...someone?"

I had to be careful of how I worded this, for Martin's sake. "That's what I was trying to find out. He did not give me any clues and I now believe he did not know of any."

Cavanaugh chuckled. "So again, I say. Dead bodies have a way of turning up around you, don't they?"

Any other time, I'd have resented the remark. Now I thought he might be on the right track.

Karen touched my elbow to remain silent. "Is that a question you need my client to answer, Detective Cavanaugh?" Karen asked. She gave him her calm face to show him that she did not, in any shape or form, appear concerned by his remark.

As my stomach did another flip, I tried to stare him down. Apart from the gritting of his teeth, he remained stoic, staring straight back at me.

People believe maintaining eye contact is a sure sign of honesty. But like most things, too much indicates an issue. Besides that, eye contact is the first thing cops learn at the academy. Module 101.

Karen sat forward, gripping my arm firmly. "Okay, Detective. My client has done everything he can to cooperate with you but if you don't have any more evidence than the insubstantial evidence and insinuations you've shown us today, then my client should be free to leave."

She hesitated before continuing. "But I'll meet you halfway, detective. Because my client would like to cooperate fully with the police, we will be willing to meet you back here tomorrow morning at the same time to check in and fill you in on what he has discovered. If you let him leave now. He is not a flight risk. He is trying to clear his name."

"Again with the bargaining," Cavanaugh smirked.

"It's called cooperation, Detective." Karen's voice was steely and I was suddenly happy to have her as my lawyer.

He sucked on his teeth, watching me. "Okay," he finally said to Karen. "We let your client leave but I'm sure you will appreciate that with this new evidence we have, we will be doing everything we can to get a warrant to search your client's house and garage."

"You'll be lucky." Karen's voice sounded firm but I knew her. She was rattled.

"What are you looking for?" I asked.

"You name it. Anything that will put the final screw in your coffin."

Cavanaugh stood up, switching the video off in one swift move. "Tomorrow at 10 am. You'd better be here."

30

My first call outside the station was to Frank. He answered on the second ring.

"I need your help, Frank."

"Anyfing, mate. Name i'."

The second one was to Sam.

We were back at Charlie's again. Same table.

"There's a mugshot of you in today's paper," Frank said as he pulled up a chair and sat down. "Fourth page. You look like a banker rather than 'Most Wanted'."

"I hope they got my best side."

I ran through everything that had happened while Sam and Frank drank their coffees. There was a lot to tell. There was the information from the red edge file, the consequent murders of the people connected to the people who were mentioned in it and Bridget Lachlan's admission that she had fabricated her statement in order to rid herself of her husband that had started the ball rolling in the first place. Then there was the interview this morning.

Sam sat still during it all. "I almost feel sorry for Jimmy," she murmured. "His whole life was ruined by his mother."

"Yes. And everything the others in the file did was based purely on her accusations," I agreed. "But don't be swayed by sentiment, Sam. What was in that file is Jimmy's motive for the murders." My statement sounded callous but innocent people had been murdered.

When it came to the night of Christine's murder and my DNA and fingerprints in her house, no one had an answer.

"They had to be planted. I don't know how, but there's no other explanation. He had my fingerprints somehow and must have broken into her office by the window and planted them. Then he killed her when she came home."

Even to my own ears, it sounded far-fetched.

"I 'ave a certain professional innerest in break-ins." Frank admitted as he smiled at Sam. Sam scowled back but remained silent as he continued. "Anyone doin' a B and E job needs to take certain precautions. The first and most obvious is ta make sure 'e or she doin' the B and E, don't leave no fingerprints. You wiv me?"

Sam nodded, letting him know she was on the same page. "You wear gloves."

"You definitely wear gloves," Frank agreed. "Nobody, no matter 'ow dumb, and this guy ain't dumb, enters a place he shouldn'ta been entering wivou' wearing gloves."

Frank's eyes went from me to Sam. "That would be careless. Very careless. And dumb. Jack ain't dumb. He'd wear gloves."

I shut my eyes. "Frank, please, you're not helping me."

"Listen to me, guv. Jimmy would 'ave worn gloves but he some'ow bough' *your* prints and DNA wiv him and left 'em for the cops to find." His eyes travelled back and forwards again from Sam to me. "It's a mystery. But are you tryin' to work it out in ya 'ead how he did tha', Jack?"

I thought for a few seconds. "He knows where I live."

Frank nodded.

"He broke in and lifted my prints."

He nodded again.

"And he hates me enough to try to frame me for murder."

He sat back. "Well done, Serpico."

I shook my head, still confused. Every time I thought about Christine's murder, Peter Marshall's name kept popping into my head.

"The big question is, how does Christine's murder and the death of Peter Marshall, the man who was writing Simon Price's book, connect? And Simon Price as well. Cavanaugh seems to think they are, and I can't help but think he's right."

I shook my head trying to work it out. "We know why Jimmy killed the others from the red edge file but did he kill Marshall or was it just an accident?" Questions were running around in my head.

"One fing at a time, mate. Solve one and the udder ones will fall inta place."

"I've got twenty-four hours to find out what I can before Cavanaugh throws the book at me."

I was staring at the dregs of my coffee when the truth came to me.

"I've been an idiot," I whispered. "I've been trying to connect Christine's murder to Peter Marshall purely because their deaths were so close together and because Simon Price's book is only being written because of Christine's involvement at the beginning." I shook my head. "But there is no connection."

I turned to Sam. "Is the Marshall case still open, Sam?"

From somewhere in the kitchen, a loud crash reverberated through the restaurant. A waitress must have dropped a few plates but it sounded like an almighty car crash. Because Sam was concentrating so hard on what was being said, she yelped and held a hand to her heart as the echoes rang in the forthcoming silence. "Jesus," she whispered, as another customer laughed and said, "Oops."

Sam giggled before continuing. "Where were we? Oh yes. The Marshall case." She nodded. "Yep. We're still trying to put the facts together. Initially, we thought it was a suicide but there was no reason for it. He was being paid a lot of money to write that book and apparently he was almost finished. We found the manuscript in the boot of his car but Price's lawyer jumped in and took it."

I was nodding as Sam spoke. "That's what Martin said." I stopped to think. "So it could have been murder?" I asked.

"Absolutely," she replied, her eyes widening.

"That's it," I stated, sitting up straight. "Jimmy had to have killed Marshall because of the manuscript. He didn't want the book published because his father's name was mentioned in it as a possible paedophile. The connection to Christine really was just a coincidence."

Things were beginning to fall into place. "After the death of Peter Marshall, Price hired a new writer to finish the book. Martin Farrow." I glanced from Frank to Sam. "Remember I met him coincidentally outside the morgue at Southport Hospital when I identified Christine's body?"

Both nodded but stayed quiet as I stared at the table trying to remember what Martin had said.

"Martin said he was at the hospital after being mugged." I looked up at Sam. "But nothing was stolen. Not his wallet, his phone or his Rolex."

Think.

I dropped my eyes to the table again as I thought. "He said whoever mugged him tried to wrench his satchel out of his hand but bystanders came to his assistance and the mugger ran." I looked up again. "That satchel held the only copy of Price's unfinished book."

It was all making sense now. "I had a couple of drinks with Martin before heading off to see Sandra to tell her about Christine. He told me that Price had devoted a whole chapter to pointing the finger at the Lachlan brothers and again I can only assume Price insinuated that David Lachlan was responsible for Jimmy's abuse, maybe even being a part of the paedophile gang. Hence Lachlan's suicide when the police were closing in on him."

David Lachlan would not have done well in prison. As vicious as some criminals are, there was nothing lower on the food chain than men who violated small children. He would not have lasted long in prison before he became a victim himself.

"If Jimmy couldn't get the manuscript from both Peter Marshall and Martin Farrow," I explained, "the next best thing to do was to get rid of the primary source. Simon Price."

Sam pushed her coffee cup aside and pulled out a notebook from her leather handbag and began scribbling everything down.

"What's Martin Farrow's phone number? Where would he be now?" she asked.

I had an uneasy feeling in the pit of my stomach. With Simon Price's murder, everything had changed once again. First Peter Marshall, now

Price. Jimmy definitely did not want this book published. He'd already tried to mug Martin for it and failed which is why he'd killed Price. So, instead of being paid by Price's lawyer to write the memoir, Martin would now have to hand the manuscript back since funding would presumably disappear. But in the meantime, Martin still had the manuscript in his possession and that could only mean he was in danger as well.

I stood up suddenly. "I don't have his number but I know where he lives. I have to get over to see Martin now. He's in danger. Hopefully he's at his home. I don't know the exact address but I can find my way back there. By now he'll know by now about Price's death."

I checked my watch. 11.45. I had to hurry. I still wanted to see Andrew Booth but that could wait until this afternoon. Right now, Martin Farrow's safety was a priority.

31

MARTIN

I am into the third day of rewriting the manuscript. Nearly everything Peter Marshall has written has now transferred onto my laptop and saved in the cloud, plus I've completed the outline and formatting of how I want the book to look. I was beginning to feel pleased at my progress.

I spent most of yesterday morning at the library getting more information on Simon Price and photocopies of photos from his early days as a politician. I then spent the rest of the day and all that evening at the dining table I use for a desk, transcribing the manuscript and making a list of questions I wanted to ask him. I don't want to be too Jekyll and Hyde but as the day progressed and the street lights flickered on, I could feel myself beginning to get into his skin. He was twenty years older than me but apart from that, our backgrounds were similar.

I always thought I could disappear and no one would miss me. All my bills are paid by direct debit and my cleaner comes twice a week and is paid through the bank. I have no appointments apart from finishing the book, I have never spoken to my neighbours and the few friends I can name have all left for greener pastures overseas. My parents are dead. I have no siblings or family and I could pack all my belongings into a couple of suitcases.

As I read the manuscript, I was struck by the resemblances. He was an only child, born in Brisbane and educated at Brisbane Grammar and possessed a law degree and a passion for drama at school. Replace law degree with journalism degree, and we were the same. I pulled a newspaper cutting from the photocopies I'd done at the library and smiled at the one of him performing as a chicken in primary school. Metaphorically speaking however, I had stayed a chicken and he had gone on to become an infamous politician. At this point the empathy vanished because nothing in his first twenty-five years could explain the second ones.

What I didn't understand was why the handsome eighteen-year-old, who spent his time acting, drinking and chasing women would suddenly choose to become a politician. It felt important somehow. It was a tiny detail but it meant he wasn't quite who we think he was. I wasn't even sure he was quite sure who *he* thought he was. What was difficult was if you're trying to write someone's memoirs, you have to feel you know the person. But I felt like I didn't know him at all. And that's the hard part if you're trying to publish someone's voice.

What I was hoping for was some mention of hardship apart from his childhood upbringing. Some sort of unhappiness. Even depression. Maybe he turned to politics because all his friends had found agents and were getting offers of work but he wasn't. Maybe he was lost because he failed in what he truly wanted to do so he turned to politics to compensate. I was trying to imagine myself in his place. In his early twenties, ambitious, talented, but not quite talented enough, looking for a path to follow, anxious and wretched. Nothing sells a memoir quite so well as a good dose of misery. Grinding poverty and depression are money in the bank.

By midmorning, I was standing in the kitchen making my fourth cup of coffee of the morning, searching through the photos for someone famous to follow up on, when a news bulletin broke on the Morning Show on television and I heard the words 'Simon Price' mentioned. To begin with it didn't sound important until the camera took in the crime scene tape and a body covered in a blanket being pushed on a gurney into an ambulance.

File footage showed him shaking hands with the mayor with a smile on his face before flicking to a policeman staring at the camera refusing to comment further. He did however state Simon Price had been found dead in his Gold Coast home yesterday under suspicious circumstances. The program moved on to the weather and that was that.

I stood in the lounge staring at the television, feeling icy shivers running up and down my spine. I had to call Rick.

And that's when the doorbell rang.

32

JACK

I pulled the car up at the address I'd dropped Martin at a couple of days ago. I did a quick glance around to make sure I hadn't been followed before walking up the path leading to the front door.

Martin opened the door wearing jeans torn at the knees and a faded blue windbreaker. Behind him the room was a mess. A MacBook stood open on the dining table surrounded by a mess of paper, books and notes. A wall dividing the dining room to what I imagined was the kitchen was covered in post-it-notes and a pile of photocopies lay strewn on the floor by a chair. Beside it lay a tray of half-eaten sandwiches and an untouched cup of coffee with film on top.

He'd been working on the book and I felt a tug of regret at the news I had to tell him. Then one glance at the shocked look on his face as he held a remote control in his hand told me he had already seen the news of Samuel Price's death.

"You've heard the news then?" I asked unnecessarily.

His mouth opened and closed as he looked from me to the morning news program and back again.

"There's something in that book you're writing that someone doesn't want published. Marshall is dead. Price is dead. And you have the only copy of the manuscript in your possession which makes you the next victim. Every instinct tells me you're in danger, Martin. You have to find somewhere else to go."

"But the book is crap!" he cried out. "There's nothing in it that's worth Price's life or all this trouble."

"Someone doesn't think so."

"Jesus Christ! I have to call my agent."

I laughed. "If you don't leave now, you'll be doing it as a ghost. You have to leave now. I'll take you somewhere where there's good security and CCTV cameras. You can call your agent from there. But my bet is whatever money was allocated for you to write this memoir is no longer available because the prime subject of the book is dead."

"But all the work I've done!" He waved his arms around the untidy room. "I've spent days and days working on this. I can't just hand the manuscript back or throw it all away!"

Sweat had broken out on his forehead and his hands were shaking.

"Have you saved your work somewhere? On your hard drive?" I asked.

His breathing slowed a little when he realised what I was saying. "Yes." He glanced over to his laptop and a slow smile came to his face. "Yes, I have! And it's on the cloud too. It's all in there."

"Then I suggest you quickly pack up the laptop and the little you'll need to take with you and let's get out of here. Now."

He didn't argue any further. He hurried to a bedroom, pulled a suitcase out of a wardrobe and started throwing clothes and underwear into it. While he packed, I pulled the curtains aside and kept a look out through the window.

Five minutes later, we were both in Christine's car and heading down the street. As we began to turn the corner, I glanced in my rear mirror and saw a white van pulling up outside Martin's house. The driver's door opened and a man dressed in jeans and a black sweat shirt with the hood pulled over his head stepped out. He stood looking at the front window through dark tinted sunglasses that hid most of his face and instinctively I knew we'd only just made it.

I was grateful we'd managed to get out of the house early because I didn't like our chances of a car chase. I still couldn't find fourth gear.

33

I stayed in the slow lane when I could from Harbour Town along the Esplanade for the forty-five minutes it took me to get to the Novotel in Surfers Paradise. Thankfully, speed is something you don't worry about when you drive on this main road.

Martin was quiet for most of the way, lost in his own thoughts as he stared at the rolling surf and the sun glistening off the ocean like diamonds to his left.

As I drove, I gazed south towards a forest of palm trees that almost obscured the restaurants, skyscrapers and fast food outlets stretching into infinity. In my peripheral vision, I could see people were beginning to move inside from garden eating areas. The wind was picking up and lightning stroked far in the distance, burning eerie images onto my retina. By nightfall, rain would be lashing the windows in silver sheets and turning the streetlights golden.

My mind raced with everything that had happened. Once again, I was like Wile E. Coyote. I kept chasing, chasing, only to end up always standing in mid-air, the edge of a cliff behind me, the bomb in my hand, the fuse burning low.

I turned to see Martin watching me, a puzzled look on his face. "I've been going through everything in my head trying to make sense of all this."

He shook his head and glanced through the windscreen. "Apart from the fact that this book has been kept a secret by just about everyone, there is absolutely nothing in it that anyone would be interested in. It's a vain man's attempt at trying to make out he's something he's not. It's more about how many toes he stood on to get to the top."

He looked back at me. "What I can't work out is how anyone found out about this book. I've been sworn to secrecy as I'm sure Peter Marshall was, so how did anyone find out about it? There is a huge campaign in the planning stages with media coverage, news coverage, press releases and a fully publicised personal appearance so secrecy is vital. He was sparing no amount of cash on this but the bottom line was it had to be kept a secret for the full effect of the book when it came out." He scowled at me. "Was it you?"

I laughed. "Don't be ridiculous. I couldn't care less about Price and his pissy book."

He stared at me some more. "I looked in the side mirror as we were leaving and saw that white van pull up outside my house. How could you possibly know that man was coming for me?"

I drove in silence for a minute, trying to put it all into a logical sequence. "You first told me about it when we had lunch at the Grand Hotel. But for me, the puzzle started before that."

Martin twisted in his seat to watch me, waiting for me to continue. "Go on," he urged.

"There's just too much for me to tell you at the moment." I indicated to merge into the right hand lane to avoid a tourist on a push bike and a car horn blared behind me. I shook my head and moved back behind the push bike, murmuring *'come on'*. "Really, I'm still piecing it all together myself."

He frowned. "You had just left the morgue when we met at the hospital. Am I right?"

I nodded. "Someone I knew was murdered and I was asked to identify the body."

"Is she connected to this somehow?"

I jiggled my head from side to side. "Indirectly. Up until this morning, I thought she was the primary cause but since then, a whole lot of other issues has come to light."

I glanced in the rear vision mirror at the line of angry motorists behind me. Thankfully, the Novotel was only another five minutes away.

"Believe it or not," I turned to Martin. "I'm the primary suspect for those murders."

He gaped at me but let me continue.

"Tell me what was in the book about the Lachlan Brothers. In particular, David Lachlan," I said before he asked me any more questions.

He shrugged. "There's a full chapter on them but all just basically finger pointing. Nothing concrete. They moved up to the Gold Coast from Sydney with money their grandfather left them while they were in their mid-thirties. Andrew was the eldest and the brains of the family. He set his sights on becoming a land developer and started buying up properties with the intention of building blocks of luxury units on them. This is where he came in touch with Price. Price says he knows a smart businessman when he sees one but my feel is Price had his hand out for cash in return for approving applications."

Martin stopped to think for a few seconds. "Andrew was the ruthless and violent one into gambling and prostitution, possibly drugs. His brother David did anything his brother told him to do. Price talked about David a few times and mentions his personal connection to the abuse of his own son."

He stopped and turned to me, a frown on his face. "It's all about David isn't it?"

I kept my eyes on the road. I didn't want him seeing that he'd hit the nail on the head. I wanted more information. "Why do you say that?" I asked.

"Because again, he was pointing the finger at everyone else and trying to make himself look like Mother Teresa. The Lachlans managed to keep it all quiet but you can't keep something like this hidden. David ended up committing suicide."

The turn off for the Novotel was coming up and I was trying to concentrate on pushing my way into the right hand lane again so I let him speak.

His eyes were shining. "I know there's more to this than the Lachlans. And there's more to all this than just the murders of Marshall and Price. I can feel it."

He was staring intently at me as I indicated to turn into the main entrance of the hotel. My silence seemed to spur him on. "This is big, isn't it? You're too quiet."

He waited for me to say something but I'd already turned off the engine and had begun unbuckling my seat belt.

"I want an exclusive from you when this is finished, Jack." He was talking fast because I'd already opened my door. "I want to write about this as a true crime book. That's what I do best. I'll give you full exposure and credit for it and your career will skyrocket because of my book."

I turned to him, one foot out of the door. "Let's just concentrate on keeping you alive, shall we?" I said.

"I hated writing this book anyway," he babbled, unclipping his own seat belt and hurrying to keep up with me. "I'm guessing Rick will want me to return this manuscript and he can have it. It's worth precious little now. But what I've done myself, I'm keeping. It's all in my computer and it's my work." He gave a nervous laugh. "This is going to be huge!"

I walked into the hotel with him scurrying behind me.

The duty manager listened attentively as I told him I wanted added security. After an initial hesitation, I added that Martin Farrow, a well-known best-selling author, would like a suite and a law firm with a big budget would be picking up the tab. Martin's eyes opened wide as I spoke but one look from me silenced him. I took two cards from the holder on the reception counter. I wrote my name and phone number on one and gave it to Martin, the other one I handed to him.

"Write your number on this for me."

His eyes lit up as he turned to the desk and grabbed a pen. As he handed me the card, he gushed, "You are going to be famous, Jack Curtis."

I left him standing in the foyer with the manager explaining the security of his hotel to Martin while a red-coated man picked up Martin's tatty suitcase, ready to lead him to the elevator.

34

Andrew Booth lived in a small, rendered house in a suburban street of Ashmore. He was perched on a ladder in his driveway, unbolting a basketball hoop from the wall. His hair was greyer now, he'd thickened around the waist and his forehead was etched with frown lines that disappeared into bushy grey eyebrows.

"Do you need a hand?" I asked as I walked towards him.

He looked down and took a moment to recognise me.

"These things are rusted on," he said, tapping the bolts.

He descended the ladder and wiped his hands on his shirtfront before shaking my hand. At the same time, he glanced at the front window nervously. Music was coming from inside and I knew his wife would be sitting by the window watching my approach. I'd spoken to her on the phone earlier to ask if I could come over and I had heard the uncertainty in her voice. She didn't want me here.

"I tell her to turn it down but she says it has to be loud. Sign of age, I guess."

He began folding up the ladder, explaining the girls didn't use the hoop any more.

"I was sorry to hear about your daughter."

I saw his hesitation and the slight turn of his head as his eyebrows raised high on his forehead. He was wondering how I knew but he pretended he didn't hear me. Tools were being packed away in a toolbox. I was about to ask which one it was who had died when he started talking.

"Kim had just won two titles at the national swimming championships and had broken a distance record," he stated. "Yet even after all that training, all those early morning laps, mile after mile, she knew she wasn't going to be good enough. There is a fine line between being good and being great."

I let him talk because I sensed he was making a point. The story unfolded. Kim Booth, not quite nineteen, dressed up for a rock concert. She went with Charlotte and a group of friends from university.

"Charlotte thinks someone gave her a white pill early on in the night," he said. "She was always so careful about medication and health supplements so why she took it is a mystery to all of us. She danced all night until her heartbeat grew rapid and her blood pressure soared. She told Charlotte she felt faint and anxious. Then she collapsed in a toilet cubicle."

While he spoke, Andrew was crouched over the toolbox as though he'd lost something, but his shoulders were shaking. In a rasping voice, he continued, "Kim spent three weeks in a coma, never regaining consciousness, while Pam and I argued over whether to turn off her life-support." He sniffled. "I wanted to remember her gliding through the water, with her smooth stroke, not this shell of a person filling the hospital bed. Pam accused me of giving up hope, of only thinking of myself, of not praying hard enough for a miracle."

He looked up at the front window. "She doesn't talk to me anymore. She just tells me when dinner is ready or when the lawn needs mowing." He turned to me. "Yesterday she saw your photograph in the paper. She'll be watching."

He was warning me that I didn't have much time before she called the police.

"Who gave Kim the tablet? Did they ever catch anyone?"

He shook his head. "Charlotte gave them a description and looked through mugshots. She couldn't see his face in any of the books they gave her."

"What did he look like?"

"Tall. Thin. But half the kids look like that these days."

"How old?"

"Maybe twenty, Charlotte said. But it was dark and she wasn't sure."

He closed the toolbox and flipped the metal catches closed, before glancing despondently at the house again, not yet ready to go inside.

"Do you remember Jimmy Lachlan?" I asked.

He turned at me and hesitated before answering. "Yes."

"When was the last time you saw him?"

He shrugged. "Nine, maybe ten years ago. He was only a kid."

"Not since then?"

He shook his head and then narrowed his eyes as if something had just occurred to him. "Kim said she knew someone called Jimmy who worked at the swimming centre."

"Could the name have been Jimmy Croft?"

He shook his head and shrugged. "I don't remember. It was just in passing."

"You never saw him?"

"No."

He glanced over to the house and saw the curtains move in the front room. "I wouldn't hang around if I were you," he said. "She'll call the police if you stay much longer. She probably already has."

The toolbox was weighing down his right hand. He swapped it for the other one and glanced up at the basketball hoop. "Guess that'll have to stay a while longer."

"I'm innocent, Andrew." I was getting tired of trying to convince people this. "Right now, the police have no solid evidence that I've done anything wrong. I'm helping them prove my innocence."

He smiled sadly. "Good luck, Jack. I think you're going to need it."

He hurried to the house and closed the door firmly behind him. The silence amplified my steps as I walked towards the car. The man who gave Kim the tainted white tablet could have been Jimmy but eyewitness accounts are notoriously unreliable. Stress and shock can alter perceptions and memory is flawed. Jimmy had made himself a chameleon, camouflaging himself, moving backwards and forwards but always blending in.

I understood what Jimmy was doing. He was trying to take away what each of us held dear: the love of a child, the closeness of a partner, the sense of belonging. He wanted us to suffer, to lose what we most loved, and to experience *his* loss.

Mel and Bill had been soulmates. Anyone who knew them could see that. Alison O'Reilly had become a schoolteacher only to have her mother die in a house fire and her father reduced to a shell in a wheelchair. She lost her family as well as her career. Christine Buchanan, the favoured child of a judge, spoiled and pampered, had been taken savagely away from her family. John Compton, a lonely widower, happy to spend his days in his garden in his retirement. Jimmy didn't give him any latitude. He left him alive long enough, four days tied to a chair, to regret what he'd done.

A small child was taken into foster care and a very different one came back. Jimmy's message was clear. We failed his father – an innocent man, arrested and questioned for hours about his sex life. His house was searched for child pornography that didn't exist and his name put on the index of sex offenders despite him never having been charged, let alone convicted. The pain alone would have ruined his father's life. All future relationships would have been ruined. Future wives and partners would have to be told. Fathering another child would become a risk. Then, as a last resort, he'd taken his own life when all else had been taken away from him.

I share the blame for Jimmy, however accidental it was. I should have taken more care and read the report. Even then, would I have questioned Mel's advice? Probably not.

35

My mobile rang almost as soon as I pulled away from the kerb. I had indicated to merge into traffic and glanced down at the screen but I didn't recognise the number and for a moment I wondered if Jimmy was finally going to call me.

I should have known it was Cavanaugh.

"I'm just calling to tell you I won $20 on a bet today."

He laughed the way he does when he's about to drop a small bomb. By the sound of traffic noise in the background, I knew he was on the motorway. "I bet the guys at the station $20 that I'd find something to finally put you behind bars."

"What are you talking about?" I asked, my voice sounding exasperated.

"We found the shovel," he said joyously. "It was buried at the gravesite under a shitload of leaves."

"Congratulations."

He ignored my sarcasm. "The boys and girls at the lab did us proud again. They matched the soil samples found on the shovel with those taken from Elizabeth's grave." He snorted. "Sorry. Christine's grave. I still get confused."

His cheeriness was alarming. Something bad was coming.

"What has this to do with me?"

He ignored my question. "Then they matched the fingerprints found on the handle with yours. You know, the ones you left at Christine's apartment on the glass?"

When does this end?

"I told you I never touched a glass at Christine's apartment. Karen and I both told you they must have been planted."

I signalled quickly to pull over to the verge. I was too involved with the conversation with Cavanaugh to concentrate on my driving. I stopped and put the hazard lights on as a car roared past, blaring its horn loudly at me.

"Oh yes, you did, didn't you," he chuckled again.

"Don't be an ass, Cavanaugh. Think about it! Why would I leave a shovel at the scene of the crime with or without my prints? Just like I wouldn't leave her mobile phone and diary at the crime scene to incriminate myself and I wouldn't leave my fingerprints on a glass in the victim's house. Everything was planted."

"Okay. I'll play along." I could hear the smile in his voice. He was enjoying this. "Who planted them?"

I sighed. "Jimmy Croft." I was trying to keep the desperation out of my voice but I knew he could hear it. "Go back to the beginning. Ask Melissa Stark for the red edge file. Read the notes. His birth name was James Lachlan. All the pieces are there. All you have to do is put them together."

"Under different circumstances I might admire your enthusiasm, but I have enough evidence already to pull you in," he said. "I have motive…"

"WHAT MOTIVE?!" I yelled over the top of him.

"… opportunity and physical evidence. You couldn't have marked your territory any better if you'd pissed in every corner."

"I told you, I can explain everything!"

"Good! Explain it to the jury! That's the beauty of our legal system. You get plenty of chances to state your case. If the jury doesn't believe you , you can appeal to the High Court. You can spend the rest of your life appealing, if you want. It obviously helps pass the time when you're banged up for life."

I had to tell him everything I'd found, however circumstantial it sounded.

I put my elbows on the steering wheel and rested my head in the palms of my hand.

"There's more," I said, trying to keep the desperation out of my voice. "I told you at the beginning that he's murdered before, and now I know for sure that he has."

"Another theory, Curtis?" He was enjoying this. His voice was light as if I had just told him a really good joke.

"Check these out. The Social Worker, Melissa Stark, was the one who pushed to have Jimmy placed in foster care. Her partner was a victim of a hit-and-run. The driver was never caught. Her boss was Andrew Booth and his daughter was a victim of a bad drug given to her at a nightclub. She never took drugs. She was an athlete. The guy who gave her the drug was never caught."

I had a feeling he wasn't listening but I couldn't stop ranting.

"John Compton was the psychologist whose report they used to take Jimmy from his parents." I took a shuddering deep breath. "Compton died in his home after a break-in where he was gagged and tied to his chair for four days before dying. Judge Buchanan, Christine's father, was the one who signed the judgement that took Jimmy from his family and made him a ward of the state. That's why Christine was killed. Because of what her father did. Alison O'Reilly was the headmistress who initially called Children's Services to report Jimmy's behaviour. She is now the full-time carer for her father who is now in a wheelchair after a house fire that killed her mother. And then there's Graham Burton, the original psychologist who stated that Jimmy was troubled and damaged. His wife died in a car crash after being run off the road. The driver of the other car was never caught."

I knew he hadn't hung up. In the silence, I could hear breathing.

I lifted my head from my hands. "Listen to me. He took them out, one by one. But instead of killing me, he's framing me for Christine's murder because I unknowingly signed the initial form to start this whole process."

I drew in a deep breath to calm myself. "I giving you the fucking pot of gold at the end of the rainbow and you can't even see it. There's a link between them all, a connecting bridge."

Still silence.

"All along, I thought Christine was murdered because of paedophile ring she exposed," I continued. "I was wrong. But that was the only connection I could see to Simon Price."

I hesitated, trying to put things in their right sequence. I knew I was babbling but my life depended on convincing Cavanaugh.

"And Peter Marshall's suicide? The guy who was writing Price's memoir? He didn't commit suicide. It was murder to stop the book from being published. Price mentions Jimmy's father in his book as being one of the paedophiles who should have been prosecuted. Now both Price and Marshall have been murdered. Not because of the paedophile ring but because Jimmy wants that book, with all reference to his father, to disappear."

The silence dragged on.

"Are you even listening to me, you pompous idiot? All you have to do is your job! Check them out. Check the red edge file. All of them were victims and all of them had something to do with Jimmy. Even me."

"I've heard enough of your rambling, Curtis. I'm putting out a warrant for your arrest, Curtis. Come in or be dragged in wearing cuffs."

I pressed the 'end call' button and turned the phone off.

36

I was hoping I'd have enough time to make a quick dash home. I needed a few changes of clothes and I needed the cash I had stashed away in my safe. I couldn't use my credit card anymore. Cavanaugh would already have frozen it, and if not, it would only be because it would be easy to track me if I used it. If he'd frozen my credit card, I was sure he'd also frozen my other accounts which left me with one alternative: the cash I had in my safe at home.

I stopped at the traffic lights at the top of my street and glanced left towards my house. Two police cars were blocking the street and another was in the driveway. Cavanaugh was leaning on an open door talking into his mobile phone, his face as black as thunder.

As the lights turned green, I imagined him looking up and seeing me saluting him as I chugged away heading towards Surfers Paradise.

I had to think of what I'd do in his situation if I wanted to catch someone. Firstly, I suddenly realised, I needed to ditch this car, which would leave me with nothing at all to get around in. I was sure I couldn't hire a car – he'd have that option covered as well.

I had no idea where to go. I couldn't go to my office, Cavanaugh would have that covered. I couldn't call Sam and I couldn't call Frank.

Cavanaugh would know to watch him as well, no doubt. I knew I should call Karen but that could wait until I had no options left.

That left me with Sandra Burton for transport.

Sandra answered after one ring. "What's going on, Jack? Frank's been under my feet for two days now waiting for Jimmy to show, which he hasn't by the way, and I've got a bad feeling about him. He's never done this before."

I explained to her about Jimmy and my current situation. I heard gasps and snorts from her end of the line and without hesitation she said I could have her car until I was able to prove my innocence.

I took the next exit and headed straight to Surfers Paradise and Adventureland, glancing in the rear vision mirror for flashing lights signally a police car.

I pulled the car into the vacant lot behind Adventureland and parked it among the weeds and tall grass. A group of teenagers watched me from the shadows beside a boarded up house but I doubted they'd steal the car, even if I left the keys in the ignition. It looked useable but it was low on petrol and they'd soon find that they could walk faster than it ran.

I took the keys out of the ignition and glanced down at the beautifully carved, wooden lizard attached to the key ring. And my heart almost stopped.

A wooden lizard. A wooden cross. And a wooden cat.

I fumbled around in my pocket for my phone and dragged it out, realising I'd switched it off after I hung up from Cavanaugh. With shaking hands, I turned the phone back on. Then I called Sally.

She answered immediately, her voice shaking. "Thank God! Where are you, Jack? The police have been here looking for you and reporters have been ringing my doorbell saying you're dangerous. They say the police are going to shoot you!"

I ignored her question. "Are you and Jazz alright? Are you safe?"

She hesitated. "We're fine. We're scared as hell but we're fine. We're worried about you."

After everything we'd been through during the divorce – the anger, the hurt, the insults – this meant more to me than I could ever have imagined.

"It wasn't me, Sally."

"I bloody know that! What's going on?"

"It's someone trying to punish me for something that happened years ago. I had no idea of any of this until a few days ago. It's not just me. He had a list of people he wanted to kill."

"My God!"

"Are the police still watching the house?"

If not, I thought, they were probably trying to trace this call right now. With mobile phones, they have to work backwards, identifying which towers are relaying the signals. There were probably half a dozen transmitters between Southport and Surfers Paradise. As each one is ticked off, the search area narrows. I had to keep the call short.

"I don't know," she mumbled. "I have no idea what's going on. JC hasn't even come to finish the work he's been doing in the back yard."

I could hear Jazz singing in the background and a rush of tenderness caught my throat.

It's funny how the little unconnected memories are the ones you remember the most. The creak of the wooden swing in our yard as I pushed Jazz. The maple tree dropping its fiery red leaves on the front lawn as four-year-old Jazz scooped them up and threw them above her head, laughing and singing. Always singing. Then I remembered sitting on the front steps the night Sally left me. Rain was falling softly onto the leaves of the Leopard tree with a soft pitter-patter. In the distance, I could hear the sorrowful barking of a dog. A baby crying in the distance. Tyres crunching down the driveway and the look Sally gave me as she reversed. As if I was a stranger. As if we hadn't been married for thirteen years and as if we didn't share a daughter staring sadly at me through the windscreen.

I swallowed the lump in my throat. She was safe. I recognised the tune Jazz was singing. It was an INXS song about all of us having wings but some of us not knowing why.

Then I froze at the realisation of where I'd heard the tune before.

"Sally. Who's JC?"

"He's a young man who was doing a door knock, wanting work. I said I needed someone to do some heavy work in the back garden and he jumped at the chance of some extra money. He's been coming and going for about a month now. Jazz thinks he's cool and they seem to really get on."

"What does he look like, Sal?"

"Why, Jack? You're scaring me."

"Tell me."

"Tall. A bit clumsy. A bit thin, I guess. Late teens. Wavy hair. Drives a white van."

Drives a white van.

JC had to be Jimmy. The initials were the same. Jimmy Croft. JC. And he'd been at Sally's house, working in the yard and getting to know them. Building up their trust in him. I didn't want to think how close he was to finishing off his list.

My mouth suddenly went dry. I tried to swallow but there was no saliva. "Was he the one who gave Jazz the wooden cat?" The words almost caught in my throat.

Her hesitation lasted for a few seconds. "How did you know that? He's good with his hands and he loves working with wood. He really likes Jazz."

It was like a hand had clutched my heart as I felt the full weight of despair. I recalled how I used to listen to Jazz breathe in her cot, how I used to watch the rise and fall of my infant daughter's chest. When she cried, I would lull her to sleep in my arms, waiting for her sobs to fade into the soft rhythms of rest. And when she was at last quiet, I would bend down slowly, carefully, my back aching from the strain of the position, and lay her in her cot. This monster, this psychopath was not going to take her from me. I will not allow him to kill any more people, especially not my precious child.

Part of me wanted to tell Sally to take Jazz and leave the house as quickly as she could and go to a friend's house. Another part, the smart part, told me it would be better for them if I didn't panic them any further and to simply call the police for help.

"Sally, listen very carefully to me." I tried to keep the panic out of my voice. "If he turns up, do not let him in. It's vital! Call OOO immediately. Lock all the doors and DO NOT LET HIM IN."

"Now I'm really scared, Jack. Is he dangerous?"

"Extremely."

At the sharp intake of her breath, I glanced at my watch. I'd been talking for close on five minutes and if Cavanaugh was trying to track me, he would be close. I had to hang up.

"I have to go, Sally. I'll call when I've sorted this out. But do as I say, call OOO if he as much as turns up in his van."

I switched my phone off again and almost ran inside the game parlour to get Sandra's keys. Five minutes later, I was sitting in Sandra's car ready to pull out into traffic on Marine Parade. My plan was to make my way back to Martin Farrow when a white van drove past. Behind the wheel was Jimmy.

37

The stretch of road leading to the Broadwater Public Boat Ramp in Southport was messy and untidy. A rusting iron fence leans at a precarious angle, separating it from the gardens behind the ramp. A caravan sat on bricks instead of wheels, missing a door, and beside it was a half-buried child's tricycle.

Jimmy hadn't looked over his shoulder since he turned down the muddy track. He parked near a boarded up bait shop and walked towards the marina, past an abandoned shed and past a sign announcing the plan to redevelop the site for a new industrial estate.

I hid the car further back towards the road under a copse of trees and followed him, scurrying from tree to tree in an effort to hide, while avoiding the pot holes full of filthy water. I waited a few seconds with my back to a tree before moving on to the next one but keeping him in sight all the way.

I had to be smart. I couldn't do this on my own and I couldn't risk calling anyone. Who would I call anyway? I'd be putting that person in danger and there'd been enough blood spilt already. I thought hard as I watched Jimmy walk purposefully towards the boats in the marina.

Then like a lightning bolt, I knew. Cavanaugh was desperately trying

Serpent

to find me. He would have been tracing my calls whenever I made them and up to now, I'd been turning off my phone to break that contact. Well, let him find me now.

I pulled my phone out of my pocket and switched it on again but before placing it at the base of the tree, I took the time to turn it to mute. I didn't want Cavanaugh ringing me again and alerting Jimmy.

I looked around the tree just as Jimmy stepped lightly on board a boat in need of a paint job moored on the dilapidated jetty. He stepped over a roll of rope and went down below deck, out of sight. I crouched out of sight for five minutes, just watching, before Jimmy finally emerged. He slid the hatch closed behind him then nimbly stepped ashore, walking slowly back along the path towards his van.

I needed to see what was inside that boat. When I heard his car engine start, I stepped out from behind the tree line and made my way hurriedly towards the boat.

The lacquered door was closed but not locked and the cabin below deck was dark. Curtains were drawn across the portholes and two steps further in I was in the galley. The stainless steel sink was clean and a lone cup sat draining on a tea towel.

Further in, as my eyes adjusted, I saw a pegboard dotted with tools. Chisels, wrenches, spanners, screwdrivers and files. There were boxes of pipes, drill bits and waterproof tape on shelves. I didn't know what I was looking for but I felt sure I'd know when I found it.

A portable generator squatted under a work bench and an old radio hung on a cord from the ceiling. Everything had its proper place.

Further on, through a bulkhead, emerged another cabin but this time everything seemed slightly askew. The mattress was too large for the bed. The lamp was too big for the table and the walls were covered in scraps of paper. It was too dark for me to see them properly so I took out my phone and used the torch.

My eyes began to adjust slowly. On the wall before me was newspaper cuttings, photographs, maps and diagrams covering the wall. To the side, I saw images of Jazz on her way to school, playing soccer, in the school yard and shopping with Sally. Others showed Sally at her yoga class, at the supermarket and painting the backyard furniture. Beside them were photos of me. Coming out of my office building. Standing closely to a smiling Sam with my hand resting on her arm. Parking my Audi in the driveway of my house.

I sat down heavily, dazed at the extent of his surveillance. On the small bedside table, ring-bound notebooks were stacked high. I took the top one and opened it. Neat concise handwriting filled each page. The left-hand margin logged the time and date. Alongside were details of my movements, including places, meetings, duration and modes of transport. It was a 'how to' manual of my life. How to be me.

There was a sound on the deck above my head. I switched off the light and sat still in the darkness, wedged between the bulkhead and the end of the bed, trying to breathe quietly as something was being dragged and poured. Seconds later, someone swung through the hatch into the saloon and began moving through the galley opening cupboards.

When the engine started up, I felt my pulse throbbing at the base of my jaw. The pistons rose and fell then settled into a steady rhythm. I saw Jimmy's legs through the portholes and felt the boat pitch as he stepped along the side, casting off.

I glanced quickly towards the galley. If I moved quickly, I could maybe get ashore before he came back to the wheelhouse. I tried to stand up and knocked over a rectangular frame leaning against the wall. As it toppled, I managed to catch it with one hand. The picture was frozen momentarily in the light leaking through the curtains: a beach scene, ice-cream stalls, beach towels. Gripped in Jazz's hand was a wooden carved cat.

I fell backwards with a groan, unable to make my legs work. They belonged to someone else.

The narrow boat rocked again as the footsteps returned. He had cast off, put the engine into gear and we were swinging away from the moorings. I could hear the water washing along the hull.

Then there was a new sound, a whooshing noise, like a strong wind. All the oxygen seemed to disappear from the air as fuel ran along the floor and soaked into my trousers. Fumes began to sting my eyes and outside the window, varnished wood crackled as it began to burn. On my hands and knees, I crawled along the boat into the gathering smoke.

I pulled myself through the galley and reached the saloon. The engine was close by and I could hear it thudding on the far side of the bulkhead. My head hit the stairs as I climbed upwards only to find the hatch had been locked from the outside. I groaned in despair and slammed my shoulder hard against it with all my strength but nothing moved. I could feel heat through the door. I needed another way out. But where?

I couldn't see a thing. All I could do was feel my way. As the air thickened with smoke, it felt like breathing molten glass into my lungs. On the benches in the workroom, my fingers closed around a hammer and a sharp, flat chisel. I hurried away from the blaze, ricocheting off walls and hammered on the portholes with the hammer. All to no avail.

Against the bulkhead in the cabin there was a small storage door. I managed to squeeze through it, flopping like a stranded fish until my legs were able to follow me. Oily tarpaulins and ropes snaked beneath me as I realised I must be in the bow. I reached above my head and felt the indentation of another hatch. I ran my fingers around the edge, searching for the latch, then tried to wedge the chisel into a corner. The angle was all wrong.

By now, the boat had started to list and water had begun to fill the stern. I lay on my back and braced both feet against the underside of the hatch, then kicked upwards – once, twice, three times – screaming and cursing with each kick. Eventually, the wood splintered and gave way and a square of blinding light filled the hold. As I dragged myself upwards into the daylight, I glanced back as the petrol in the cabin ignited and a ball of orange flame erupted towards me. Fresh air engulfed me for a split second as I was propelled through the air and then freezing water wrapped itself around me. I sank slowly, exhausted, still screaming in my head, until I felt my feet hit the silt on the bottom. I wasn't thinking of drowning. I was just embracing the feeling of coolness in the dark green shadows knowing the boat would be blazing above me.

When my lungs began to hurt, I pushed upwards, grasping for lungfuls of air. When my head broke the surface, I sucked air in greedily as the stern of the boat slipped under the surface. The engine had stopped but drums in the workroom were exploding like grenades.

I waded towards the bank as mud sucked at my shoes and pulled myself upwards using handfuls of reeds. My legs bumped on the edge of the canal just as a hand reached out and grabbed me.

I recognised Jimmy's Nike shoes instantly. He reached under my arms and grabbed me around the chest, lifting me with his chin digging into the top of my head. I could smell petrol on his clothes, and maybe on mine, as he dragged me through the silt towards the abandoned shed. I didn't cry out. I was too exhausted.

A heavy stench of decay rose from the inside of the shed, causing my stomach to churn. Wooden pallets were stacked against a wall and sheets of roofing iron had fallen in a storm. Water leaked down the walls, weaving a tapestry of black and green slime and from the darkness of a corner, I could hear rats scurrying in alarm. Even breathing through my mouth, the smell of putrefaction was overwhelming.

Jimmy looped a rope around my neck with a knot pressing into my windpipe and tied the other end to something above me, forcing me up onto my toes. My legs jerked like a puppet because I couldn't get much purchase on the ground to stop myself from choking. I managed to squeeze my fingers inside the rope and hold it away from my throat.

Jimmy shifted away from me, his face damp with sweat.

"I know why you're doing this," I gulped.

He didn't answer me. He stripped off his jacket and rolled up the sleeves of his shirt as if there was business to be taken care of. Then he sat down on a packing crate and stared at me. His stillness was remarkable.

"You won't get away with killing me," I managed.

He smiled. A smile the Grim Reaper would have produced. "What makes you think I want to kill you?" He pushed long strands of wet hair behind his ears. "You're a wanted man. They'll probably give me a reward."

He was trying to sound confident but his voice betrayed him. It came out shaky and a little high pitched, a sure giveaway that he was nervous and out of his comfort zone. After all the killings he'd done, I wondered why killing me felt different.

In the distance I heard a siren. The fire brigade was coming and hopefully Cavanaugh behind them.

"By now, Cavanaugh will have examined the details of the events I've told him."

I didn't know this for a fact, it was pure hope and speculation, but I had to keep Jimmy off balance and feeling nervous. As I talked, I tried to wedge my hand further inside the rope.

"He will cross-reference the times, dates and places by putting my name into the sequence of events and you know what he'll discover?" I asked. "That I couldn't have killed them. I was elsewhere every single time. Then maybe, just maybe, they'll run *your* name into the same equation. How many alibis have you tucked away? How well did you cover his tracks?"

I had to keep him off-balance but listening, praying Cavanaugh would know to hurry. I hurried on. "I visited your mother yesterday. She asked about you."

Jimmy stiffened slightly and his breathing quickened.

"I haven't met Bridget before but she must have been very beautiful once. Alcohol and cigarettes aren't very kind to the skin. I never met your father either, but I think I would have liked him."

"You know nothing about him," he spat at me.

"Not true," I said. "I know a lot about David Lachlan. And you. But I need to understand how things work. That's why I came looking for you. I thought you might help me figure something out."

He squinted at me, his eyes barely open, but didn't answer.

"I worked out most of it. I know about John Compton, Judge Buchanan, Melissa Stark, Andrew Booth, Graham Burton and Alison O'Reilly. But what I can't fathom out if why you punished everyone except the one person you hate the most."

Jimmy was on his feet, blowing himself up like one of those fish with poisonous spikes. He shoved his face close to mine and I could see a vein, faint and pulsing blue above his left eyelid.

"Your mother says you look like your father but that's not entirely true," I continued. I could smell his fetid breath inches from my face. "Every time you look in the mirror you must see your mother's eyes."

I waited for a reaction that never came. "You can't even say her name," I taunted, pushing hard for a reaction. People make mistakes when they're angry. They do things they would normally think twice about and in that split second, they leave themselves vulnerable. I was hoping he'd make a mistake so I could take full advantage of it.

What I hadn't expected was a knife to suddenly appear, glinting in the darkness. He held the point of the blade against my bottom lip so close that if I opened my mouth it would draw blood. But I had to risk it. I couldn't stop now and show fear.

"Let me tell you what I've worked out so far, Jimmy. I see a small boy, suckled on his father's dreams of a grand future but polluted by his mother's violence. She was the one who abused you, wasn't she? Not your father."

The blade was so sharp, I didn't feel the nick until I felt blood leaking down my chin and dripping on to my fingers that were still pressed against my neck trying to relieve the pressure.

"This little boy blamed himself," I gasped. "Most victims of abuse do. He saw himself as a clumsy oaf – always running, tripping, falling, breaking things, mumbling excuses, never good enough, always late, born to disappoint. He thought he should have been able to save his father, but he didn't understand that he was just a little boy and that what was happening was not his fault."

"SHUT THE FUCK UP! You were one of them! *You* helped to kill him!"

I managed to shake my head. "I didn't even know him."

He snorted. "Yeah. That's right. You condemned an innocent man you didn't even know. How arbitrary is that? At least I choose who I killed."

Jimmy face was still inches from mine, I could feel spit on my face. I could see the hurt in his eyes and almost feel the hatred in his heart.

"So he blamed himself, this little boy," I continued, "who was already growing too quickly and becoming more awkward and uncoordinated. He was tender and shy but slowly becoming angry and bitter. He couldn't untangle these feelings and he couldn't forgive. He hated the world, but no more than he hated himself. He clung to the memories of his father and of how things used to be. Not perfect, but OK. Together."

His eyes blazed at me but he let me talk.

Serpent

"So what did he do? He withdrew from his surroundings and isolated himself. He made himself smaller, hoping to be forgotten, and took himself to a fantasy world. It must have been nice to have somewhere to go, Jimmy."

The knife pressed deeper into my lip and I gasped in pain. He pulled it away and waved it in front of my eyes. "I told you to shut your mouth," he warned through gritted teeth. "Why can't people just keep their mouths shut? You're no better than Simon Price and his bloody book," he spat.

I tried to move my head to make it easier to breathe. The rope held firm. "I can understand why you killed the ones on your list," I pressed. "But why Simon Price? And Peter Marshall? They had nothing to do with what happened to you as a child."

I watched contempt radiate from his eyes and the pulse in his neck throbbing with blood.

"Tell me," I asked, watching the pulse in his neck pound in time with his heartbeat. "Was it purely because of the book Price was publishing?"

Cats, both wild and domestic, watch unblinkingly, alert for the smallest variation in posture, the tiniest shift of attention. As he watched me, I saw the hate slowly turn to something else as a slow smile came to his lips.

"You don't know," he began to laugh. Then he threw his head back and laughed hard as if I was the greatest fool ever. "The great detective, Jack Curtis, doesn't know!"

I stared at him in confusion. "What do you mean, Jimmy? What don't I know?"

He sniggered some more, ignoring my question. "That writer on Stradbroke Island. All it took was a bottle of scotch for him to tell me everything. It was just so easy to shove him off the boat."

I tried to swallow but saliva filled my mouth, dribbling out from the corner of my mouth. "How did you know about the book in the first place?" I asked in a garbled voice.

He snickered. "That stupid bitch, Amelia," he spat. "Price's secretary told me. We were both attending the same night class and most nights afterwards, we got to talking. She had just started working part-time for Price and mentioned he had hired a journalist to write his stupid memoirs." He snarled. "I knew straight away what he was writing about. You didn't have to be a rocket scientist to know that. She told me Marshall was on Stradbroke Island writing the book and I followed him. He told me the rest."

There it was. The last piece of the puzzle.

He was still watching me, a smirk on his face. "You think you've worked it all out, don't you? You think you're so damned clever," he snarled. "Well, smart-ass, you know nothing!"

I closed my eyes, hoping Cavanaugh would hurry. "What don't I know Jimmy?" I repeated. I had to keep him talking.

He shook his head as he smiled. "I'll give you a clue." He poked me in the chest. "Are you ready?"

He waited for me to say something but I could barely breathe. All I could do was nod as I glanced at the door, willing Cavanaugh to burst through.

He stepped forward so our noses were almost touching. "There's nothing worse than someone who turns on old friends."

He wiggled his eyebrows and smirked. "Think about it genius."

I had no idea what he meant but I had to keep his attention focussed on me and not the door.

"How does it feel to be judge, jury and executioner, Jimmy? Punishing all those who deserve to be punished. You must have spent years rehearsing all of this." I tried to shake my head but the rope dug deep. "Amazing. But who are you doing it for exactly?"

Jimmy reached down and picked up a plank. He mumbled something at me, sounding like shut up.

"Oh, that's right. Your father. A man you can hardly remember. I bet you don't know his favourite song or what movies he liked or who his heroes were. Was he right or left handed? Which side did he part his hair?"

Emotions are by nature erratic. When put into words, our passions often come out sounding melodramatic, even pathetic. I closed my eyes and breathed through my nose, making a horsy noise.

"I told you to SHUT YOUR MOUTH!"

The plank swung in a wide arc striking me across the chest. Air blasted out of my lungs and my body spun, tightening the rope like a tourniquet. I kicked my legs trying to spin back as my mouth flapped like the gills of a stranded fish, trying to suck in air.

Jimmy tossed the plank aside and watched me with a smirk on his face.

My ribs felt broken, but my lungs were beginning to work again. "Why are you such a coward, Jimmy?" I coughed, then gasped as pain stabbed my chest. "I mean, it's pretty obvious who deserved all this hatred. Look at what your mother did. She belittled and tormented your father. She slept with other men and made him a figure of pity, even to his friends. And then, to top it all off, she accused him of abusing his own son."

Jimmy turned away from me but even the silence was speaking to him.

"She ripped up the letters he wrote to you," I lied. "I bet she even found the photographs you kept of him and destroyed them. She wanted him out of her life and out of yours. She even hated hearing his name."

Jimmy was growing smaller, as if collapsing in on himself. His anger was turning to grief.

"Let me guess. She was going to be the first. You went looking for her and found her easily enough. Bridget had never been the shy, retiring type. You watched her and waited. You had it all planned. Down to every detail. The woman who had destroyed your life was just a few feet away, close enough for you to put those fingers around her throat. She was right there, *right there,* but you hesitated. You couldn't do it. You were standing right there and she had no weapon. You could have crushed her so easily."

I paused, letting the moment live in his mind. "Nothing happened. You couldn't do it. You were scared. When you saw her again, you became that little boy, with his trembling bottom lip and his stutter and she terrified you."

Jimmy's face was twisted in pain. At the same time, he wanted to wipe me from his world.

"Has her cancer done the job for you or has it robbed you?"

"Robbed me," he whispered.

"She's dying in terrible pain. I've seen her."

He exploded. "It's not enough! She's a MONSTER."

He kicked at a metal drum, sending it spinning across the gravel. "She destroyed my life. *She* made me do this." Spittle hung from his lips.

"I'm not going to give you any bullshit excuses, Jimmy." If I did that, I would be sanctioning everything he'd done. "Terrible things happened to you. I wish things could have been different. But look at the world around you. There are children starving in Africa. Jets are being flown into buildings. Bombs are being dropped on civilians. People are dying of disease. Prisoners are being tortured. Women are being raped. Some of these things we can change but others we can't. Sometimes we just have to accept what happened to us and get on with our lives."

He laughed bitterly. "How can you even say that?"

"Because it's true. You know it is."

"I'll tell you what's true." He was staring at me unblinkingly, his voice a low rumble. "There is a shed on the coast road about eight miles south of Kingscliff. It's on a dirt road set back from the road."

His voice was ragged. "I was six when she first took me there. I had no idea what was happening. She would lay down on the bed and let strange men run their hands over her. Every week there was a different man. I watched them tie her up and I watched the enjoyment she got from it. And every time she opened her eyes, she looked directly at me, smiling."

He rocked slightly, back and forth, staring straight ahead, picturing the scene in his mind. "Private clubs and swingers bars were too middle class for my mother. She preferred her orgy to be anonymous and unsophisticated. I lost count of how many men she let into that shed." He swallowed. "Sometimes she let them touch me and eventually, she let them tie me up too."

His eyes were brimming with tears. "She told them it was my father." He gulped. "But he never touched me. Never. It was them. Always them. *They* caused the bruises. Then she lied and she let them take my father away."

As he sobbed quietly, I didn't know what to say. My tongue had gone thick and my peripheral vision had started to fail because I couldn't get enough oxygen to my brain. I had failed.

I wanted to say something but the words wouldn't form. I wanted to say he wasn't alone. There were other people who had suffered as he had and had reached out for help. I knew he was lost and damaged but everyone has choices. Not every abused child turns out like this.

As I struggled to breathe through gritted teeth, the stench of decay felt like a dead hand over my mouth and nostrils. I felt vomit rising and I forced it down. If I stopped trying for even a moment I knew I would die.

"Let me down, Jimmy. I can't breathe properly."

I could see the back of his head and his badly trimmed hair. He turned in slow motion, not looking at my face. The blade swept above my head and I collapsed forwards, still clutching the remnants of the rope. The muscles in my legs spasmed and I tasted concrete dust, mingled with blood.

Lifting myself painfully and slowly to my knees, I started crawling over metal shavings and broken concrete towards the door. It felt like an obstacle course. The door was partly open and through the gap, I saw a fire engine beside the canal and the flashing lights of a police car. I tried to shout but no sound emerged.

Something was wrong. I'd stopped moving. I turned to see Jimmy standing on the leg of my pants.

"Your fucking arrogance blows me away," he growled, grasping my collar and lifting me to my feet.

He pulled me backwards and I gasped in pain. "Do you think I'd fall for your cereal box psychology?" he snarled. "I've seen more therapists, counsellors and psychiatrist than you've had crappy birthday presents."

He put his face close to mine once again. "You don't know me. You think you're inside my head," he smiled a terrible grin that became a snarl, "but you're not even close."

We were breathing the same air as he placed the blade under my ear. I could feel the metal against my neck, his breath warm on my neck, the blade cold, and I could do nothing about it. A flick of his wrist and my throat would open like a dropped melon. That's what he was going to do. He was going to end it now.

I closed my eyes and took a shaky breath, readying myself, when the sound of screeching wood filled the small room. My eyes flew open and flicked towards the sound. Standing in the doorway was Cavanaugh, a torch in one hand and a gun pointed at Jimmy chest in the other one.

"DROP THE KNIFE!" he screamed. "Drop it now or I'll shoot!"

38

"You took your damn time getting here," I grumbled as I tried to swallow the taste of blood, bile and petrol from my mouth.

I was sitting in the front seat of his squad car, shivering and aching all over, as I held a cup of water in both hands in the vain attempt to stop them from trembling. "I thought you'd given up."

"It was your own damn fault," he said, placing my mobile phone on the seat beside me. "You kept turning your phone on and off all the time. If you hadn't we'd have been here earlier."

"You talked to Mel and had a look at the red edge file?"

"Yeah." He spoke the word quietly and I was hoping he felt bad about doubting me.

"What about the other names in the file?" I asked.

He leaned against the open door, studying me thoughtfully. The glint of sunlight off the channel picked up the Tower of Pisa pin on his tie. His distant blue eyes were fixed on the ambulance parked a hundred feet away, framed against the shed.

"We'll look into them," he said, nodding. "We're checking the details from the file and running the names through the computer."

"I spoke to Andrew Booth," I admitted.

"I know," he grinned. "We had an interesting call from his wife. She gave us the registration number of the car you were driving and we traced it to Christine Buchanan. Up until then, we had no idea how you were getting around since we had your car. We were just lucky a patrol car spotted it fifteen kilometres away. We found two fourteen-year-olds and a kid of eleven in it and the only reason we did was became it ran out of petrol." He shook his head with a wry look on his face.

"Andrew said there was a Jimmy who worked at the swimming centre where Kim trained."

"I'll check it out."

"I also saw Jimmy's mother in the Hospice."

His eyes flicked to me. "I know that too."

Cavanaugh could see I was struggling. The pain in my chest and throat was making me light-headed and I winced as I pulled the grey blanket around my shoulders.

"When did you start to believe me about Jimmy?" I asked.

"It was becoming obvious someone didn't like you. Anyone who met you, I imagine." He grinned. "My job was to find the most persistent one who disliked you the most."

A car was speeding down the narrow driveway, tyres crunching on the loose stones. It came to an abrupt halt with stones hurtling towards the trees as the driver's side door flew open. Sam jumped out and almost ran towards us, coming to a halt in front of me.

She glanced quickly at Cavanaugh before dropping to her knees. "Are you alright?" she asked, running her eyes over my face. She couldn't help but notice the bloody, swollen lip and ligature mark around my neck.

"I'm fine, Sam. Really. I'm okay."

What I didn't know was blood was running down my chin from the lip that was swollen to twice its size and my eyes had gone bloodshot from the restriction around my neck.

Her eyes glinted as she ran her index finger along the cut. "You try so hard to be tough." She was looking at me with soft eyes and I felt my heart twinge. "But you're not. You won't admit it but you're tender and vulnerable. And that's what makes you special to me." She swallowed audibly and whispered, "Let me look after you."

Love is an amazing emotion. It can send you higher than a bird, it can rip your heart out and it can make you sit at the feet of the one you love with their hands in yours while your jaw trembles.

She clamped her hands on either side of my face and turned it, first one way then the other, her eyes raking over my face.

"Hey!" I yelped. "Take it easy. That hurts!"

"Okay. Enough of this," Cavanaugh muttered." You should get the paramedics to look at the lip while they're here. You look like you could use stitches in it."

"I'm not going to the hospital in that ambulance," I stated. "I'll only go to the hospital after I've spoken to you."

Sam reached out to touch my lip again, pursing her lips and making a cooing noise while Cavanaugh turned away his gaze towards the ambulance and the police car, shaking his head. Jimmy was sitting between two police officers in the back seat reading him his rights.

"At the beginning you told me the killer was going to be older and more practiced," Cavanaugh said over his shoulder.

"I thought he would be."

"And you said it was sexual," he reminded me.

"I said pain aroused him, but the motive wasn't clear at that stage. Revenge was one of the possibilities, I remember saying." I winced as I turned my head away from Sam and towards him. "Are you nit-picking?"

He grinned as he turned back to me. "Just making sure we're on the same page. I will admit however, you saw him before anyone else did."

"I tripped over him," I said. "Metaphorically speaking."

The ambulance pulled away making the water birds lift off the reeds in a wild flap of wings. They twisted and turned across the pale sky through the skeletal trees stretching along the bank. It almost looked like they were reaching out to the birds as they flew into the air.

"Come on," Cavanaugh said. "Let's get you to the hospital." He turned to Sam. "I'll take him. Can you get started on the names in the red edge file?"

"Why can't I take Jack to the hospital?" she whined.

"Because you're too close and I still have to get the statement from him. Let's keep this on a professional level, Sam. It's no skin off my nose if

Curtis is the best you can find but if you and Curtis are a couple, we have to leave the personal side out of it and do our jobs."

I stood up slowly, groaning and cradling my chest, while I put my phone back into the pocket of my wet jacket. "He's right, Sam. When I'm finished, I'll call you and you can pick me up. Call Frank for me please and fill him in on what happened. He'll know what to do."

She glanced slyly at Cavanaugh and nodded. She knew Frank was meant to call Sandra Burton as well.

Cavanaugh snorted. "I'll pretend I didn't see and hear that."

"And ask him to keep the animals for another day," I added. "When he comes by tomorrow, we can talk."

In the end, Sam gave in and Cavanaugh gave me a lift to the hospital. He turned into the emergency bay and as I tried to step out of the car, my legs seized up as the adrenalin drained out of them. Cavanaugh grabbed a wheelchair and pushed me into the familiar white-tiled emergency section then straight through to an empty bay.

He called out to a passing triage nurse, getting off on the wrong foot by calling her 'sweetheart' and telling her to get her 'priorities sorted.' She took her annoyance out on me, shoving her fingers between my ribs with unnecessary zeal, making me feel like I was going to pass out. I was glad Sam wasn't here to see it. She was already in a panic. This would have put her over the edge.

A young female doctor with bleached blond hair came into the cubicle and peered at my lip for a second. She glanced over at Cavanaugh leaning against the wall with his arms folded over his chest and said, "I don't want to hear anything from you, please," then turned back to me.

I heard him mumble something that sounded like 'precious' but he remained silent.

"You'll need a stitch or two in that lip," she told me. "The anaesthetic needle in the wound to kill the pain will hurt more than the stitches, I'm sorry."

She was right. Lying on the bed with my eyes watering from the anaesthetic, I tried to keep my head still as I felt the needle slide into my lip and the thread tug at the skin. Scissors snipped the ends and she stood back to appraise her work.

Serpent

"And my mother said I would never be good at needlework," she grinned.

"How does it look?"

"You could have waited for a plastic surgeon but I've done alright. You'll have a slight scar, just there." She touched the hollow beneath the bottom lip then tossed the latex gloves into a bin. "You still need an x-ray for the ribs so I'm sending you to Radiology. Do you need someone," she jerked her head sideways towards Cavanaugh without looking at him, "to push you or can you walk?"

"I'll walk," I said.

She pointed down the corridor and told me to follow the green line to Radiology. "Not you," she turned to Cavanaugh. "I'd like a word with you."

Half an hour later, Cavanaugh found me in the waiting room, hanging around for the radiologist to confirm what I already suspected. Two fractured ribs but no internal bleeding.

"When can you give me a statement?" he asked.

"When they strap me up."

"It can wait till tomorrow then. Come on. I'll give you a lift home. You can call Sam from there once you're settled in."

Downstairs, he continued to boss people around until my chest was strapped and my stomach rattling with painkillers and anti-inflammatories. I floated along the corridor in a wheelchair, pushed along by Cavanaugh to his car.

As we drove along the M1 to my home, questions were running around in my head still. When I spoke to him after seeing Andrew Booth, I gave him everything I had discovered and still he wanted to issue a warrant for my arrest. I needed to know what finally made him believe in my innocence.

I turned my head carefully to face him. He looked pleased with himself, a smile on his face.

"I need to know why you finally believed me. For days, I've tried telling you it was Jimmy and you still wanted to arrest me. What changed?" I asked.

I allowed him a moment with the self-satisfied chuckle because he'd saved my life.

"Come on. What was it?"

"The glass," he stated simply.

I blinked. "What glass?"

"The glass in Christine Buchanan's kitchen."

He took his eyes off the road for a second to squint at me. "And don't think I don't remember that you were withholding information from me about her identity. I haven't forgotten that and I'm tossing up whether to charge you for it. I also don't know the whys and hows of your relationship with her."

I tsked loudly. "Shut up and tell me about the glass."

He turned back to the road again. "That glass has always bothered me. Her house was immaculate. Everything beautifully arranged and clean. Nothing out of place except the vase of dead flowers on the coffee table that were probably fresh when she was murdered."

He thought for a while. "But that glass in the drainer." He shook his head. "It bothered me." He nodded and smiled to himself. Again, I let him pat himself on the back.

"I went back to her house," he continued, "just to have another look around. I checked the kitchen cupboards for glassware and there were six matching water glasses in one, along with six matching wine glasses and five coffee cups. The sixth coffee cup was on the bench with grounds in it."

He glanced in the rear vision mirror and indicated to turn left and take the Oxenford turnoff that would lead us to Coomera.

"So if there were full matching sets of glassware in the cupboard, where did this odd glass come from?" He turned to face me. "The only answer to that is the killer brought it with him with your prints on it."

I stared at him open mouthed. "That's it? That's how you knew I was innocent? Not the facts I kept feeding you? Not Mel's file? A bloody glass left in the drainer?"

I couldn't believe it. My life had depended on Cavanaugh's idea of a House and Garden catalogue.

"That and the potpourri on the pavers outside the study window," he added. "That's when I knew the killer had broken in through that window and waited for her in the study. And why had he waited? Because he knew she wasn't home and she was at the Star Casino waiting for someone to arrive."

He manoeuvred his way in silence around the spaghetti of the Oxenford overpass then turned onto Foxwell Road. We were twenty minutes from my home and there were still questions I needed answered.

"You saw the CCTV footage of Christine at the Star Casino?" I asked.

"Of course I did." He glanced at me and frowned. "What sort of detective would I be if I hadn't?"

I put the palm of my hand in the air in apology and nodded. "Go on."

"I knew when she was there and I knew she called you." He glanced at me. "And I believe you tried to call her back."

I opened my mouth to deny it but he interrupted me.

"Don't bother, Curtis. I know. All right?" He let the statement hang in the air. "She probably didn't answer when you called because he already had her drugged and restrained."

He drove in silence while he thought. "What I couldn't figure out was how he got your prints on the glass and how the GPS in your car registered that you had driven to her house on the night of her murder. You said you were alone and asleep that night but I began thinking, if that's was the case, and if you were innocent, how did those prints get on the glass?"

It was rhetorical question meant to show me how clever he was. He wasn't looking for an answer. He was explaining his logic.

"Then I remembered your nosy neighbour, the Neighbourhood Watch guy."

"Gary?" I asked bewildered.

"Gary." He smiled. "You owe him and his wife an expensive dinner to his favourite restaurant because he was the lynch pin who helped me put this all together."

I blinked. "Gary?" I repeated. "From next door?"

"One and the same," he grinned. "I remembered him coming up to me on the morning I was looking for you to come to the morgue to identify Christine's body. He baled me up for about half an hour while he told me about the a series of minor burglaries around your street."

He'd told me the same thing and mentioned telling Cavanaugh about them.

"I told him to report them if he wanted to but there wasn't much the police could do without proof of identity." He smiled. "On the off chance he may have seen something or someone on the night of Christine's murder, I went to see him about the burglaries around your area. What I didn't know was he had installed security cameras on his property a year ago." He shook his head. "That man is fanatical about his neighbourhood watch role."

He glanced quickly at me again. "He has four cameras facing all directions. Did you know that?"

I shook my head, stunned at what he was telling me.

He snorted. "Four bloody cameras." He laughed, shaking his head. "Lucky for you, one of those cameras is facing your house and he keeps everything. And I mean everything. The footage is linked up to his computer and is saved in a file."

He indicated to turn right to enter Coomera Waters estate, then continued talking. "I asked him if he had the footage from the 24th August and he looked affronted. He took me inside his house to show me the file and there it was, backed up on his computer. I asked if he was able to transfer the complete file to the station and he did it while I was standing there." He shook his head. "That guy should work for Wormald."

"Is that why you were at my house?" I asked. *Was it really only a few hours ago?*

He turned sharply. "You saw me?"

I pulled a face. "You looked furious. I thought you were angry because I wasn't at my house."

"Well, there was that too," he smirked. "But it was mainly because I was told the techs were still at lunch and my request was in a queue. I said a few choice words to the right people and within an hour, I was looking at the footage I needed as it ran through for that night."

He drove in silence, a smirk spreading across his face.

"Well come on!" I finally yelled. "Stop gloating and tell me what you saw!"

He glanced at me, his eyebrows high on head and a grin on his face.

"On the night of Christine's murder, a man was seen entering your house. Three times."

"What?"

I thought hard. My routine has always been irregular although Jimmy would have known that I was having a meeting with Sandra for most of that afternoon and night. He knew the house would be empty.

"Yep," Cavanaugh replied with a grin. "It's all in the file. The first time was at 6.18 pm. A guy wearing a backpack entered through the front door, bold as you like. He was only inside for about five minutes before he left the same way." He threw me a look. "James Croft must have known everything about you. When you would be there, where you hid the key and how to drug you. He was only in the house for a few minutes and then he was gone again. I'd say in that time he managed to place a drug somewhere that he knew you would take unknowingly. Then at 9.33 pm, we have you entering the house. Half an hour later, the lights were turned out and the house was in darkness. At 10.55 pm, he entered the house again. The house remained in darkness except for what I believe to be a torch shining. Ten minutes later, your garage door went up and your Audi drove away."

He glanced quickly at me. "I'm assuming you were sound asleep because one and a half hours later, almost to the minute, the car returned and the same man entered and exited by the front door and left." He turned and his eyes bored into mine. "But this time he left with a shovel in his hand."

I gasped. I know I did. I was totally stunned. "But can you prove it was Jimmy? I'm assuming he hid his face and it was dark."

In every court case, it is the job of the defence attorney to make mincemeat of every damning testimony delivered by the prosecution. I've seen it done many times. When the prosecution thought they had proven the guilt of the criminal by some piece of evidence, the defence attorney had that same evidence thrown out because of a minor technicality. It was wrong but that's the way the justice system works.

"Don't worry. There is no way this is being thrown out of court. Down the road was a white van into which he entered before driving away. The registration plate was blurry on the camera but we enlarged it and it's registered to one James Croft."

"You caught all that?"

He nodded and grinned. "Every last second of it. And to add icing to the cake, that same white van was at the boat ramp when we arrived at the crime scene. I'm having forensics run it for fingerprints right now to match it to Croft's."

The rain that had been threatening for most of the day was almost upon us. The sky was darkening and the drive through the leafy area of Foxwell Road looked almost eerie. As if reading my thoughts, Cavanaugh switched his head lights on.

I turned to him. "He drugged my Jack Daniels. That's all it could be. I didn't eat at home that night but when I came home, I spent some time with the dog and had a drink as usual before going to bed."

"Well, you need to get a better watch dog because there wasn't a peep out of him. I would say both of you were heavily drugged."

"He lifted my prints and put them onto a glass while I was asleep? That was some drug."

"You're lucky to have Gary next door," he repeated with an edge to his voice. "Criminals think they're so smart. They watch shows like CSI and Criminal Intent and they think they know all the tricks and the pitfalls. Then they forget about the simple things that can put them away for life."

We'd pulled into my driveway and it took me several minutes to step gingerly out from the front seat, cradling my chest the whole time.

Before I had limped to the front door, Gary came marching over to me, a shocked look on his face. "What the hell happened to you?" he asked.

I slapped him on the back. "Gary, I owe you. But right now, I need to get inside and lie down before I fall down."

He turned to Cavanaugh. "I helped?"

"You, my friend, were instrumental in exonerating this man."

Gary puffed out his chest and smiled from ear to ear as Cavanaugh turned to me.

"I'll call Sam but I would suggest you throw that Jack Daniels down the sink. And I would wait for a few days before having another drink. You're drugged to the eyeballs with painkillers."

"Alcohol is the last thing I want right now." I said as I turned back to face him. All I wanted was to lie down and sleep for the next two days but first I had to let him know how much I appreciated his diligence, even if he was trying his best to put me behind bars.

"Thank you, Cavanaugh. For everything."

"Don't get gushy on me, Curtis. I'll see you down at the station tomorrow for that statement. Ring me in the morning and we'll set up a time."

He turned, clapped Gary on the back and walked towards his car.

39

MARTIN

I may have mentioned before that the sweet poison of vanity is in my blood and I love seeing my name, Martin Farrow, on the bestseller list in bookstores. It's been a while since I've had that pleasure, but if things work out, I may have that opportunity once again.

I spoke to Rick twice on the day I arrived at the Novotel. Once to tell him I was being pursued by a deranged murderer and the second time to give him news of my proposed true crime book.

He seemed uninterested in the crime book. "Do you want to hear the good news or the bad news," Rick asked instead.

"I'm not sure your idea of good news is the same a mine."

He chuckled. "Preston Crane just called. Price Inc still wants you to finish the memoirs and they will give you an extra month to work on the manuscript."

"And the good news is?"

"Oh. Very cute. Listen, don't be so goddamned snooty about it. You aren't hurt, are you? And you're holed up in the Novotel gratis, right? This is a really hot book now. This is Simon Price's voice from the grave. The whole situation is rich with possibilities."

"What possibilities?" I scoffed.

"You can write what you like, is what! Within reason, of course. Nobody's going to stop you. And you liked him, didn't you?"

I thought about that. Had I actually liked the man who was involved with paedophiles, gangsters and criminals?

"I never met the man," I said instead, hedging.

"You owe it to him, Martin. And besides, there's another consideration."

"Which is?"

"Crane said that if you don't fulfil your contractual obligations and finish the book, they'll sue your ass off."

And so, I sat down at the desk positioned in front of a window overlooking the ocean. I watched the clouds drift across the sky and the seagulls float on the wind currents while I thought of how I would do it. Normally, I would work better in such an environment but this time, guilt plagued me. Did I really want to finish a book exonerating this evil man? Could I sleep at night if I made him look innocent of crimes I knew he was guilty off? Where were my morals?

I flipped through Marshall's manuscript again. The truth is I was almost finished except for the finale. I felt the need to rush through this book in order to start my own book but I had a couple of days spare before Jack either called me back or came to see me. In that time, I planned to work through the days and nights to finish Price's book.

I'd completed the basic structure of the story, heavily editing the chapters Marshall had finished. My method has been to work with his manuscript on my left and retype it completely and in the process of passing it through my brain and fingers and on to my computer, to strain out any of my predecessor's lumpy clichés. Although I reckoned it was still useful to have a page or two of heroic struggle against inner demons, etc, etc.

That is when I came across a scrap of paper between the last few pages of the manuscript.

'The key to everything is in the beginnings.'

I have never been good at puzzles but I was intrigued with the message Marshall had left. I took the manuscript, now tattered from use and barely legible in places, and started flicking through the opening chapters to see what he had meant by the cryptic note. I ran my finger swiftly down the centre of the pages, sweeping my eyes over all the made-up feelings and half-true memories. Marshall's professional prose had rendered the roughness of a human life and made it as smooth as a plastered wall. A truly worthless piece of junk.

Then I looked at the words again. 'The key to everything is in the beginnings.' Not 'beginning' but 'beginnings'.

I had cut all of Marshall's deathless chapter beginnings from my book because every single one of them had been particularly dreadful. I hadn't left one of them in my book as I rewrote it. Could that be the clue to Marshall's note?

I opened the desk drawer and took out one of those pens and notepads high-end hotels leave for your use and started at the beginning of the manuscript.

I took all thirteen chapter openings and fanned them across the desk.

Chapter One: Simon Price's family were so poor.....

Chapter Two: Price is a British name...

Chapter Three: And as always, Alice, my first wife, saw my future...

Chapter Four: Andrew, my first child, turned five when I began my career...

Chapter Five: Lachlan is not a common name in Queensland, but is well known...

Chapter Six: Are any of us guiltless? Haven't we all done things we...

Chapter Seven: The main ideology was to try and become a better person than...

Chapter Eight: Ring in hand, I knelt at my second wife's feet and proposed...

Chapter Nine: Leaders in our world should be ready to stand up and face ...

Chapter Ten: Of all the times I wished I could change my course...

Chapter Eleven: The time was now. It was do it now or forever regret...

Chapter Twelve: Paedophile gangs were rife in Surfers when I came to power...

Chapter Thirteen: Gang warfare started in earnest during the final years of my...

. . .

I reread the words again. *'The key to everything is in the beginnings.'* Then I went through the pages and circled the first word of each chapter. That's when I saw it. I couldn't help but see it.

The sentence that Marshall, fearful for his safety and life, had embedded in the manuscript, like a message from the grave was:

'Simon Price And Andrew Lachlan Are The Ring Leaders Of The Paedophile Gang.'

40

I left the Novotel that night when it was dark, never to return. Since then, a month has passed and neither Rick nor Jack Curtis have tried to contact me to talk about my book. As far as I know, I haven't been missed. There were times, especially the first week, sitting alone in my scruffy hotel room – I've stayed in four so far – when I thought I'd go mad. I ought to ring Rick, I told myself, but was my phone tapped? Could I be traced?

There is no going back. I know that now. I can't tell you how precisely Marshall uncovered the truth. I presume it must have started back when he began working for Price many years ago. He would have seen and heard things but hidden that knowledge. He knew better than anyone that Price never made a decision unless he consulted with Andrew Lachlan. In most of the photos I had photocopied at the library, Lachlan was standing in the background, smug and silent, but always there. If you had to pick which of them would have been the brains, the callous one, the ruthless one, there was only ever one choice. Marshall would have suspected early on, but I believe he eventually put together enough of the picture to know for certain when he was writing the book.

As you can appreciate, I don't care to linger in any place for long. Already I sense that strangers are starting to take too much interest in me. I'm sure Andrew Lachlan has men everywhere. That's his style. He would never get his hands dirty and risk a personal connection to any crime, but he's there, as always, in the background. He will not halt until he stops me from publishing this book just like he tried to stop Peter Marshall and Simon Price by having them murdered. Of that I am sure. His sole purpose is to protect his family's reputation at any cost. I know that now after researching him. I've had plenty of time to do that.

My plan has been to parcel the manuscript up and post it to Jack Curtis, along with the note from Marshall and my acknowledgement of what it meant. I scurried out yesterday and sent it via Express Post to his office, with the authorisation for him to sign for it upon delivery. He will know I am not being melodramatic when he reads the letter I enclosed. If anyone is stubborn enough and bloody-minded enough to get this thing into print, it is Jack Curtis.

I wonder where I will go next. It puts me in somewhat of a dilemma now that you have read this final paragraph. Am I supposed to be pleased that you've read it or not? Pleased, of course, to speak at last in my own voice. Disappointed, obviously, because it means that I'm dead.

But as my mother used to say, in this life, I'm afraid you can't have everything.

Milton Keynes UK
Ingram Content Group UK Ltd.
UKHW021926151124
451262UK00014B/1618